The Assistant

Other Avon Books by
Bernard Malamud

GOD'S GRACE
THE NATURAL

BERNARD MALAMUD

The Assistant

AVON BOOKS ◆ NEW YORK

AVON BOOKS
A division of
The Hearst Corporation
1350 Avenue of the Americas
New York, New York 10019

Copyright © 1957 by Bernard Malamud
Cover art by Sarah Waldron
Published by arrangement with Farrar, Straus & Giroux, Inc.
Library of Congress Catalog Card Number: 57-7397
ISBN: 0-380-72085-X

First Avon Books Trade Printing: December 1993
First Avon Books Mass Market Printing: September 1980

AVON TRADEMARK REG. U.S. PAT. OFF. AND IN OTHER COUNTRIES, MARCA REGISTRADA, HECHO EN U.S.A.

Printed in the U.S.A.

OPM 10 9 8 7 6 5 4 3 2 1

For Ann with Love

The early November street was dark though night had ended, but the wind, to the grocer's surprise, already clawed. It flung his apron into his face as he bent for the two milk cases at the curb. Morris Bober dragged the heavy boxes to the door, panting. A large brown bag of hard rolls stood in the doorway along with the sour-faced, gray-haired Poilisheh huddled there, who wanted one.

"What's the matter so late?"

"Ten after six," said the grocer.

"Is cold," she complained.

Turning the key in the lock he let her in. Usually he lugged in the milk and lit the gas radiators, but the Polish woman was impatient. Morris poured the bag of rolls into a wire basket on the counter and found an unseeded one for her. Slicing it in halves, he wrapped it in white store paper. She tucked the roll into her cord market bag and left three pennies on the counter. He rang up the sale on an old noisy cash register, smoothed and put away the bag the rolls had come in, finished pulling in the milk, and stored the bottles at the bottom of the refrigerator. He lit the gas radiator at the front of the store and went into the back to light the one there.

He boiled up coffee in a blackened enamel pot and sipped it, chewing on a roll, not tasting what he was eating. After he had cleaned up he waited; he waited for Nick Fuso, the upstairs tenant, a young mechanic who worked in a garage in the neighborhood. Nick came in every morning around seven for twenty cents' worth of ham and a loaf of bread.

But the front door opened and a girl of ten entered, her face pinched and eyes excited. His heart held no welcome for her.

"My mother says," she said quickly, "can you trust her till tomorrow for a pound of butter, loaf of rye bread and a small bottle of cider vinegar?"

He knew the mother. "No more trust."

The girl burst into tears.

Morris gave her a quarter-pound of butter, the bread and vinegar. He found a penciled spot on the worn counter, near the cash register, and wrote a sum under "Drunk Woman." The total now came to $2.03, which he never hoped to see. But Ida would nag if she noticed a new figure, so he reduced the amount to $1.61. His peace—the little he lived with—was worth forty-two cents.

He sat in a chair at the round wooden table in the rear of the store and scanned, with raised brows, yesterday's Jewish paper that he had already thoroughly read. From time to time he looked absently through the square windowless window cut through the wall, to see if anybody had by chance come into the store. Sometimes when he looked up from his newspaper, he was startled to see a customer standing silently at the counter.

Now the store looked like a long dark tunnel.

The grocer sighed and waited. Waiting he did poorly. When times were bad time was bad. It died as he waited, stinking in his nose.

A workman came in for a fifteen-cent can of King Oscar Norwegian sardines.

Morris went back to waiting. In twenty-one years the store had changed little. Twice he had painted all over, once added new shelving. The old-fashioned double windows at the front a carpenter had made into a large single one. Ten years ago the sign hanging outside fell to the ground but he had never replaced it. Once, when business hit a long good spell, he had had the wooden icebox ripped out and a new white refrigerated showcase put in. The showcase stood at the front in line with the old counter and he often leaned against it as he stared out of the window. Otherwise the store was the same. Years ago it was more a delicatessen; now, though he still sold a little delicatessen, it was more a poor grocery.

A half-hour passed. When Nick Fuso failed to appear, Morris got up and stationed himself at the front window, behind a large cardboard display sign the beer people had rigged up in an otherwise empty window. After a while the hall door opened, and Nick came out in a thick, hand-knitted green sweater. He trotted around the corner and soon returned carrying a bag of groceries. Morris was now visible at the window. Nick saw the look on his face but didn't look long. He ran into the house, trying to make it seem it was the wind that was chasing him. The door slammed behind him, a loud door.

The grocer gazed into the street. He wished

fleetingly that he could once more be out in the
open as when he was a boy—never in the house,
but the sound of the blustery wind frightened him.
He thought again of selling the store but who
would buy? Ida still hoped to sell. Every day she
hoped. The thought caused him grimly to smile,
although he did not feel like smiling. It was an
impossible idea so he tried to put it out of his
mind. Still, there were times when he went into
the back, poured himself a spout of coffee and
pleasantly thought of selling. Yet if he miraculously did, where would he go, where? He had a moment of uneasiness as he pictured himself without
a roof over his head. There he stood in all kinds of
weather, drenched in rain, and the snow froze on
his head. No, not for an age had he lived a whole
day in the open. As a boy, always running in the
muddy, rutted streets of the village, or across the
fields, or bathing with the other boys in the river;
but as a man, in America, he rarely saw the sky. In
the early days when he drove a horse and wagon,
yes, but not since his first store. In a store you
were entombed.

The milkman drove up to the door in his truck
and hurried in, a bull, for his empties. He lugged
out a caseful and returned with two half-pints of
light cream. Then Otto Vogel, the meat provisions
man, entered, a bush-mustached German carrying
a smoked liverwurst and string of wieners in his
oily meat basket. Morris paid cash for the liverwurst; from a German he wanted no favors. Otto
left with the wieners. The bread driver, new on
the route, exchanged three fresh loaves for three
stale and walked out without a word. Leo, the cake
man, glanced hastily at the package cake on top of

the refrigerator and called, "See you Monday, Morris."

Morris didn't answer.

Leo hesitated. "Bad all over, Morris."

"Here is the worst."

"See you Monday."

A young housewife from close by bought sixty-three cents' worth; another came in for forty-one cents'. He had earned his first cash dollar for the day.

Breitbart, the bulb peddler, laid down his two enormous cartons of light bulbs and diffidently entered the back.

"Go in," Morris urged. He boiled up some tea and served it in a thick glass, with a slice of lemon. The peddler eased himself into a chair, derby hat and coat on, and gulped the hot tea, his Adam's apple bobbing.

"So how goes now?" asked the grocer.

"Slow," shrugged Breitbart.

Morris sighed. "How is your boy?"

Breitbart nodded absently, then picked up the Jewish paper and read. After ten minutes he got up, scratched all over, lifted across his thin shoulders the two large cartons tied together with clothesline and left.

Morris watched him go.

The world suffers. *He* felt every schmerz.

At lunchtime Ida came down. She had cleaned the whole house.

Morris was standing before the faded couch, looking out of the rear window at the back yards. He had been thinking of Ephraim.

His wife saw his wet eyes.

"So stop sometime, please." Her own grew wet.

He went to the sink, caught cold water in his cupped palms and dipped his face into it.

"The Italyener," he said, drying himself, "bought this morning across the street."

She was irritated. "Give him for twenty-nine dollars five rooms so he should spit in your face."

"A cold water flat," he reminded her.

"You put in gas radiators."

"Who says he spits? This I didn't say."

"You said something to him not nice?"

"Me?"

"Then why he went across the street?"

"Why? Go ask him," he said angrily.

"How much you took in till now?"

"Dirt."

She turned away.

He absent-mindedly scratched a match and lit a cigarette.

"Stop with the smoking," she nagged.

He took a quick drag, clipped the butt with his thumb nail and quickly thrust it under his apron into his pants pocket. The smoke made him cough. He coughed harshly, his face lit like a tomato. Ida held her hands over her ears. Finally he brought up a gob of phlegm and wiped his mouth with his handkerchief, then his eyes.

"Cigarettes," she said bitterly. "Why don't you listen what the doctor tells you?"

"Doctors," he remarked.

Afterward he noticed the dress she was wearing. "What is the picnic?"

Ida said, embarrassed, "I thought to myself maybe will come today the buyer."

She was fifty-one, nine years younger than he,

her thick hair still almost all black. But her face was lined, and her legs hurt when she stood too long on them, although she now wore shoes with arch supports. She had waked that morning resenting the grocer for having dragged her, so many years ago, out of a Jewish neighborhood into this. She missed to this day their old friends and landsleit—lost for parnusseh unrealized. That was bad enough, but on top of their isolation, the endless worry about money embittered her. She shared unwillingly the grocer's fate though she did not show it and her dissatisfaction went no farther than nagging—her guilt that she had talked him into a grocery store when he was in the first year of evening high school, preparing, he had said, for pharmacy. He was, through the years, a hard man to move. In the past she could sometimes resist him, but the weight of his endurance was too much for her now.

"A buyer," Morris grunted, "will come next Purim."

"Don't be so smart. Karp telephoned him."

"Karp," he said in disgust. "Where he telephoned—the cheapskate?"

"Here."

"When?"

"Yesterday. You were sleeping."

"What did he told him?"

"For sale a store—yours, cheap."

"What do you mean cheap?"

"The key is worth now nothing. For the stock and the fixtures that they are worth also nothing, maybe three thousand, maybe less."

"I paid four."

"Twenty-one years ago," she said irritably. "So don't sell, go in auction."

"He wants the house too?"

"Karp don't know. Maybe."

"Big mouth. Imagine a man that they held him up four times in the last three years and he still don't take in a telephone. What he says ain't worth a cent. He promised me he wouldn't put in a grocery around the corner, but what did he put?—a grocery. Why does he bring me buyers? Why didn't he keep out the German around the corner?"

She sighed. "He tries to help you now because he feels sorry for you."

"Who needs his sorrow?" Morris said. "Who needs him?"

"So why *you* didn't have the sense to make out of your grocery a wine and liquor store when came out the licenses?"

"Who had cash for stock?"

"So if you don't have, don't talk."

"A business for drunken bums."

"A business is a business. What Julius Karp takes in next door in a day we don't take in in two weeks."

But Ida saw he was annoyed and changed the subject.

"I told you to oil the floor."

"I forgot."

"I asked you special. By now would be dry."

"I will do later."

"Later the customers will walk in the oil and make everything dirty."

"What customers?" he shouted. "Who customers? Who comes in here?"

"Go," she said quietly. "Go upstairs and sleep. I will oil myself."

But he got out the oil can and mop and oiled the floor until the wood shone darkly. No one had come in.

She had prepared his soup. "Helen left this morning without breakfast."

"She wasn't hungry."

"Something worries her."

He said with sarcasm, "What worries her?" Meaning: the store, his health, that most of her meager wages went to keep up payments on the house; that she had wanted a college education but had got instead a job she disliked. Her father's daughter, no wonder she didn't feel like eating.

"If she will only get married," Ida murmured.

"She will get."

"Soon." She was on the verge of tears.

He grunted.

"I don't understand why she don't see Nat Pearl anymore. All summer they went together like lovers."

"A showoff."

"He'll be someday a rich lawyer."

"I don't like him."

"Louis Karp also likes her. I wish she will give him a chance."

"A stupe," Morris said, "like the father."

"Everybody is a stupe but not Morris Bober."

He was staring out at the back yards.

"Eat already and go to sleep," she said impatiently.

He finished the soup and went upstairs. The going up was easier than coming down. In the bedroom, sighing, he drew down the black window shades. He was half asleep, so pleasant was the anticipation. Sleep was his one true refreshment: it excited him to go to sleep. Morris took off his apron, tie and trousers, and laid them on a chair. Sitting at the edge of the sagging wide bed, he unlaced his misshapen shoes and slid under the cold covers in shirt, long underwear and white socks. He nudged his eye into the pillow and waited to grow warm. He crawled toward sleep. But upstairs Tessie Fuso was running the vacuum cleaner, and though the grocer tried to blot the incident out of his mind, he remembered Nick's visit to the German and on the verge of sleep felt bad.

He recalled the bad times he had lived through, but now times were worse than in the past; now they were impossible. His store was always a marginal one, up today, down tomorrow—as the wind blew. Overnight business could go down enough to hurt; yet as a rule it slowly recovered—sometimes it seemed to take forever—went up, not high enough to be really *up*, only not down. When he had first bought the grocery it was all right for the neighborhood; it had got worse as the neighborhood had. Yet even a year ago, staying open seven days a week, sixteen hours a day, he could still eke out a living. What kind of living?—a living; you lived. Now, though he toiled the same hard hours, he was close to bankruptcy, his patience torn. In the past when bad times came he had somehow lived through them, and when good times returned, they more or less returned to him. But now, since the appearance of H. Schmitz across the street ten months ago, all times were bad.

Last year a broken tailor, a poor man with a sick

wife, had locked up his shop and gone away, and from the minute of the store's emptiness Morris had felt a gnawing anxiety. He went with hesitation to Karp, who owned the building, and asked him to please keep out another grocery. In this kind of neighborhood one was more than enough. If another squeezed in they would both starve. Karp answered that the neighborhood was better than Morris gave it credit (for schnapps, thought the grocer), but he promised he would look for another tailor or maybe a shoemaker, to rent to. He said so but the grocer didn't believe him. Yet weeks went by and the store stayed empty. Though Ida pooh-poohed his worries, Morris could not overcome his underlying dread. Then one day, as he daily expected, there appeared a sign in the empty store window, announcing the coming of a new fancy delicatessen and grocery.

Morris ran to Karp. "What did you do to me?"

The liquor dealer said with a one-shouldered shrug. "You saw how long stayed empty the store. Who will pay my taxes? But don't worry," he added, "he'll sell more delicatessen but you'll sell more groceries. Wait, you'll see he'll bring you in customers."

Morris groaned; he knew his fate.

Yet as the days went by, the store still sitting empty—emptier, he found himself thinking maybe the new business would never materialize. Maybe the man had changed his mind. It was possible he had seen how poor the neighborhood was and would not attempt to open the new place. Morris wanted to ask Karp if he had guessed right but could not bear to humiliate himself further.

Often after he had locked his grocery at night,

he would go secretly around the corner and cross
the quiet street. The empty store, dark and deserted, was one door to the left of the corner drugstore; and if no one was looking the grocer would
peer through its dusty window, trying to see
through shadows whether the emptiness had
changed. For two months it stayed the same, and
every night he went away reprieved. Then one
time—after he saw that Karp was, for once,
avoiding him—he spied a web of shelves sprouting
from the rear wall, and that shattered the hope he
had climbed into.

In a few days the shelves stretched many arms
along the other walls, and soon the whole tiered
and layered place glowed with new paint. Morris
told himself to stay away but he could not help
coming nightly to inspect, appraise, then guess the
damage, in dollars, to himself. Each night as he
looked, in his mind he destroyed what had been
built, tried to make of it nothing, but the growth
was too quick. Every day the place flowered with
new fixtures—streamlined counters, the latest refrigerator, fluorescent lights, a fruit stall, a chromium cash register; then from the wholesalers arrived a mountain of cartons and wooden boxes
of all sizes, and one night there appeared in the
white light a stranger, a gaunt German with a German pompadour, who spent the silent night hours,
a dead cigar stuck in his teeth, packing out sym-
metrical rows of brightly labeled cans, jars, gleam-
ing bottles. Though Morris hated the new store,
in a curious way he loved it too, so that sometimes
as he entered his own old-fashioned place of business, he could not stand the sight of it; and now he
understood why Nick Fuso had that morning

run around the corner and crossed the street—to taste the newness of the place and be waited on by Heinrich Schmitz, an energetic German dressed like a doctor, in a white duck jacket. And that was where many of his other customers had gone, and stayed, so that his own poor living was cut in impossible half.

Morris tried hard to sleep but couldn't and grew restless in bed. After another quarter of an hour he decided to dress and go downstairs, but there drifted into his mind, with ease and no sorrow, the form and image of his boy Ephraim, gone so long from him, and he fell deeply and calmly asleep.

Helen Bober squeezed into a subway seat between two women and was on the last page of a chapter when a man dissolved in front of her and another appeared; she knew without looking that Nat Pearl was standing there. She thought she would go on reading, but couldn't, and shut her book.

"Hello, Helen." Nat touched a gloved hand to a new hat. He was cordial but as usual held back something—his future. He carried a fat law book, so she was glad to be protected with a book of her own. But not enough protected, for her hat and coat felt suddenly shabby, a trick of the mind, because on her they would still do.

"Don Quixote"?

She nodded.

He seemed respectful, then said in an undertone, "I haven't seen you a long time. Where've you been keeping yourself?"

She blushed under her clothes.

"Did I offend you in some way or other?"

Both of the women beside her seemed stolidly deaf. One held a rosary in her heavy hand.

"No." The offense was hers against herself.

"So what's the score?" Nat's voice was low, his gray eyes annoyed.

"No score," she murmured.

"How so?"

"You're you, I'm me."

This he considered a minute, then remarked, "I haven't much of a head for oracles."

But she felt she had said enough.

He tried another way. "Betty asks for you."

"Give her my best." She had not meant it but this sounded funny because they all lived on the same block, separated by one house.

Tight-jawed, he opened his book. She returned to hers, hiding her thoughts behind the antics of a madman until memory overthrew him and she found herself ensnared in scenes of summer that she would gladly undo, although she loved the season; but how could you undo what you had done again in the fall, unwillingly willing? Virginity she thought she had parted with without sorrow, yet was surprised by torments of conscience, or was it disappointment at being valued under her expectations? Nat Pearl, handsome, cleft-chinned, gifted, ambitious, had wanted without too much trouble a lay and she, half in love, had obliged and regretted. Not the loving, but that it had taken her so long to realize how little he wanted. Not her, Helen Bober.

Why should he?—magna cum laude, Columbia, now in his second year at law school, she only a high school graduate with a year's evening col-

lege credit mostly in lit; he with first-rate prospects, also rich friends he had never bothered to
introduce her to; she as poor as her name sounded,
with little promise of a better future. She had
more than once asked herself if she had meant by
her favors to work up a claim on him. Always she
denied it. She had wanted, admittedly, satisfaction, but more than that—respect for the giver of
what she had to give, had hoped desire would become more than just that. She wanted, simply, a
future in love. Enjoyment she had somehow had,
felt very moving the freedom of fundamental in-
timacy with a man. Though she wished for more
of the same, she wanted it without aftermath of
conscience, or pride, or sense of waste. So she
promised herself next time it would go the other
way; first mutual love, then loving, harder maybe
on the nerves, but easier in memory. Thus she had
reasoned, until one night in September, when coming up to see his sister Betty, she had found herself
alone in the house with Nat and had done again
what she had promised herself she wouldn't. Afterward she fought self-hatred. Since then, to this day,
without telling him why, she had avoided Nat
Pearl.

Two stations before their stop, Helen shut her
book, got up in silence and left the train. On the
platform, as the train moved away, she caught a
glimpse of Nat standing before her empty seat,
calmly reading. She walked on, lacking, wanting,
not wanting, not happy.

Coming up the subway steps, she went into the
park by a side entrance, and despite the sharp wind
and her threadbare coat, took the long way home.
The leafless trees left her with unearned sadness.

She mourned the long age before spring and feared loneliness in winter. Wishing she hadn't come, she left the park, searching the faces of strangers although she couldn't stand their stares. She went quickly along the Parkway, glancing with envy into the lighted depths of private houses that were, for no reason she could give, except experience, not for her. She promised herself she would save every cent possible and register next fall for a full program at NYU, night.

When she reached her block, a row of faded yellow brick houses, two stories squatting on ancient stores, Sam Pearl, stifling a yawn, was reaching into his corner candy store window to put on the lamp. He snapped the string and the dull glow from the fly-specked globe fell upon her. Helen quickened her step. Sam, always sociable, a former cabbie, bulky, wearing bifocals and chewing gum, beamed at her but she pretended no see. Most of the day he sat hunched over dope sheets spread out on the soda fountain counter, smoking as he chewed gum, making smeary marks with a pencil stub under horses' names. He neglected the store; his wife Goldie was the broad-backed one, yet she did not much complain, because Sam's luck with the nags was exceptional and he had nicely supported Nat in college until the scholarships started rolling in.

Around the corner, through the many-bottled window that blinked in neon "KARP wines and liquors," she glimpsed paunchy Julius Karp, with bushy eyebrows and an ambitious mouth, blowing imaginary dust off a bottle as he slipped a deft fifth of something into a paper bag, while Louis, slightly popeyed son and heir, looking up from clipping to the quick his poor fingernails, smiled amiably upon a sale. The Karps, Pearls and Bobers, representing attached houses and stores, but otherwise detachment, made up the small Jewish segment of this gentile community. They had somehow, her father first, then Karp, later Pearl, drifted together here where no other Jews dwelt, except on the far fringes of the neighborhood. None of them did well and were too poor to move elsewhere until Karp, who with a shoe store that barely made him a living, got the brilliant idea after Prohibition gurgled down the drain and liquor licenses were offered to the public, to borrow cash from a white-bearded rich uncle and put in for one. To everybody's surprise he got the license, though Karp, when asked how, winked a heavy-lidded eye and answered nothing. Within a short time after cheap shoes had become expensive bottles, in spite of the poor neighborhood—or maybe because of it, Helen supposed—he became astonishingly successful and retired his overweight wife from the meager railroad flat above the store to a big house on the Parkway—from which she hardly ever stepped forth—the house complete with two-car garage and Mercury; and at the same time as Karp changed his luck—to hear her father tell it—he became wise without brains.

The grocer, on the other hand, had never altered his fortune, unless degrees of poverty meant alteration, for luck and he were, if not natural enemies, not good friends. He labored long hours, was the soul of honesty—he could not escape his honesty, it was bedrock; to cheat would cause an explosion in him, yet he trusted cheaters—

coveted nobody's nothing and always got poorer.
The harder he worked—his toil was a form of time
devouring time—the less he seemed to have. He was
Morris Bober and could be nobody more fortu-
nate. With that name you had no sure sense of
property, as if it were in your blood and history
not to possess, or if by some miracle to own something, to do so on the verge of loss. At the end
you were sixty and had less than at thirty. It was,
she thought, surely a talent.

Helen removed her hat as she entered the grocery. "Me," she called, as she had from childhood.
It meant that whoever was sitting in the back
should sit and not suddenly think he was going to
get rich.

Morris awoke, soured by the long afternoon
sleep. He dressed, combed his hair with a broken
comb and trudged downstairs, a heavy-bodied man
with sloping shoulders and bushy gray hair in need
of a haircut. He came down with his apron on.
Although he felt chilly he poured out a cup of cold
coffee, and backed against the radiator, slowly
sipped it. Ida sat at the table, reading.

"Why you let me sleep so long?" the grocer complained.

She didn't answer.

"Yesterday or today's paper?"

"Yesterday."

He rinsed the cup and set it on the top of the
gas range. In the store he rang up "no sale" and
took a nickel out of the drawer. Morris lifted the
lid of the cash register, struck a match on the un-
derside of the counter, and holding the flame
cupped in his palm, peered at the figure of his

earnings. Ida had taken in three dollars. Who could afford a paper?

Nevertheless he went for one, doubting the small pleasure he would get from it. What was so worth reading about the world? Through Karp's window, as he passed, he saw Louis waiting on a customer while four others crowded the counter. Der oilem iz a goilem. Morris took the *Forward* from the newsstand and dropped a nickel into the cigar box. Sam Pearl, working over a green racing sheet, gave him a wave of his hammy hand. They never bothered to talk. What did he know about race horses? What did the other know of the tragic quality of life? Wisdom flew over his hard head.

The grocer returned to the rear of his store and sat on the couch, letting the diminishing light in the yard fall upon the paper. He read nearsightedly, with eyes stretched wide, but his thoughts would not let him read long. He put down the newspaper.

"So where is your buyer?" he asked Ida.

Looking absently into the store she did not reply.

"You should sell long ago the store," she remarked after a minute.

"When the store was good, who wanted to sell? After came bad times, who wanted to buy?"

"Everything we did too late. The store we didn't sell in time. I said, 'Morris, sell now the store.' You said, 'Wait.' What for? The house we bought too late, so we have still a big mortgage that it's hard to pay every month. 'Don't buy,' I said, 'times are bad.' 'Buy,' you said, 'will get better. We will save rent.' "

He answered nothing. If you had failed to do the right thing, talk was useless.

When Helen entered, she asked if the buyer had come. She had forgotten about him but remembered when she saw her mother's dress.

Opening her purse, she took out her pay check and handed it to her father. The grocer, without a word, slipped it under his apron into his pants pocket.

"Not yet," Ida answered, also embarrassed. "Maybe later."

"Nobody goes in the night to buy a store," Morris said. "The time to go is in the day to see how many customers. If this man comes here he will see with one eye the store is dead, then he will run home."

"Did you eat lunch?" Ida asked Helen.

"Yes."

"What did you eat?"

"I don't save menus, Mama."

"Your supper is ready." Ida lit the flame under the pot on the gas range.

"What makes you think he'll come today?" Helen asked her.

"Karp told me yesterday. He knows a refugee that he looks to buy a grocery. He works in the Bronx, so he will be here late."

Morris shook his head.

"He's a young man," Ida went on, "maybe thirty —thirty-two. Karp says he saved a little cash. He can make alterations, buy new goods, fix up modern, advertise a little and make here a nice business."

"Karp should live so long," the grocer said.

"Let's eat." Helen sat at the table.

Ida said she would eat later.

"What about you, Papa?"

"I am not hungry." He picked up his paper.

She ate alone. It would be wonderful to sell out and move but the possibility struck her as remote. If you had lived so long in one place, all but two years of your life, you didn't move out overnight.

Afterward she got up to help with the dishes but Ida wouldn't let her. "Go rest," she said.

Helen took her things and went upstairs.

She hated the drab five-room flat; a gray kitchen she used for breakfast so she could quickly get out to work in the morning. The living room was colorless and cramped; for all its overstuffed furniture of twenty years ago it seemed barren because it was lived in so little, her parents being seven days out of seven in the store; even their rare visitors, when invited upstairs, preferred to remain in the back. Sometimes Helen asked a friend up, but she went to other people's houses if she had a choice. Her bedroom was another impossibility, tiny, dark, despite the two by three foot opening in the wall, through which she could see the living room windows; and at night Morris and Ida had to pass through her room to get to theirs, and from their bedroom back to the bathroom. They had several times talked of giving her the big room, the only comfortable one in the house, but there was no place else that would hold their double bed. The fifth room was a small icebox off the second floor stairs, in which Ida stored a few odds and ends of clothes and furniture. Such was home. Helen had once in anger remarked that the place was awful to live in, and it had made her feel bad that her father had felt so bad.

She heard Morris's slow footsteps on the stairs. He came aimlessly into the living room and tried to relax in a stiff armchair. He sat with sad eyes, saying nothing, which was how he began when he wanted to say something.

When she and her brother were kids, at least on Jewish holidays Morris would close the store and venture forth to Second Avenue to see a Yiddish play, or take the family visiting; but after Ephraim died he rarely went beyond the corner. Thinking about his life always left her with a sense of the waste of her own.

She looks like a little bird, Morris thought. Why should she be lonely? Look how pretty she looks. Whoever saw such blue eyes?

He reached into his pants pocket and took out a five-dollar bill.

"Take," he said, rising and embarrassedly handing her the money. "You will need for shoes."

"You just gave me five dollars downstairs."

"Here is five more."

"Wednesday was the first of the month, Pa."

"I can't take away from you all your pay."

"You're not taking, I'm giving."

She made him put the five away. He did, with renewed shame. "What did I ever give you? Even your college education I took away."

"It was my own decision not to go, yet maybe I will yet. You can never tell."

"How can you go? You are twenty-three years old."

"Aren't you always saying a person's never too old to go to school?"

"My child," he sighed, "for myself I don't care, for you I want the best but what did I give you?"

"I'll give myself," she smiled. "There's hope."

With this he had to be satisfied. He still conceded her a future.

But before he went down, he said gently, "What's the matter you stay home so much lately? You had a fight with Nat?"

"No." Blushing, she answered, "I don't think we see things in the same way."

He hadn't the heart to ask more.

Going down, he met Ida on the stairs and knew she would cover the same ground.

In the evening there was a flurry of business. Morris's mood quickened and he exchanged pleasantries with the customers. Carl Johnsen, the Swedish painter, whom he hadn't seen in weeks, came in with a wet smile and bought two dollars' worth of beer, cold cuts and sliced Swiss cheese. The grocer was at first worried he would ask to charge —he had never paid what he owed on the books before Morris had stopped giving trust—but the painter had the cash. Mrs. Anderson, an old loyal customer, bought for a dollar. A stranger then came in and left eighty-eight cents. After him two more customers appeared. Morris felt a little surge of hope. Maybe things were picking up. But after half-past eight his hands grew heavy with nothing to do. For years he had been the only one for miles around who stayed open at night and had just about made a living from it, but now Schmitz matched him hour for hour. Morris sneaked a little smoke, then began to cough. Ida pounded on the floor upstairs, so he clipped the butt and put it away. He felt restless and stood at the front window, watching the street. He watched a trolley go

by. Mr. Lawler, formerly a customer, good for at
least a fiver on Friday nights, passed the store.
Morris hadn't seen him for months but knew
where he was going. Mr. Lawler averted his gaze
and hurried along. Morris watched him disappear
around the corner. He lit a match and again
checked the register—nine and a half dollars, not
even expenses.

Julius Karp opened the front door and poked
his foolish head in.

"Podolsky came?"

"Who Podolsky?"

"The refugee."

Morris said in annoyance, "What refugee?"

With a grunt Karp shut the door behind him.
He was short, pompous, a natty dresser in his ad-
vanced age. In the past, like Morris, he had toiled
long hours in his shoe store, now he stayed all day
in silk pajamas until it came time to relieve Louis
before supper. Though the little man was insensi-
tive and a blunderer, Morris had got along fairly
well with him, but since Karp had rented the tailor shop to another grocer, sometimes they did not
speak. Years ago Karp had spent much time in the
back of the grocery, complaining of his poverty as
if it were a new invention and he its first victim.
Since his success with wines and liquors he came
in less often, but he still visited Morris more than
his welcome entitled him to, usually to run down
the grocery and spout unwanted advice. His ticket
of admission was his luck, which he gathered wherever he reached, at a loss, Morris thought, to
somebody else. Once a drunk had heaved a rock at
Karp's window, but it had shattered his. Another
time, Sam Pearl gave the liquor dealer a tip on a

horse, then forgot to place a bet himself. Karp collected five hundred for his ten-dollar bill. For years the grocer had escaped resenting the man's good luck, but lately he had caught himself wishing on him some small misfortune.

"Podolsky is the one I called up to take a look at your gesheft," Karp answered.

"Who is this refugee, tell me, an enemy yours?"

Karp stared at him unpleasantly.

"Does a man," Morris insisted, "send a friend he should buy such a store that you yourself took away from it the best business?"

"Podolsky ain't you," the liquor dealer replied. "I told him about this place. I said, 'the neighborhood is improving. You can buy cheap and build up this store. It's run down for years, nobody changed anything there for twenty years.'"

"You should live so long how much I changed—" Morris began but he didn't finish, for Karp was at the window, peering nervously into the dark street.

"You saw that gray car that just passed," the liquor dealer said. "This is the third time I saw it in the last twenty minutes." His eyes were restless.

Morris knew what worried him. "Put in a telephone in your store," he advised, "so you will feel better."

Karp watched the street for another minute and worriedly replied, "Not for a liquor store in this neighborhood. If I had a telephone, every drunken bum would call me to make deliveries, and when you go there they don't have a cent."

He opened the door but shut it in afterthought. "Listen, Morris," he said, lowering his voice, "if they come back again, I will lock my front door and put out my lights. Then I will call you from the back window so you can telephone the police."

"This will cost you five cents," Morris said grimly.

"My credit is class A."

Karp left the grocery, disturbed.

God bless Julius Karp, the grocer thought. Without him I would have my life too easy. God made Karp so a poor grocery man will not forget his life is hard. For Karp, he thought, it was miraculously not so hard, but what was there to envy? He would allow the liquor dealer his bottles and gelt just not to be him. Life was bad enough.

At nine-thirty a stranger came in for a box of matches. Fifteen minutes later Morris put out the lights in his window. The street was deserted except for an automobile parked in front of the laundry across the car tracks. Morris peered at it sharply but could see nobody in it. He considered locking up and going to bed, then decided to stay open the last few minutes. Sometimes a person came in at a minute to ten. A dime was a dime.

A noise at the side door which led into the hall frightened him.

"Ida?"

The door opened slowly. Tessie Fuso came in in her housecoat, a homely Italian girl with a big face.

"Are you closed, Mr. Bober?" she asked embarrassedly.

"Come in," said Morris.

"I'm sorry I came through the back way but I was undressed and didn't want to go out in the street."

"Don't worry."

"Please give me twenty cents' ham for Nick's lunch tomorrow."

He understood. She was making amends for Nick's trip around the corner that morning. He cut her an extra slice of ham.

Tessie bought also a quart of milk, package of paper napkins and loaf of bread. When she had gone he lifted the register lid. Ten dollars. He thought he had long ago touched bottom but now knew there was none.

I slaved my whole life for nothing, he thought.

Then he heard Karp calling him from the rear. The grocer went inside, worn out.

Raising the window he called harshly, "What's the matter there?"

"Telephone the police," cried Karp. "The car is parked across the street."

"What car?"

"The holdupniks."

"There is nobody in this car, I saw myself."

"For God's sake, I tell you call the police. I will pay for the telephone."

Morris shut the window. He looked up the phone number and was about to dial the police when the store door opened and he hurried inside.

Two men were standing at the other side of the counter, with handkerchiefs over their faces. One wore a dirty yellow clotted one, the other's was white. The one with the white one began pulling out the store lights. It took the grocer a half-minute to comprehend that he, not Karp, was their victim.

Morris sat at the table, the dark light of the dusty bulb falling on his head, gazing dully at

the few crumpled bills before him, including
Helen's check, and the small pile of silver. The
gunman with the dirty handkerchief, fleshy, wearing a fuzzy black hat, waved a pistol at the grocer's head. His pimply brow was thick with sweat;
from time to time with furtive eyes he glanced into the darkened store. The other, a taller man in
an old cap and torn sneakers, to control his trembling leaned against the sink, cleaning his fingernails with a matchstick. A cracked mirror hung
behind him on the wall above the sink and every
so often he turned to stare into it.

"I know damn well this ain't everything you
took in," said the heavy one to Morris, in a hoarse,
unnatural voice. "Where've you got the rest hid?"

Morris, sick to his stomach, couldn't speak.

"Tell the goddam truth." He aimed the gun
at the grocer's mouth.

"Times are bad," Morris muttered.

"You're a Jew liar."

The man at the sink fluttered his hand, catching
the other's attention. They met in the center of
the room, the other with the cap hunched awkwardly over the one in the fuzzy hat, whispering
into his ear.

"No," snapped the heavy one sullenly.

His partner bent lower, whispering earnestly
through his handkerchief.

"I say he hid it," the heavy one snarled, "and
I'm gonna get it if I have to crack his goddam
head."

At the table he whacked the grocer across the
face.

Morris moaned.

The one at the sink hastily rinsed a cup and

filled it with water. He brought it to the grocer,
spilling some on his apron as he raised the cup to
his lips.

Morris tried to swallow but managed only a dry
sip. His frightened eyes sought the man's but he
was looking elsewhere.

"Please," murmured the grocer.

"Hurry up," warned the one with the gun.

The tall one straightened up and gulped down
the water. He rinsed the cup and placed it on a
cupboard shelf.

He then began to hunt among the cups and
dishes there and pulled out the pots on the bottom. Next, he went hurriedly through the drawers
of an old bureau in the room, and on hands and
knees searched under the couch. He ducked into
the store, removed the empty cash drawer from the
register and thrust his hand into the slot, but came
up with nothing.

The heavy one elbowed him aside.

"We better scram out of here."

"Are you gonna go chicken on me?"

"That's all the dough he has, let's beat it."

"Business is bad," Morris muttered.

"Your Jew ass is bad, you understand?"

"Don't hurt me."

"I will give you your last chance. Where have
you got it hid?"

"I am a poor man." He spoke through cracked
lips.

The one in the dirty handkerchief raised his
gun. The other, staring into the mirror, waved
frantically, his black eyes bulging, but Morris saw
the blow descend and felt sick of himself, of
soured expectations, endless frustration, the years

gone up in smoke, he could not begin to count
how many. He had hoped for much in America
and got little. And because of him Helen and
Ida had less. He had defrauded them, he and the
bloodsucking store.

He fell without a cry. The end fitted the day. It
was his luck, others had better.

During the week that Morris lay in bed with a thickly bandaged head, Ida tended the store fitfully. She went up and down twenty times a day until her bones ached and her head hurt with all her worries. Helen stayed home Saturday, a half-day in her place, and Monday, to help her mother, but she could not risk longer than that, so Ida, who ate in snatches and worked up a massive nervousness, had to shut the store for a full day, although Morris angrily protested. He needed no attention, he insisted, and urged her to keep open at least half the day or he would lose his remaining few customers; but Ida, short of breath, said she hadn't the strength, her legs hurt. The grocer attempted to get up and pull on his pants but was struck by a violent headache and had to drag himself back to bed.

On the Tuesday the store was closed a man appeared in the neighborhood, a stranger who spent much of his time standing on Sam Pearl's corner with a toothpick in his teeth, intently observing the people who passed by; or he would drift down the long block of stores, some empty, from Pearl's to the bar at the far end of the street. Beyond that was a freight yard, and in the distance, a bulky

warehouse. After an occasional slow beer in the
tavern, the stranger turned the corner and wandered past the high-fenced coal yard; he would go
around the block until he got back to Sam's candy
store. Once in a while the man would walk over to
Morris's closed grocery, and with both hands shad-
ing his brow, stare through the window; sighing,
he went back to Sam's. When he had as much as he
could take of the corner he walked around the
block again, or elsewhere in the neighborhood.

Helen had pasted a paper on the window of the
front door, that said her father wasn't well but the
store would open on Wednesday. The man spent
a good deal of time studying this paper. He was
young, dark-bearded, wore an old brown rain-
stained hat, cracked patent leather shoes and a
long black overcoat that looked as if it had been
lived in. He was tall and not bad looking, except
for a nose that had been broken and badly set, un-
balancing his face. His eyes were melancholy.
Sometimes he sat at the fountain with Sam Pearl,
lost in his thoughts, smoking from a crumpled
pack of cigarettes he had bought with pennies.
Sam, who was used to all kinds of people, and
had in his time seen many strangers appear in the
neighborhood and as quickly disappear, showed no
special concern for the man, though Goldie, after
a full day of his presence complained that too
much was too much; he didn't pay rent. Sam did
notice that the stranger sometimes seemed to be
under stress, sighed much and muttered inaudibly
to himself. However, he paid the man scant attention—everybody to their own troubles. Other times
the stranger, as if he had somehow squared himself
with himself, seemed relaxed, even satisfied with

his existence. He read through Sam's magazines, strolled around in the neighborhood and when he returned, lit a fresh cigarette as he opened a paperbound book from the rack in the store. Sam served him coffee when he asked for it, and the stranger, squinting from the smoke of the butt in his mouth, carefully counted out five pennies to pay. Though nobody had asked him he said his name was Frank Alpine and he had lately come from the West, looking for a better opportunity. Sam advised if he could qualify for a chauffeur's license, to try for work as a hack driver. It wasn't a bad life. The man agreed but stayed around as if he was expecting something else to open up.

The day Ida reopened the grocery the stranger disappeared but he returned to the candy store the next morning, and seating himself at the fountain, asked for coffee. He looked bleary, unhappy, his beard hard, dark, contrasting with the pallor of his face; his nostrils were inflamed and his voice was husky. He looks half in his grave, Sam thought. God knows what hole he slept in last night.

As Frank Alpine was stirring his coffee, with his free hand he opened a magazine lying on the counter, and his eye was caught by a picture in color of a monk. He lifted the coffee cup to drink but had to put it down, and he stared at the picture for five minutes.

Sam, out of curiosity, went behind him with a broom, to see what he was looking at. The picture was of a thin-faced, dark-bearded monk in a coarse brown garment, standing barefooted on a sunny country road. His skinny, hairy arms were raised to a flock of birds that dipped over his head. In the background was a grove of leafy trees; and in the far distance a church in sunlight.

"He looks like some kind of a priest," Sam said cautiously.

"No, it's St. Francis of Assisi. You can tell from that brown robe he's wearing and all those birds in the air. That's the time he was preaching to them. When I was a kid, an old priest used to come to the orphans' home where I was raised, and every time he came he read us a different story about St. Francis. They are clear in my mind to this day."

"Stories are stories," Sam said.

"Don't ask me why I never forgot them."

Sam took a closer squint at the picture. "Talking to the birds? What was he—crazy? I don't say this out of any harm."

The stranger smiled at the Jew. "He was a great man. The way I look at it, it takes a certain kind of a nerve to preach to birds."

"That makes him great, because he talked to birds?"

"Also for other things. For instance, he gave everything away that he owned, every cent, all his clothes off his back. He enjoyed to be poor. He said poverty was a queen and he loved her like she was a beautiful woman."

Sam shook his head. "It ain't beautiful, kiddo. To be poor is dirty work."

"He took a fresh view of things."

The candy store owner glanced again at St. Francis, then poked his broom into a dirty corner. Frank, as he drank his coffee, continued to study the picture. He said to Sam, "Every time I read about somebody like him I get a feeling inside of me I have to fight to keep from crying. He was born good, which is a talent if you have it."

He spoke with embarrassment, embarrassing Sam.

Frank drained his cup and left.

That night as he was wandering past Morris's store he glanced through the door and saw Helen inside, relieving her mother. She looked up and noticed him staring at her through the plate glass. His appearance startled her; his eyes were haunted, hungry, sad; she got the impression he would come in and ask for a handout and had made up her mind to give him a dime, but instead he disappeared.

On Friday Morris weakly descended the stairs at six A.M., and Ida, nagging, came after him. She had been opening at eight o'clock and had begged him to stay in bed until then, but he had refused, saying he had to give the Poilisheh her roll.

"Why does three cents for a lousy roll mean more to you than another hour sleep?" Ida complained.

"Who can sleep?"

"You need rest, the doctor said."

"Rest I will take in my grave."

She shuddered. Morris said, "For fifteen years she gets here her roll, so let her get."

"All right, but let me open up. I will give her and you go back to bed."

"I stayed in bed too long. Makes me feel weak."

But the woman wasn't there and Morris feared he had lost her to the German. Ida insisted on dragging in the milk boxes, threatening to shout if he made a move for them. She packed the bottles into the refrigerator. After Nick Fuso they waited hours for another customer. Morris sat at the table, reading the paper, occasionally raising his hand gently to feel the bandage around his head. When he shut his eyes he still experienced moments of weakness. By noon he was glad to go upstairs and crawl into bed and he didn't get up until Helen came home.

The next morning he insisted on opening alone. The Poilisheh was there. He did not know her name. She worked somewhere in a laundry and had a little dog called Polaschaya. When she came home at night she took the little Polish dog for a walk around the block. He liked to run loose in the coal yard. She lived in one of the stucco houses nearby. Ida called her die antisemitke, but that part of her didn't bother Morris. She had come with it from the old country, a different kind of anti-Semitism from in America. Sometimes he suspected she needled him a little by asking for a "Jewish roll," and once or twice, with an odd smile, she wanted a "Jewish pickle." Generally she said nothing at all. This morning Morris handed her her roll and she said nothing. She didn't ask him about his bandaged head though her quick beady eyes stared at it, nor why he had not been there for a week; but she put six pennies on the counter instead of three. He figured she had taken a roll from the bag one of the days the store hadn't opened on time. He rang up the six-cent sale.

Morris went outside to pull in the two milk cases. He gripped the boxes but they were like rocks, so he let one go and tugged at the other. A storm cloud formed in his head and blew up to the size of a house. Morris reeled and almost fell into

the gutter, but he was caught by Frank Alpine, in
his long coat, steadied and led back into the store.
Frank then hauled in the milk cases and refrigerated the bottles. He quickly swept up behind the
counter and went into the back. Morris, recovered,
warmly thanked him.

Frank said huskily, his eyes on his scarred and
heavy hands, that he was new to the neighborhood but living here now with a married sister.
He had lately come from the West and was looking
for a better job.

The grocer offered him a cup of coffee, which he
at once accepted. As he sat down Frank placed
his hat on the floor at his feet, and he drank the
coffee with three heaping spoonfuls of sugar, to
get warm quick, he said. When Morris offered him
a seeded hard roll, he bit into it hungrily. "Jesus,
this is good bread." After he had finished he wiped
his mouth with his handkerchief, then swept the
crumbs off the table with one hand into the other,
and though Morris protested, he rinsed the cup
and saucer at the sink, dried them and set them on
top of the gas range, where the grocer had got
them.

"Much obliged for everything." He had picked
up his hat but made no move to leave.

"Once in San Francisco I worked in a grocery
for a couple of months," he remarked after a
minute, "only it was one of those supermarket
chain store deals."

"The chain store kills the small man."

"Personally I like a small store myself. I might
someday have one."

"A store is a prison. Look for something better."

"At least you're your own boss."

"To be a boss of nothing is nothing."

"Still and all, the idea of it appeals to me. The only thing is I would need experience on what goods to order. I mean about brand names, et cetera. I guess I ought to look for a job in a store and get more experience."

"Try the A&P," advised the grocer.

"I might."

Morris dropped the subject. The man put on his hat.

"What's the matter," he said, staring at the grocer's bandage, "did you have some kind of an accident to your head?"

Morris nodded. He didn't care to talk about it, so the stranger, somehow disappointed, left.

He happened to be in the street very early on Monday when Morris was again struggling with the milk cases. The stranger tipped his hat and said he was off to the city to find a job but he had time to help him pull in the milk. This he did and quickly left. However, the grocer thought he saw him pass by in the other direction about an hour later. That afternoon when he went for his *Forward* he noticed him sitting at the fountain with Sam Pearl. The next morning, just after six, Frank was there to help him haul in the milk bottles and he willingly accepted when Morris, who knew a poor man when he saw one, invited him for coffee.

"How is going now the job?" Morris asked as they were eating.

"So-so," said Frank, his glance shifting. He seemed preoccupied, nervous. Every few minutes he would set down his cup and uneasily look around. His lips parted as if to speak, his eyes took on a tormented expression, but then he shut his jaw as if he had decided it was better never to say what he intended. He seemed to need to talk, broke into sweat—his brow gleamed with it—his pupils widening as he struggled. He looked to Morris like someone who had to retch—no matter where; but after a brutal interval his eyes grew dull. He sighed heavily and gulped down the last of his coffee. After, he brought up a belch. This for a moment satisfied him.

Whatever he wants to say, Morris thought, let him say it to somebody else. I am only a grocer. He shifted in his chair, fearing to catch some illness.

Again the tall man leaned forward, drew a breath and once more was at the point of speaking, but now a shudder passed through him, followed by a fit of shivering.

The grocer hastened to the stove and poured out a cup of steaming coffee. Frank swallowed it in two terrible gulps. He soon stopped shaking, but looked defeated, humiliated, like somebody, the grocer felt, who had lost out on something he had wanted badly.

"You caught a cold?" he asked sympathetically.

The stranger nodded, scratched up a match on the sole of his cracked shoe, lit a cigarette and sat there, listless.

"I had a rough life," he muttered, and lapsed into silence.

Neither of them spoke. Then the grocer, to ease the other's mood, casually inquired, "Where in the neighborhood lives your sister? Maybe I know her."

Frank answered in a monotone. "I forget the exact address. Near the park somewheres."

"What is her name?"

"Mrs. Garibaldi."

"What kind name is this?"

"What do you mean?" Frank stared at him.

"I mean the nationality?"

"Italian. I am of Italian extraction. My name is Frank Alpine—Alpino in Italian."

The smell of Frank Alpine's cigarette compelled Morris to light his butt. He thought he could control his cough and tried but couldn't. He coughed till he feared his head would pop off. Frank watched with interest. Ida banged on the floor upstairs, and the grocer ashamedly pinched his cigarette and dropped it into the garbage pail.

"She don't like me to smoke," he explained between coughs. "My lungs ain't so healthy."

"Who don't?"

"My wife. It's a catarrh some kind. My mother had it all her life and lived till eighty-four. But they took a picture of my chest last year and found two dried spots. This frightened my wife."

Frank slowly put out his cigarette. "What I started out to say before about my life," he said heavily, "is that I have had a funny one, only I don't mean funny. I mean I've been through a lot. I've been close to some wonderful things—jobs, for instance, education, women, but close is as far as I go." His hands were tightly clasped between his knees. "Don't ask me why, but sooner or later everything I think is worth having gets away from me in some way or other. I work like a mule for what I want, and just when it looks like I am going to get it I make some kind of a stupid move, and everything that is just about nailed down tight blows up in my face."

"Don't throw away your chance for education," Morris advised. "It's the best thing for a young man."

"I could've been a college graduate by now, but when the time came to start going, I missed out because something else turned up that I took instead. With me one wrong thing leads to another and it ends in a trap. I want the moon so all I get is cheese."

"You are young yet."

"Twenty-five," he said bitterly.

"You look older."

"I feel old—damn old."

Morris shook his head.

"Sometimes I think your life keeps going the way it starts out on you," Frank went on. "The week after I was born my mother was dead and buried. I never saw her face, not even a picture. When I was five years old, one day my old man leaves this furnished room where we were staying, to get a pack of butts. He takes off and that was the last I ever saw of him. They traced him years later but by then he was dead. I was raised in an orphans' home and when I was eight they farmed me out to a tough family. I ran away ten times, also from the next people I lived with. I think about my life a lot. I say to myself, 'What do you expect to happen after all of that?' Of course, every now and again, you understand, I hit some nice good spots in between, but they are few and far, and usually I end up like I started out, with nothing."

The grocer was moved. Poor boy.

"I've often tried to change the way things work out for me but I don't know how, even when I think I do. I have it in my heart to do more than I can remember." He paused, cleared his throat and said, "That makes me sound stupid but it's not as easy as that. What I mean to say is that when I need it most something is missing in me, in me or on account of me. I always have this dream where I want to tell somebody something on the telephone so bad it hurts, but then when I am in the booth, instead of a phone being there, a bunch of bananas is hanging on a hook."

He gazed at the grocer then at the floor. "All my life I wanted to accomplish something worthwhile —a thing people will say took a little doing, but I don't. I am too restless—six months in any one place is too much for me. Also I grab at everything too quick—too impatient. I don't do what I have to—that's what I mean. The result is I move into a place with nothing, and I move out with nothing. You understand me?"

"Yes," said Morris.

Frank fell into silence. After a while he said, "I don't understand myself. I don't really know what I'm saying to you or why I am saying it."

"Rest yourself," said Morris.

"What kind of a life is that for a man my age?"

He waited for the grocer to reply—to tell him how to live his life, but Morris was thinking, I am sixty and he talks like me.

"Take some more coffee," he said.

"No, thanks." Frank lit another cigarette and smoked it to the tip. He seemed eased yet not eased, as though he had accomplished something (What? wondered the grocer) yet had not. His face was relaxed, almost sleepy, but he cracked the knuckles of both hands and silently sighed.

Why don't he go home? the grocer thought. I am a working man.

"I'm going." Frank got up but stayed.

"What happened to your head?" he asked again.

Morris felt the bandage. "This Friday before last I had here a holdup."

"You mean they slugged you?"

The grocer nodded.

"Bastards like that ought to die." Frank spoke vehemently.

Morris stared at him.

Frank brushed his sleeve. "You people are Jews, aren't you?"

"Yes," said the grocer, still watching him.

"I always liked Jews." His eyes were downcast.

Morris did not speak.

"I suppose you have some kids?" Frank asked.

"Me?"

"Excuse me for being curious."

"A girl." Morris sighed. "I had once a wonderful boy but he died from an ear sickness that they had in those days."

"Too bad." Frank blew his nose.

A gentleman, Morris thought with a watery eye.

"Is the girl the one that was here behind the counter a couple of nights last week?"

"Yes," the grocer replied, a little uneasily.

"Well, thanks for all the coffee."

"Let me make you a sandwich. Maybe you'll be hungry later."

"No thanks."

The Jew insisted, but Frank felt he had all he wanted from him at the moment.

Left alone, Morris began to worry about his health. He felt dizzy at times, often headachy.

Murderers, he thought. Standing before the cracked and faded mirror at the sink he unwound the bandage from his head. He wanted to leave it off but the scar was still ugly, not nice for the customers, so he tied a fresh bandage around his skull. As he did this he thought of that night with bitterness, recalling the buyer who hadn't come, nor had since then, nor ever would. Since his recovery, Morris had not spoken to Karp. Against words the liquor dealer had other words, but silence silenced him.

Afterward the grocer looked up from his paper and was startled to see somebody out front washing his window with a brush on a stick. He ran out with a roar to drive the intruder away, for there were nervy window cleaners who did the job without asking permission, then held out their palms to collect. But when Morris came out of the store he saw the window washer was Frank Alpine.

"Just to show my thanks and appreciation." Frank explained he had borrowed the pail from Sam Pearl and the brush and squeegee from the butcher next door.

Ida then entered the store by the inside door, and seeing the window being washed, hurried outside.

"You got rich all of a sudden?" she asked Morris, her face inflamed.

"He does me a favor," the grocer replied.

"That's right," said Frank, bearing down on the squeegee.

"Come inside, it's cold." In the store Ida asked, "Who is this goy?"

"A poor boy, an Italyener he looks for a job. He

gives me a help in the morning with the cases milk."

"If you sold containers like I told you a thousand times, you wouldn't need help."

"Containers leak. I like bottles."

"Talk to the wind," Ida said.

Frank came in blowing his breath on water-reddened fists. "How's it look now, folks, though you can't really tell till I do the inside."

Ida remarked under her breath, "Pay now for your favor."

"Fine," Morris said to Frank. He went to the register and rang up "no sale."

"No, thanks," Frank said, holding up his hand. "For services already rendered."

Ida reddened.

"Another cup coffee?" Morris asked.

"Thanks. Not as of now."

"Let me make you a sandwich?"

"I just ate."

He walked out, threw the dirty water into the gutter, returned the pail and brush, then came back to the grocery. He went behind the counter and into the rear, pausing to rap on the doorjamb.

"How do you like the clean window?" he asked Ida.

"Clean is clean." She was cool.

"I don't want to intrude here but your husband was nice to me, so I just thought maybe I could ask for one more small favor. I am looking for work and I want to try some kind of a grocery job just for size. Maybe I might like it, who knows? It happens I forgot some of the things about cutting and weighing and such, so I am wondering if you would mind me working around here for a couple-

three weeks without wages just so I could learn
again? It won't cost you a red cent. I know I am
a stranger but I am an honest guy. Whoever keeps
an eye on me will find that out in no time. That's
fair enough, isn't it?"

Ida said, "Mister, isn't here a school."

"What do you say, pop?" Frank asked Morris.

"Because somebody is a stranger don't mean
they ain't honest," answered the grocer. "This subject don't interest me. Interests me what you can
learn here. Only one thing"—he pressed his hand
to his chest—"a heartache."

"You got nothing to lose on my proposition, has
he now, Mrs?" Frank said. "I understand he don't
feel so hot yet, and if I helped him out a short
week or two it would be good for his health,
wouldn't it?"

Ida didn't answer.

But Morris said flatly, "No. It's a small, poor
store. Three people would be too much."

Frank flipped an apron off a hook behind the
door and before either of them could say a word,
removed his hat and dropped the loop over his
head. He tied the apron strings around him.

"How's that for fit?"

Ida flushed, and Morris ordered him to take it
off and put it back on the hook.

"No bad feelings, I hope," Frank said on his
way out.

Helen Bober and Louis Karp walked, no hands
touching, in the windy dark on the Coney Island
boardwalk.

Louis had, on his way home for supper that evening, stopped her in front of the liquor store, on her way in from work.

"How's about a ride in the Mercury, Helen? I never see you much anymore. Things were better in the bygone days in high school."

Helen smiled. "Honestly, Louis, that's so far away." A sense of mourning at once oppressed her, which she fought to a practiced draw.

"Near or far, it's all the same for me." He was built with broad back and narrow head, and despite prominent eyes was presentable. In high school, before he quit, he had worn his wet hair slicked straight back. One day, after studying a picture of a movie actor in the *Daily News,* he had run a part across his head. This was as much change as she had known in him. If Nat Pearl was ambitious, Louis made a relaxed living letting the fruit of his father's investment fall into his lap.

"Anyway," he said, "why not a ride for old-times' sake?"

She thought a minute, a gloved finger pressed into her cheek; but it was a fake gesture because she was lonely.

"For old-times' sake, where?"

"Name your scenery—continuous performance."

"The Island?"

He raised his coat collar. "Brr, it's a cold, windy night. You wanna freeze?"

Seeing her hesitation, he said, "But I'll die game. When'll I pick you up?"

"Ring my bell after eight and I'll come down."

"Check," Louis said. "Eight bells."

They walked to Seagate, where the boardwalk ended. She gazed with envy through a wire fence at the large lit houses fronting the ocean. The Island was deserted, except here and there an open hamburger joint or pinball machine concession. Gone from the sky was the umbrella of rosy light that glowed over the place in summertime. A few cold stars gleamed down. In the distance a dark Ferris wheel looked like a stopped clock. They stood at the rail of the boardwalk, watching the black, restless sea.

All during their walk she had been thinking about her life, the difference between her aloneness now and the fun when she was young and spending every day of summer in a lively crowd of kids on the beach. But as her high school friends had got married, she had one by one given them up; and as others of them graduated from college, envious, ashamed of how little she was accomplishing, she stopped seeing them too. At first it hurt to drop people but after a time it became a not too difficult habit. Now she saw almost no one, occasionally Betty Pearl, who understood, but not enough to make much difference.

Louis, his face reddened by the wind, sensed her mood.

"What's got in you, Helen?" he said, putting his arm around her.

"I can't really explain it. All night I've been thinking of the swell times we had on this beach when we were kids. And do you remember the parties? I suppose I'm blue that I'm no longer seventeen."

"What's so wrong about twenty-three?"

"It's old, Louis. Our lives change so quickly. You know what youth means?"

"Sure I know. You don't catch me giving away nothing for nothing. I got my youth yet."

"When a person is young he's privileged," Helen said, "with all kinds of possibilities. Wonderful things might happen, and when you get up in the morning you feel they will. That's what youth means, and that's what I've lost. Nowadays I feel that every day is like the day before, and what's worse, like the day after."

"So now you're a grandmother?"

"The world has shrunk for me."

"What do you wanna be—Miss Rheingold?"

"I want a larger and better life. I want the return of my possibilities."

"Such as which ones?"

She clutched the rail, cold through her gloves. "Education," she said, "prospects. Things I've wanted but never had."

"Also a man?"

"Also a man."

His arm tightened around her waist. "Talk is too cold, baby, how's about a kiss?"

She brushed his cold lips, then averted her head. He did not press her.

"Louis," she said, watching a far-off light on the water, "what do you want out of your life?"

He kept his arm around her. "The same thing I got—plus."

"Plus what?"

"Plus more, so my wife and family can have also."

"What if she wanted something different than you do?"

"Whatever she wanted I would gladly give her."

"But what if she wanted to make herself a better

person, have bigger ideas, live a more worthwhile life? We die so quickly, so helplessly. Life *has* to have some meaning."

"I ain't gonna stop anybody from being better," Louis said, "That's up to them."

"I suppose," she said.

"Say, baby, let's drop this deep philosophy and go trap a hamburger. My stomach complains."

"Just a little longer. It's been ages since I came here this late in the year."

He pumped his arms. "Jesus, this wind, it flies up my pants. At least gimme another kiss." He unbuttoned his overcoat.

She let him kiss her. He felt her breast. Helen stepped back out of his embrace. "Don't, Louis."

"Why not?" He stood there awkwardly, annoyed.

"It gives me no pleasure."

"I suppose I'm the first guy that ever gave it a nip?"

"Are you collecting statistics?"

"Okay," he said, "I'm sorry. You know I ain't a bad guy, Helen."

"I know you're not, but please don't do what I don't like."

"There was a time you treated me a whole lot better."

"That was the past, we were kids."

It's funny, she remembered, how necking made glorious dreams.

"We were older than that, up till the time Nat Pearl started in college, then you got interested in him. I suppose you got him in mind for the future?"

"If I do, I don't know it."

"But he's the one you want, ain't he? I like to know what that stuck up has got beside a college education? I work for my living."

"No, I don't want him, Louis." But she thought, Suppose Nat said I love you? For magic words a girl might do magic tricks.

"So if that's so, what's wrong with me?"

"Nothing. We're friends."

"Friends I got all I need."

"What do you need, Louis?"

"Cut out the wisecracks, Helen. Would it interest you that I would honestly like to marry you?" He paled at his nerve.

She was surprised, touched.

"Thank you," she murmured.

"Thank you ain't good enough. Give me yes or no."

"No, Louis."

"That's what I thought." He gazed blankly at the ocean.

"I never guessed you were at all remotely interested. You go with girls who are so different from me."

"Please, when I go with them you can't see my thoughts."

"No," she admitted.

"I can give you a whole lot better than you got."

"I know you can, but I want a different life from mine now, or yours. I don't want a storekeeper for a husband."

"Wines and liquors ain't exactly pisher groceries."

"I know."

"It ain't because your old man don't like mine?"

"No."

She listened to the wind-driven, sobbing surf. Louis said, "Let's go get the hamburgers."

"Gladly." She took his arm but could tell from the stiff way he walked that he was hurt.

As they drove home on the Parkway, Louis said, "If you can't have everything you want, at least take something. Don't be so goddam proud."

Touché. "What shall I take, Louis?"

He paused. "Take less."

"Less I'll never take."

"People got to compromise."

"I won't with my ideals."

"So what'll you be then, a dried-up prune of an old maid? What's the percentage of that?"

"None."

"So what'll you do?"

"I'll wait. I'll dream. Something will happen."

"Nuts," he said.

He let her off in front of the grocery.

"Thanks for everything."

"You'll make me laugh." Louis drove off.

The store was closed, upstairs dark. She pictured her father asleep after his long day, dreaming of Ephraim. What am I saving myself for? she asked herself. What unhappy Bober fate?

It snowed lightly the next day—too early in the year, complained Ida, and when the snow had melted it snowed again. The grocer remarked, as he was dressing in the dark, that he would shovel after he had opened the store. He enjoyed shoveling snow. It reminded him that he had practically lived in it in his boyhood; but Ida forbade him to exert himself because he still complained

of dizziness. Later, when he tried to lug the milk
cases through the snow, he found it all but impossible. And there was no Frank Alpine to help
him, for he had disappeared after washing the
window.

Ida came down shortly after her husband, in a
heavy cloth coat, a woolen scarf pinned around
her head and wearing galoshes. She shoveled a
path through the snow and together they pulled
in the milk. Only then did Morris notice that a
quart bottle was missing from one of the cases.

"Who took it?" Ida cried.

"How do I know?"

"Did you count yet the rolls?"

"No."

"I told you always to count right away."

"The baker will steal from me? I know him
twenty years."

"Count what everybody delivers, I told you a
thousand times."

He dumped the rolls out of the basket and
counted them. Three were missing and he had
sold only one to the Poilisheh. To appease Ida he
said they were all there.

The next morning another quart of milk and
two rolls were gone. He was worried but didn't
tell Ida the truth when she asked him if anything
else was missing. He often hid unpleasant news
from her because she made it worse. He mentioned the missing bottle to the milkman, who answered, "Morris, I swear I left every bottle in that
case. Am I responsible for this lousy neighborhood?"

He promised to cart the milk cases into the vestibule for a few days. Maybe whoever was stealing

the bottles would be afraid to go in there. Morris considered asking the milk company for a storage box. Years ago he had had one at the curb, a large wooden box in which the milk was padlocked; but he had given it up after developing a hernia lifting the heavy cases out, so he decided against a box.

On the third day, when a quart of milk and two rolls had again been taken, the grocer, much disturbed, considered calling the police. It wasn't the first time he had lost milk and rolls in this neighborhood. That had happened more than once—usually some poor person stealing a breakfast. For this reason Morris preferred not to call the police but to get rid of the thief by himself. To do it, he would usually wake up very early and wait at his bedroom window in the dark. Then when the man—sometimes it was a woman—showed up and was helping himself to the milk, Morris would quickly raise the window and shout down, "Get outa here, you thief you." The thief, startled—sometimes it was a customer who could afford to buy the milk he was stealing—would drop the bottle and run. Usually he never appeared again—a lost customer cut another way —and the next goniff was somebody else.

So this morning Morris arose at four-thirty, a little before the milk was delivered, and sat in the cold in his long underwear, to wait. The street was heavy with darkness as he peered down. Soon the milk truck came, and the milkman, his breath foggy, lugged the two cases of milk into the vestibule. Then the street was silent again, the night dark, the snow white. One or two people trudged by. An hour later, Witzig, the baker, delivered the rolls, but no one else stopped at the door. Just before six Morris dressed hastily and went downstairs. A bottle of milk was gone, and when he counted the rolls, so were two of them.

He still kept the truth from Ida. The next night she awoke and found him at the window in the dark.

"What's the matter?" she asked, sitting up in bed.

"I can't sleep."

"So don't sit in your underwear in the cold. Come back to bed."

He did as she said. Later, the milk and rolls were missing.

In the store he asked the Poilisheh whether she had seen anyone sneak into the vestibule and steal a quart of milk. She stared at him with small eyes, grabbed the sliced roll and slammed the door.

Morris had a theory that the thief lived on the block. Nick Fuso wouldn't do such a thing; if he did Morris would have heard him going down the stairs, then coming up again. The thief was somebody from outside. He sneaked along the street close to the houses, where Morris couldn't see him because of the cornice that hung over the store; then he softly opened the hall door, took the milk, two rolls from the bag, and stole away, hugging the house fronts.

The grocer suspected Mike Papadopolous, the Greek boy who lived on the floor above Karp's store. He had served a reformatory sentence at eighteen. A year later he had in the dead of night climbed down the fire escape overhanging Karp's back yard, boosted himself up on the fence and forced a window into the grocery. There he stole three cartons of cigarettes, and a roll of dimes that Morris had left in the cash register. In the morning, as the grocer was opening the store, Mike's mother, a thin, old-looking woman, returned the cigarettes and dimes to him. She had caught her son coming in with them and had walloped his head with a shoe. She clawed his face, making him confess what he had done. Returning the cigarettes and dimes, she had begged Morris not to have the boy arrested and he had assured her he wouldn't do such a thing.

On this day that he had guessed it might be Mike taking the milk and rolls, shortly after eight A.M., Morris went up the stairs and knocked reluctantly on Mrs. Papadopolous' door.

"Excuse me that I bother you," he said, and told her what had been happening to his milk and rolls.

"Mike work all nights in restaurants," she said. "No come home till nine o'clock in mornings. Sleep all days." Her eyes smoldered. The grocer left.

Now he was greatly troubled. Should he tell Ida and let her call the police? They were bothering him at least once a week with questions about the holdup but had produced nobody. Still, maybe it would be best to call them, for this stealing had gone on for almost a week. Who could afford it? Yet he waited, and that night as he was leaving the store by the side door, which he always padlocked after shutting the front door from inside, he flicked on the cellar light and as he peered down the stairs, his nightly habit, his heart tightened with foreboding that somebody was down there. Morris unlocked the lock, went back into the store and got a hatchet. Forcing his courage, he slowly descended the wooden steps. The cellar was empty. He searched in the dusty storage bins, poked around all over, but there was no sign of anybody.

In the morning he told Ida what was going on and she, calling him big fool, telephoned the police. A stocky, red-faced detective came, Mr. Minogue, from a nearby precinct, who was in charge of investigating Morris's holdup. He was a soft-spoken, unsmiling man, bald, a widower who had once lived in this neighborhood. He had a son Ward, who had gone to Helen's junior high school, a wild boy, always in trouble for manhandling girls. When he saw one he knew playing in front of her house, or on the stoop, he would come swooping down and chase her into the hall. There, no matter how desperately the girl struggled, or tenderly begged him to stop, Ward forced his hand down her dress and squeezed her breast till she screamed. Then by the time her mother came running down the stairs he had ducked out of the hall, leaving the girl sobbing. The detective, when he heard of these happenings, regularly beat up his son, but it didn't do much good. Then one day, about eight years ago, Ward was canned from his job for stealing from the company. His father beat him sick and bloody with his billy and drove him out of the neighborhood. After that, Ward disappeared and nobody knew where he had gone. People felt sorry for the detective, for he was a strict man and they knew what it meant to him to have such a son.

Mr. Minogue seated himself at the table in the rear and listened to Ida's complaint. He slipped on his glasses and wrote in a little black notebook. The detective said he would have a cop watch the store mornings after the milk was delivered, and if there was any more trouble to let him know.

As he was leaving, he said, "Morris, would you recognize Ward Minogue if you happened to see him again? I hear he's been seen around but whereabouts I don't know."

"I don't know," said Morris. "Maybe yes or maybe no. I didn't see him for years."

"If I ever meet up with him," said the detective, "I might bring him in to you for identification."

"What for?"

"I don't know myself—just for possible identification."

Ida said afterward that if Morris had called the police in the first place, he might have saved himself a few bottles of milk that they could hardly afford to lose.

That night, on an impulse, the grocer closed the store an hour later than usual. He snapped on the cellar light and cautiously descended the stairs, gripping his hatchet. Near the bottom he uttered a cry and the hatchet fell from his hands. A man's drawn and haggard face stared up at him in dismay. It was Frank Alpine, gray and unshaven. He had been asleep with his hat and coat on, sitting on a box against the wall. The light had awakened him.

"What do you want here?" Morris cried out.

"Nothing," Frank said dully. "I have just been sleeping in the cellar. No harm done."

"Did you steal from me my milk and rolls?"

"Yes," he confessed. "On account of I was hungry."

"Why didn't you ask me?"

Frank got up. "Nobody has any responsibility to take care of me but myself. I couldn't find any job. I used up every last cent I had. My coat is too thin for this cold and lousy climate. The snow and the rain get in my shoes so I am always shivering. Also, I had no place to sleep. That's why I came down here."

"Don't you stay any more with your sister?"

"I have no sister. That was a lie I told you. I am alone by myself."

"Why you told me you had a sister?"

"I didn't want you to think I was a bum."

Morris regarded the man silently. "Were you ever in prison sometimes?"

"Never, I swear to Christ."

"How you came to me in my cellar?"

"By accident. One night I was walking around in the snow so I tried the cellar door and found out you left it unlocked, then I started coming down at night about an hour after you closed the store. In the morning, when they delivered the milk and rolls, I sneaked up through the hall, opened the door and took what I needed for breakfast. That's practically all I ate all day. After you came down and got busy with some customer or a salesman, I left by the hallway with the empty milk bottle under my coat. Later I threw it away in a lot. That's all there is to it. Tonight I took a chance and came in while you were still in the back of the store, because I have a cold and don't feel too good."

"How can you sleep in such a cold and drafty cellar?"

"I slept in worse."

"Are you hungry now?"

"I'm always hungry."

"Come upstairs."

Morris picked up his hatchet, and Frank, blowing his nose in his damp handkerchief, followed him up the stairs.

Morris lit a light in the store and made two fat liverwurst sandwiches with mustard, and in the back heated up a can of bean soup. Frank sat at the table in his coat, his hat lying at his feet. He ate with great hunger, his hand trembling as he brought the spoon to his mouth. The grocer had to look away.

As the man was finishing his meal, with coffee and cup cakes, Ida came down in felt slippers and bathrobe.

"What happened?" she asked in fright, when she saw Frank Alpine.

"He's hungry," Morris said.

She guessed at once. "He stole the milk!"

"He was hungry," explained Morris. "He slept in the cellar."

"I was practically starving," said Frank.

"Why didn't you look for a job?" Ida asked.

"I looked all over."

After, Ida said to Frank, "When you finish, please go someplace else." She turned to her husband. "Morris, tell him to go someplace else. We are poor people."

"This he knows."

"I'll go away," Frank said, "as the lady wishes."

"Tonight is already too late," Morris said. "Who wants he should walk all night in the streets?"

"I don't want him here." She was tense.

"Where you want him to go?"

Frank set his coffee cup on the saucer and listened with interest.

"This ain't my business," Ida answered.

"Don't anybody worry," said Frank. "I'll leave in ten minutes' time. You got a cigarette, Morris?"

The grocer went to the bureau and took out of the drawer a crumpled pack of cigarettes.

"It's stale," he apologized.

"Don't make any difference." Frank lit a stale cigarette, inhaling with pleasure.

"I'll go after a short while," he said to Ida.

"I don't like trouble," she explained.

"I won't make any. I might look like a bum in these clothes, but I am not. All my life I lived with good people."

"Let him stay here tonight on the couch," Morris said to Ida.

"No. Give him better a dollar he should go someplace else."

"The cellar would be fine," Frank remarked.

"It's too damp. Also rats."

"If you let me stay there one more night I promise I will get out the first thing in the morning. You don't have to be afraid to trust me. I am an honest man."

"You can sleep here," Morris said.

"Morris, you crazy," shouted Ida.

"I'll work it off for you," Frank said. "Whatever I cost you I'll pay you back. Anything you want me to do, I'll do it."

"We will see," Morris said.

"No," insisted Ida.

But Morris won out, and they went up, leaving Frank in the back, the gas radiator left lit.

"He will clean out the store," Ida said wrathfully.

"Where is his truck?" Morris asked, smiling. Seriously he said, "He's a poor boy. I feel sorry for him."

They went to bed. Ida slept badly. Sometimes she was racked by awful dreams. Then she awoke and sat up in bed, straining to hear noises in the store—of Frank packing huge bags of groceries to steal. But there was no sound. She dreamed she came down in the morning and all the stock was gone, the shelves as barren as the picked bones of dead birds. She dreamed, too, that the Italyener had sneaked up into the house and was peeking through the keyhole of Helen's door. Only when Morris got up to open the store did Ida fall fitfully asleep.

The grocer trudged down the stairs with a dull pain in his head. His legs felt weak. His sleep had not been refreshing.

The snow was gone from the streets and the milk boxes were again lying on the sidewalk near the curb. None of the bottles were missing. The grocer was about to drag in the milk cases when the Poilisheh came by. She went inside and placed three pennies on the counter. He entered with a brown bag of rolls, cut up one and wrapped it. She took it wordlessly and left.

Morris looked through the window in the wall. Frank was asleep on the couch in his clothes, his coat covering him. His beard was black, his mouth loosely opened.

The grocer went out into the street, grabbed both milk boxes and yanked. The shape of a black hat blew up in his head, flared into hissing light, and exploded. He thought he was rising but felt himself fall.

Frank dragged him in and laid him on the couch. He ran upstairs and banged on the door. Helen, holding a housecoat over her nightdress, opened it. She suppressed a cry.

"Tell your mother your father just passed out. I called the ambulance."

She screamed. As he ran down the stairs he could hear Ida moaning. Frank hurried into the back of the store. The Jew lay white and motionless on the couch. Frank gently removed his apron. Draping the loop over his own head, he tied the tapes around him.

"I need the experience," he muttered.

Morris had reopened the wound on his head. The ambulance doctor, the same who had treated him after the holdup, said he had got up too soon last time and worn himself out. He again bandaged the grocer's head, saying to Ida, "This time let him lay in bed a good couple of weeks till his strength comes back." "You tell him, doctor," she begged, "he don't listen to me." So the doctor told Morris, and Morris weakly nodded. Ida, in a gray state of collapse, remained with the patient all day. So did Helen, after calling the ladies' underthings concern where she worked. Frank Alpine stayed competently downstairs in the store. At noon Ida remembered him and came down to tell him to leave. Recalling her dreams, she connected him with their new misfortune. She felt that if he had not stayed the night, this might not have happened.

Frank was clean-shaven in the back, having borrowed Morris's safety razor, his thick hair neatly combed, and when she appeared he hopped up to ring open the cash register, showing her a pile of puffy bills.

"Fifteen," he said, "count every one."

She was astonished. "How is so much?"

He explained, "We had a busy morning. A lot of people stopped in to ask about Morris's accident."

Ida had planned to replace him with Helen for the time being, until she herself could take over, but she was now of two minds.

"Maybe you can stay," she faltered, "if you want to, till tomorrow."

"I'll sleep in the cellar, Mrs. You don't have to worry about me. I am as honest as the day."

"Don't sleep in the cellar," she said with a tremble to her voice, "my husband said on the couch. What can anybody steal here? We have nothing."

"How is he now?" Frank asked in a low voice.

She blew her nose.

The next morning Helen went reluctantly to work. Ida came down at ten to see how things were. This time there were only eight dollars in the drawer, but still better than lately. He apologized, "Not so good today, but I wrote down every article I sold so you'll know nothing stuck to my fingers." He produced a list of goods sold, written on wrapping paper. She happened to notice that it began with three cents for a roll. Glancing around, Ida saw he had packed out the few cartons delivered yesterday, swept up, washed the window from the inside and had straightened the cans on the shelves.

The place looked a little less dreary.

During the day he also kept himself busy with odd jobs. He cleaned the trap of the kitchen sink, which swallowed water slowly, and in the store fixed a light whose chain wouldn't pull, making useless one lamp. Neither of them mentioned his

leaving. Ida, still uneasy, wanted to tell him to go
but she couldn't ask Helen to stay home any
more, and the prospect of two weeks alone in the
store, with her feet and a sick man in the bargain
to attend upstairs, was too much for her. Maybe
she would let the Italian stay ten days or so. With
Morris fairly well recovered there would be no
reason to keep him after that. In the meantime he
would have three good meals a day and a bed, for
being little more than a watchman. What business, after all, did they do here? And while Morris
was not around she would change a thing or two
she should have done before. So when the milkman stopped by for yesterday's empties, she ordered containers brought from now on. Frank Alpine heartily approved. "Why should we bother
with bottles?" he said.

Despite all she had to do upstairs, and her recent good impressions of him, Ida haunted the
store, watching his every move. She was worried
because, now, not Morris but she was responsible
for the man's presence in the store. If something
bad happened, it would be her fault. Therefore,
though she climbed the stairs often to tend to her
husband's needs, she hurried back down, arriving
pale and breathless to see what Frank was up to.
But anything he happened to be doing was help-
ful. Her suspicions died slowly, though they never
wholly died.

She tried not to be too friendly to him, to make
him feel that a distant relationship meant a short
one. When they were in the back or for a few minutes together behind the counter she discouraged
conversation, took up something to do, or clean,
or her paper to read. And in the matter of teach-

ing him the business there was also little to say.
Morris had price tags displayed under all items on
the shelves, and Ida supplied Frank with a list of
prices for meats and salads and for the miscel-
laneous unmarked things like loose coffee, rice or
beans. She taught him how to wrap neatly and
efficiently, as Morris had long ago taught her, how
to read the scale and to set and handle the electric
meat slicer. He caught on quickly; she suspected
he knew more than he said he did. He added rap-
idly and accurately, did not overcut meats or over-
load the scale on bulk items, as she had urged him
not to do, and judged well the length of paper
needed to wrap with, and what number bag to
pack goods into, conserving the larger bags which
cost more money. Since he learned so fast, and
since she had seen in him not the least evidence
of dishonesty (a hungry man who took milk and
rolls, though not above suspicion, was not the
same as a thief), Ida forced herself to remain upstairs with more calm, in order to give Morris his
medicine, bathe her aching feet and keep up the
house, which was always dusty from the coal yard.
Yet she felt, whenever she thought of it, always a
little troubled at the thought of a stranger's presence below, a goy, after all, and she looked forward to the time when he was gone.

Although his hours were long—six to six, at
which time she served him his supper—Frank
was content. In the store he was quits with the
outside world, safe from cold, hunger and a damp
bed. He had cigarettes when he wanted them and
was comfortable in clean clothes Morris had sent
down, even a pair of pants that fitted him after
Ida lengthened and pressed the cuffs. The store

was fixed, a cave, motionless. He had all his life
been on the move, no matter where he was; here
he somehow couldn't be. Here he could stand at
the window and watch the world go by, content
to be here.

It wasn't a bad life. He woke before dawn. The
Polish dame was planted at the door like a statue,
distrusting him with beady eyes to open the place
in time for her to get to work. Her he didn't like;
he would gladly have slept longer. To get up in
the middle of the night for three lousy cents was
a joke but he did it for the Jew. After packing
away the milk containers, turning bottomside up
the occasional one that leaked, he swept the store
and then the sidewalk. In the back he washed,
shaved, had coffee and a sandwich, at first made
with meat from a ham or roast pork butt, then
after a few days, from the best cut. As he smoked
after coffee he thought of everything he could do
to improve this dump if it were his. When somebody came into the store he was up with a bound,
offering service with a smile. Nick Fuso, on
Frank's first day, was surprised to see him there,
knowing Morris could not afford a clerk. But
Frank said that though the pay was scarce there
were other advantages. They spoke about this and
that, and when the upstairs tenant learned Frank
Alpine was a paisan, he told him to come up and
meet Tessie. She cordially invited him for maca-
roni that same night, and he said he would come
if they let him bring the macs.

Ida, after the first few days, began to go down at
her regular hour, around ten, after she had finished the housework; and she busied herself with
writing in a notebook which bills they had got

and which paid. She also wrote out, in a halting hand, a few meager special-account checks for bills that could not be paid in cash directly to the drivers, mopped the kitchen floor, emptied the garbage pail into the metal can on the curb outside and prepared salad if it was needed. Frank watched her shred cabbage on the meat slicer for coleslaw, which she made in careful quantity, because if it turned sour it had to be dumped into the garbage. Potato salad was a bigger job, and she cooked up a large pot of new potatoes, which Frank helped her peel hot in their steaming jackets. Every Friday she prepared fish cakes and a panful of homemade baked beans, first soaking the little beans overnight, pouring out the water, then spreading brown sugar on top before baking. Her expression as she dipped in among the soggy beans pieces of ham from a butt she had cut up caught his eye, and he felt for her repugnance for hating to touch the ham, and some for himself because he had never lived this close to Jews before. At lunchtime there was a little "rush," which meant that a few dirty-faced laborers from the coal yard and a couple of store clerks from on the block wanted sandwiches and containers of hot coffee. But the "rush," for which they both went behind the counter, petered out in a matter of minutes and then came the dead hours of the afternoon. Ida said he ought to take some time off, but he answered that he had nowhere special to go and stayed in the back, reading the *Daily News* on the couch, or flipping through some magazines that he had got out of the public library, which he had discovered during one of his solitary walks in the neighborhood.

At three, when Ida departed for an hour or so to see if Morris needed something, and to rest, Frank felt relieved. Alone, he did a lot of casual eating, sometimes with unexpected pleasure. He sampled nuts, raisins, and small boxes of stale dates or dried figs, which he liked anyway; he also opened packages of crackers, macaroons, cupcakes and doughnuts, tearing up their wrappers into small pieces and flushing them down the toilet. Sometimes in the middle of eating sweets he would get very hungry for something more substantial, so he made a thick meat and Swiss cheese sandwich on a seeded hard roll spread with mustard, and swallowed it down with a bottle of ice-cold beer. Satisfied, he stopped roaming in the store.

Now and then there were sudden unlooked-for flurries of customers, mostly women, whom he waited on attentively, talking to them about all kinds of things. The drivers, too, liked his sociability and cheery manner and stayed to chew the fat. Otto Vogel, once when he was weighing a ham, warned him in a low voice, "Don't work for a Yid, kiddo. They will steal your ass while you are sitting on it." Frank, though he said he didn't expect to stay long, felt embarrassed for being there; then, to his surprise, he got another warning, from an apologetic Jew salesman of paper products, Al Marcus, a prosperous, yet very sick and solemn character who wouldn't stop working. "This kind of a store is a death tomb, positive," Al Marcus said. "Run out while you can. Take my word, if you stay six months, you'll stay forever."

"Don't worry about that," answered Frank.

Alone afterward, he stood at the window, thinking thoughts about his past, and wanting a new life. Would he ever get what he wanted? Sometimes he stared out of the back yard window at nothing at all, or at the clothesline above, moving idly in the wind, flying Morris's scarecrow union suits, Ida's hefty bloomers, modestly folded lengthwise, and her housedresses guarding her daughter's flower-like panties and restless brassières.

In the evening, whether he wanted to or not, he was "off." Ida insisted, fair was fair. She fed him a quick supper and allowed him, with apologies because she couldn't afford more, fifty cents spending money. He occasionally passed the time upstairs with the Fusos or went with them to a picture at the local movie house. Sometimes he walked, in spite of the cold, and stopped off at a poolroom he knew, about a mile and a half from the grocery store. When he got back, always before closing, for Ida wouldn't let him keep a key to the store in his pocket, she counted up the day's receipts, put most of the cash into a small paper bag and took it with her, leaving Frank five dollars to open up with in the morning. After she had gone, he turned the key in the front door lock, hooked the side door through which she had left, put out the store lights and sat in his undershirt in the rear, reading tomorrow's pink-sheeted paper that he had picked off Sam Pearl's stand on his way home. Then he undressed and went restlessly to bed in a pair of Morris's bulky, rarely used, flannel pajamas.

The old dame, he thought with disgust, always hurried him out of the joint before her daughter came down for supper.

The girl was in his mind a lot. He couldn't help it, imagined seeing her in the things that were hanging on the line—he had always had a good imagination. He pictured her as she came down the stairs in the morning; also saw himself standing in the hall after she came home, watching her skirts go flying as she ran up the stairs. He rarely saw her around, had never spoken to her but twice, on the day her father had passed out. She had kept her distance—who could blame her, dressed as he was and what he looked like then? He had the feeling as he spoke to her, a few hurried words, that he knew more about her than anybody would give him credit for. He had got this thought the first time he had ever laid eyes on her, that night he saw her through the grocery window. When she had looked at him he was at once aware of something starved about her, a hunger in her eyes he couldn't forget because it made him remember his own, so he knew how wide open she must be. But he wouldn't try to push anything, for he had heard that these Jewish babes could be troublemakers and he was not looking for any of that now—at least no more than usual; besides, he didn't want to spoil anything before it got started. There were some dames you had to wait for—for them to come to you.

His desire grew to get to know her, he supposed because she had never once come into the store in all the time he was there except after he left at night. There was no way to see and talk to her to

her face, and this increased his curiosity. He felt
they were both lonely but her old lady kept her
away from him as if he had a dirty disease; the result was he grew more impatient to find out what
she was like, get to be friends with her for whatever it was worth. So, since she was never around,
he listened and watched for her. When he heard
her walking down the stairs he went to the front
window and stood there waiting for her to come
out; he tried to look casual, as if he weren't watching, just in case she happened to glance back and
see him; but she never did, as if she liked nothing about the place enough to look back on. She
had a pretty face and a good figure, small-breasted,
neat, as if she had meant herself to look that way.
He liked to watch her brisk, awkward walk till
she turned the corner. It was a sexy walk, with a
wobble in it, a strange movement, as though she
might dart sideways although she was walking
forward. Her legs were just a bit bowed, and maybe
that was the sexy part of it. She stayed in his mind
after she had turned the corner; her legs and
small breasts and the pink brassières that covered
them. He would be reading something or lying on
his back on the couch, smoking, and she would appear in his mind, walking to the corner. He did
not have to shut his eyes to see her. Turn around,
he said out loud, but in his thoughts she wouldn't.

To see her coming toward him he stood at the
lit grocery window at night, but often before he
could catch sight of her she was on her way upstairs, or already changing her dress in her room,
and his chance was over for the day. She came
home about a quarter to six, sometimes a little
earlier, so he tried to be at the window around

then, which wasn't so easy because that was the time for Morris's few supper customers to come in. So he rarely saw her come home from work, though he always heard her on the stairs. One day things were slower than usual in the store, it was dead at five-thirty, and Frank said to himself, Today I will see her. He combed his hair in the toilet so that Ida wouldn't notice, changed into a clean apron, lit a cigarette, and stood at the window, visible in its light. At twenty to six, just after he had practically shoved a woman out of the joint, a dame who had happened to walk in off the trolley, he saw Helen turn Sam Pearl's corner. Her face was prettier than he had remembered and his throat tightened as she walked to within a couple of feet of him, her eyes blue, her hair, which she wore fairly long, brown, and she had an absent-minded way of smoothing it back off the side of her face. He thought she didn't look Jewish, which was all to the good. But her expression was discontented, and her mouth a little drawn. She seemed to be thinking of something she had no hope of ever getting. This moved him, so that when she glanced up and saw his eyes on her, his face plainly showed his emotion. It must have bothered her because she quickly walked, without noticing him further, to the hall and disappeared inside.

The next morning he didn't see her—as if she had sneaked out on him—and at night he was waiting on somebody when she returned from work; regretfully he heard the door slam behind her. Afterward he felt downhearted; every sight lost to a guy who lived with his eyes was lost for all time. He thought up different ways to meet her and exchange a few words. What he had on his mind to say to her about himself was beginning to weigh on him, though he hadn't clearly figured out the words. Once he thought of coming in on her unexpectedly while she was eating her supper, but then he would have Ida to deal with. He also had the idea of opening the door the next time he saw her and calling her into the store; he could say that some guy had telephoned her, and after that talk about something else, but nobody did call her. She was in her way a lone bird, which suited him fine, though why she should be with her looks he couldn't figure out. He got the feeling that she wanted something big out of life, and this scared him. Still, he tried to think of schemes of getting her inside the store, even planning to ask her something like did she know where her old man kept his saw; only she mightn't like that, her mother being around all day to tell him. He had to watch out not to scare her any farther away than the old dame had done.

For a couple of nights after work he stood in a hallway next door to the laundry across the street in the hope that she would come out to do some errand, then he would cross over, tip his hat and ask if he could keep her company to where she was going. But this did not pay off either, because she didn't leave the house. The second night he waited fruitlessly until Ida put out the lights in the grocery window.

One evening toward the end of the second week after Morris's accident, Frank's loneliness burdened him to the point of irritation. He was eating his supper a few minutes after Helen had returned from work, while Ida happened to be up-

stairs with Morris. He had seen Helen come round
the corner and had nodded to her as she approached the house. Caught by surprise, she half-
smiled, then entered the hall. It was then the lonely feeling gripped him. While he was eating, he
felt he had to get her into the store before her old
lady came down and it was time for him to leave.
The only excuse he could think of was to call
Helen to answer the phone and after he would
say that the guy must've hung up. It was a trick
but he had to do it. He warned himself not to,
because it would be starting out the wrong way
with her and he might someday regret it. He tried
to think of a better way but time was pressing
him and he couldn't.

Frank got up, went over to the bureau, and took
the phone off its cradle. He then walked out into
the hall, opened the vestibule door, and holding
his breath, pressed the Bober bell.

Ida looked over the banister. "What's the matter?"

"Telephone for Helen."

He could see her hesitate, so he returned quickly to the store. He sat down, pretending to be eating, his heart whamming so hard it hurt. All he
wanted, he told himself, was to talk to her a minute so the next time would be easier.

Helen eagerly entered the kitchen. On the
stairs she had noticed the excitement that flowed
through her. My God, it's gotten to be that a
phone call is an event.

If it's Nat, she thought, I might give him another chance.

Frank half-rose as she entered, then sat down.

"Thanks," she said to him as she picked up the phone.

"Hello." While she waited he could hear the buzz in the receiver.

"There's nobody there," she said mystified.

He laid down his fork. "This girl called you," he said gently.

But when he saw the disappointment in her eyes, how bad she felt, he felt bad.

"You must've been cut off."

She gave him a long look. She was wearing a white blouse that showed the firmness of her small breasts. He wet his dry lips, trying to figure out some quick way to square himself, but his mind, usually crowded with all sorts of schemes, had gone blank. He felt very bad, as he had known he would, that he had done what he had. If he had it to do over he wouldn't do it this way.

"Did she leave you her name?" Helen asked.

"No."

"It wasn't Betty Pearl?"

"No."

She absently brushed back her hair. "Did she say anything to you?"

"Only to call you." He paused. "Her voice was nice—like yours. Maybe she didn't get me straight when I said you were upstairs but I would ring your doorbell, and that's why she hung up."

"I don't know why anybody would do that."

Neither did he. He wanted to step clear of his mess but saw no way other than to keep on lying. But lying made their talk useless. When he lied he was somebody else lying to somebody else. It wasn't the two of them as they were. He should have kept that in his mind.

She stood at the bureau, holding the telephone in her hand as if still expecting the buzz to become a voice; so he waited for the same thing, a voice to speak and say he had been telling the truth, that he was a man of fine character. Only that didn't happen either.

He gazed at her with dignity as he considered saying the simple truth, starting from there, come what would, but the thought of confessing what he had done almost panicked him.

"I'm sorry," he said brokenly, but by then she was gone, and he was attempting to fix in his memory what she had looked like so close.

Helen too was troubled. Not only could she not explain why she believed yet did not fully believe him, nor why she had lately become so conscious of his presence among them, though he never strayed from the store, but she was also disturbed by her mother's efforts to keep her away from him. "Eat when he leaves," Ida had said. "I am not used to goyim in my house." This annoyed Helen because of the assumption that she would keel over for somebody just because he happened to be a gentile. It meant, obviously, her mother didn't trust her. If she had been casual about him, Helen doubted she would have paid him any attention to speak of. He was interesting looking, true, but what except a poor grocery clerk? Out of nothing Ida was trying to make something.

Though Ida was still concerned at having the young Italian around the place, she observed with pleased surprise how practically from the day of his appearance, the store had improved. During the first week there were days when they had taken

in from five to seven dollars more than they were
averaging daily in the months since summer. And
the same held for the second week. The store
was of course still a poor store, but with this forty
to fifty a week more they might at least limp along
until a buyer appeared. She could at first not understand why more people were coming in, why
more goods were being sold. True, the same thing
had happened before. Without warning, after a
long season of dearth, three or four customers,
lost faces, straggled in one day, as if they had been
let out of their poor rooms with a few pennies in
their pockets. And others, who had skimped on
food, began to buy more. A storekeeper could tell
almost at once when times were getting better.
People seemed less worried and irritable, less in
competition for the little sunlight in the world.
Yet the curious thing was that business, according
to most of the drivers, had not very much improved anywhere. One of them said that Schmitz
around the corner was having his troubles too;
furthermore he wasn't feeling so good. So the sudden pickup of business in the store, Ida thought,
would not have happened without Frank Alpine.
It took her a while to admit this to herself.

The customers seemed to like him. He talked a
lot as he waited on them, sometimes saying things
that embarrassed Ida but made the customers, the
gentile housewives, laugh. He somehow drew in
people she had never before seen in the neighborhood, not only women, men too. Frank tried things
that Morris and she could never do, such as attempting to sell people more than they asked for,
and usually he succeeded. "What can you do with
a quarter of a pound?" he would say. "A quarter

is for the birds—not even a mouthful. Better
make it a half." So they would make it a half. Or
he would say, "Here's a new brand of mustard
that we just got in today. It weighs two ounces
more than the stuff they sell you in the super-
markets for the same price. Why don't you give it
a try? If you don't like it, bring it back and I will
gargle it." And they laughed and bought it. This
made Ida wonder if Morris and she were really
suited to the grocery business. They had never
been salesmen.

One of the women customers 'called Frank a
supersalesman, a word that brought a pleased
smile to his lips. He was clever and worked hard.
Ida's respect for him reluctantly grew; gradually
she became more relaxed in his presence. Morris
was right in recognizing that he was not a bum
but a boy who had gone through bad times. She
pitied him for having lived in an orphan asylum.
He did his work quickly, never complained, kept
himself neat and clean now that he had soap and
water around, and answered her politely. The one
or two times, just lately, that he had briefly talked
to Helen in her presence, he had spoken like a
gentleman and didn't try to stretch a word into a
mouthful. Ida discussed the situation with Morris
and they raised his "spending money" from fifty
cents a day to five dollars for the week. Despite
her good will to him, this worried Ida, but, after
all, he was bringing more money into the store,
the place looked spic and span—let him keep five
dollars of their poor profit. Bad as things still
were, he willingly did so much extra around the
store—how could they not pay him a little some-

thing? Besides, she thought, he would soon be leaving.

Frank accepted the little raise with an embarrassed smile. "You don't have to pay me anything more, Mrs, I said I would work for nothing to make up for past favors from your husband and also to learn the business. Besides that, you give me my bed and board, so you don't owe me a thing."

"Take," she said, handing him a crumpled five-dollar bill. He let the money lie on the counter till she urged him to put it into his pocket. Frank felt troubled about the raise because he was earning something for his labor that Ida knew nothing of, for business was a little better than she thought. During the day, while she was not around, he sold at least a buck's worth, or a buck and a half, that he made no attempt to ring up on the register. Ida guessed nothing; the list of sold items he had supplied her with in the beginning they had discontinued as impractical. It wasn't hard for him to scrape up here a bit of change, there a bit. At the end of the second week he had ten dollars in his pocket. With this and the five she gave him he bought a shaving kit, a pair of cheap brown suede shoes, a couple of shirts and a tie or two; he figured that if he stayed around two more weeks he would own an inexpensive suit. He had nothing to be ashamed of, he thought—it was practically his own dough he was taking. The grocer and his wife wouldn't miss it because they didn't know they had it, and they wouldn't have it if it wasn't for his hard work. If he weren't working there, they would have less than they had with him taking what he took.

Thus he settled it in his mind only to find himself remorseful. He groaned, scratching the backs
of his hands with his thick nails. Sometimes he felt
short of breath and sweated profusely. He talked
aloud to himself when he was alone, usually when
he was shaving or in the toilet, exhorted himself
to be honest. Yet he felt a curious pleasure in his
misery, as he had at times in the past when he was
doing something he knew he oughtn't to, so he
kept on dropping quarters into his pants pocket.

One night he felt very bad about all the wrong
he was doing and vowed to set himself straight. If
I could do one right thing, he thought, maybe
that would start me off; then he thought if he
could get the gun and get rid of it he would at
least feel better. He left the grocery after supper
and wandered restlessly in the foggy streets, feeling cramped in the chest from his long days in the
store and because his life hadn't changed much
since he had come here. As he passed by the cemetery, he tried to keep out of his mind the memory
of the holdup but it kept coming back in. He saw
himself sitting with Ward Minogue in the parked
car, waiting for Karp to come out of the grocery,
but when he did his store lights went out and he
hid in the back among the bottles. Ward said to
drive quick around the block so they would flush
the Jew out, and he would slug him on the sidewalk and take his fat wallet away; but when they
got back, Karp's car was gone with him in it, and
Ward cursed him into an early grave. Frank said
Karp had beat it, so they ought to scram, but
Ward sat there with heartburn, watching with his

small eyes, the grocery store, the one lit place on the block besides the candy store on the corner.

"No," Frank urged, "it's just a little joint, I got my doubts if they took in thirty bucks today."

"Thirty is thirty," Ward said. "I don't care if it's Karp or Bober, a Jew is a Jew."

"Why not the candy store?"

Ward made a face. "I can't stand penny candy."

"How do you know his name?" asked Frank.

"Who?"

"The Jew grocer."

"I used to go to school with his daughter. She has a nice ass."

"Then if that's so, he will recognize you."

"Not with a rag around my snoot, and I will rough up my voice. He ain't seen me for eight or nine years. I was a skinny kid then."

"Have it your way. I will keep the car running."

"Come in with me," Ward said. "The block is dead. Nobody will expect a stickup in this dump."

But Frank hesitated. "I thought you said Karp was the one you were out after?"

"I will take Karp some other time. Come on."

Frank put on his cap and crossed the car tracks with Ward Minogue. "It's your funeral," he said, but it was really his own.

He remembered thinking as they went into the store, a Jew is a Jew, what difference does it make? Now he thought, I held him up because he was a Jew. What the hell are they to me so that I gave them credit for it?

But he didn't know the answer and walked faster, from time to time glancing through the spiked iron fence at the shrouded gravestones. Once he felt he was being followed and his heart

picked up a hard beat. He hurried past the cemetery and turned right on the first street after it,
hugging the stoops of the stone houses as he went
quickly down the dark street. When he reached
the poolroom he felt relieved.

Pop's poolroom was a dreary four-table joint,
owned by a glum old Italian with a blue-veined
bald head and droopy hands, who sat close to his
cash register.

"Seen Ward yet?" Frank said.

Pop pointed to the rear where Ward Minogue,
in his fuzzy black hat and a bulky overcoat, was
practicing shots alone at a table. Frank watched
him place a black ball at a corner pocket and aim
a white at it. Ward leaned tensely forward, his
face strained, a dead butt hanging from his sick
mouth. He shot but missed. He banged his cue on
the floor.

Frank had drifted past the players at the other
tables. When Ward looked up and saw him, his
eyes lit with fear. The fear drained after he recognized who it was. But his pimply face was covered with sweat.

He spat his butt to the floor. "What have you
got on your feet, you bastard, gumshoes?"

"I didn't want to spoil your shot."

"Anyway you did."

"I've been looking for you about a week."

"I was on my vacation." Ward smiled in the
corner of his mouth.

"On a drunk?"

Ward put his hand to his chest and brought up
a belch. "I wish to hell it was. Somebody tipped
my old man I was around here, so I hid out for a
while. I had a rough time. My heartburn is acting

up." He hung up his cue, then wiped his face with a dirty handkerchief.

"Why don't you go to a doctor?" Frank said.

"The hell with them."

"Some medicine might help you."

"What will help me is if my goddam father drops dead."

"I want to talk to you, Ward," Frank said in a low voice.

"So talk."

Frank nodded toward the players at the next table.

"Come out in the yard," Ward said. "I got something I want to say to you."

Frank followed him out the rear door into a small enclosed back yard with a wooden bench against the building. A weak bulb shone down on them from the top of the doorjamb.

Ward sat down on the bench and lit a cigarette. Frank did the same, from his own pack. He puffed but got no pleasure from the butt, so he threw it away.

"Sit down," said Ward.

Frank sat on the bench. Even in the fog he stinks, he thought.

"What do you want me for?" Ward asked, his small eyes restless.

"I want my gun, Ward. Where is it?"

"What for?"

"I want to throw it in the ocean."

Ward snickered. "Cat got your nuts?"

"I don't want some dick coming around and asking me do I own it."

"I thought you said you bought the rod off a fence."

"That's right."

"Then nobody's got a record of it, so what are you scared of?"

"If you lost it," Frank said, "they trace them even without a record."

"I won't lose it," Ward said. After a minute he ground his cigarette into the dirt. "I will give it back to you after we do this job I have on my mind."

Frank looked at him. "What kind of a job?"

"Karp. I want to stick him up."

"Why Karp?—there are bigger liquor stores."

"I hate that Jew son of a bitch and his popeyed Louis. When I was a kid all I had to do was go near banjo eyes and they would complain to my old man and get me beat up."

"They would recognize you if you go in there."

"Bober didn't. I will use a handkerchief and wear some different clothes. Tomorrow I will go out and pick up a car. All you got to do is drive and I will make the heist."

"You better stay away from that block," Frank warned. "Somebody might recognize you."

Ward moodily rubbed his chest. "All right, you sold me. We will go somewheres else."

"Not with me," Frank said.

"Think it over."

"I've had all I want."

Ward showed his disgust. "The minute I saw you I knew you would puke all over."

Frank didn't answer.

"Don't act so innocent," Ward said angrily. "You're hot, the same as me."

"I know," Frank said.

"I slugged him because he was lying where he hid the rest of the dough," Ward argued.

"He didn't hide it. It's a poor, lousy store."

"I guess you know all about that."

"What do you mean?"

"Can the crud. I know you been working there."

Frank drew a breath. "You following me again, Ward?"

Ward smiled. "I followed you one night after you left the poolroom. I found out you were working for a Jew and living on bird crap."

Frank slowly got up. "I felt sorry for him after you slugged him, so I went back to give him a hand while he was in a weak condition. But I won't be staying there long."

"That was real sweet of you. I suppose you gave him back the lousy seven and a half bucks that was your part of the take?"

"I put it back in the cash register. I told the Mrs. the business was getting better."

"I never thought I would meet up with a goddam Salvation Army soldier."

"I did it to quiet my conscience," Frank said.

Ward rose. "That ain't your conscience you are worried about."

"No?"

"It's something else. I hear those Jew girls make nice ripe lays."

Frank went back without his gun.

Helen was with her mother as Ida counted the cash.

Frank stood behind the counter, cleaning his

fingernails with his jackknife blade, waiting for them to leave so he could close up.

"I think I'll take a hot shower before I go to bed," Helen said to her mother. "I've felt chilled all night."

"Good night," Ida said to Frank. "I left five dollars change for the morning."

"Good night," said Frank.

They left by the rear door and he heard them go up the stairs. Frank closed the store and went into the back. He thumbed through tomorrow's *News,* then got restless.

After a while he went into the store and listened at the side door; he unlatched the lock, snapped on the cellar light, closed the cellar door behind him so no light would leak out into the hall, then quietly descended the stairs.

He found the air shaft where an old unused dumb-waiter stood, pushed the dusty box back and gazed up the vertical shaft. It was pitch-dark. Neither the Bobers' bathroom window nor the Fusos' showed any light.

Frank struggled against himself but not for long. Shoving the dumb-waiter back as far as it would go, he squeezed into the shaft and then boosted himself up on top of the box. His heart shook him with its beating.

When his eyes got used to the dark he saw that her bathroom window was only a couple of feet above his head. He felt along the wall as high as he could reach and touched a narrow ledge around the air shaft. He thought he could anchor himself on it and see into the bathroom.

But if you do it, he told himself, you will suffer.

Though his throat hurt and his clothes were

drenched in sweat, the excitement of what he might see forced him to go up.

Crossing himself, Frank grabbed both of the dumb-waiter ropes and slowly pulled himself up, praying the pulley at the skylight wouldn't squeak too much.

A light went on over his head.

Holding his breath, he crouched motionless, clinging to the swaying ropes. Then the bathroom window was shut with a bang. For a while he couldn't move, the strength gone out of him. He thought he might lose his grip and fall, and he thought of her opening the bathroom window and seeing him lying at the bottom of the shaft in a broken, filthy heap.

It was a mistake to do it, he thought.

But she might be in the shower before he could get a look at her, so, trembling, he began again to pull himself up. In a few minutes he was straddling the ledge, holding onto the ropes to steady himself yet keep his full weight off the wood.

Leaning forward, though not too far, he could see through the uncurtained crossed sash window into the old-fashioned bathroom. Helen was there looking with sad eyes at herself in the mirror. He thought she would stand there forever, but at last she unzipped her housecoat, stepping out of it.

He felt a throb of pain at her nakedness, an overwhelming desire to love her, at the same time an awareness of loss, of never having had what he had wanted most, and other such memories he didn't care to recall.

Her body was young, soft, lovely, the breasts like small birds in flight, her ass like a flower. Yet it was a lonely body in spite of its lovely form, lonelier. Bodies are lonely, he thought, but in bed she wouldn't be. She seemed realer to him now than she had been, revealed without clothes, personal, possible. He felt greedy as he gazed, all eyes at a banquet, hungry so long as he must look. But in looking he was forcing her out of reach, making her into a thing only of his seeing, her eyes reflecting his sins, rotten past, spoiled ideals, his passion poisoned by his shame.

Frank's eyes grew moist and he wiped them with one hand. When he gazed up again she seemed, to his horror, to be staring at him through the window, a mocking smile on her lips, her eyes filled with scorn, pitiless. He thought wildly of jumping, bolting, broken-boned, out of the house; but she turned on the shower and stepped into the tub, drawing the flowered plastic curtain around her.

The window was quickly covered with steam. For this he was relieved, grateful. He let himself down silently. In the cellar, instead of the grinding remorse he had expected to suffer, he felt a moving joy.

On a Saturday morning in December, Morris, after a little more than two impatient weeks upstairs, came down with his head healed. The night before, Ida told Frank he would have to leave in the morning, but when Morris later learned this they had an argument. Although he hadn't said so to Ida, the grocer, after his long layoff, was depressed at the prospect of having to take up his dreary existence in the store. He dreaded the deadweight of hours, mostly sad memories of his lost years of youth. That business was better gave him some comfort but not enough, for he was convinced from all Ida had told him that business was better only because of their assistant, whom he remembered as a stranger with hungry eyes, a man to be pitied. Yet the why of it was simple enough—the store had improved not because this cellar dweller was a magician, but because he was not Jewish. The goyim in the neighborhood were happier with one of their own. A Jew stuck in their throats. Yes, they had, on and off, patronized his store, called him by his first name and asked for credit as if he were obliged to give it, which he had, in the past, often foolishly done; but in their hearts they hated him. If it weren't so, Frank's presence could not have made such a quick difference in income. He was afraid that the extra forty-five dollars weekly would melt away overnight if the Italian left and he vehemently said so to Ida. She, though she feared he was right, still argued that Frank must be let go. How could they, she asked, keep him working seven days a week, twelve hours a day, for a miserable five dollars? It was unjust. The grocer agreed, but why push the boy into the street if he wanted to stay longer? The five dollars, he admitted, was nothing, but what of the bed and board, the free packs of cigarettes, the bottles of beer she said he guzzled in the store? If things went on well, he would offer him more, maybe even a small commission, very small—maybe on all they took in over a hundred and fifty a week, a sum they had not realized since Schmitz had opened up around the corner; meantime he would give him his Sundays off and otherwise reduce his hours. Since Morris was now able to open the store, Frank could stay in bed till nine. This proposition was no great bargain but the grocer insisted that the man have the chance to take or refuse it.

Ida, a red flush spreading on her neck, said, "Are you crazy, Morris? Even with the forty more that comes in, which we give him away five dollars, our little profit, who can afford to keep him here? Look what he eats. It's impossible."

"We can't afford to keep him but we can't afford to lose him, on account he might improve more the business if he stays," Morris answered.

"How can three people work in such a small store?" she cried.

"Rest your sick feet," he answered. "Sleep longer in the morning and stay more upstairs in the house. Who needs you should be so tired every night?"

"Also," Ida argued, "who wants him in the back all night so we can't go inside after the store is closed when we forget something?"

"This I thought about also. I think I will take off from Nick's rent upstairs a couple dollars and tell him he should give Frank the little room to sleep in. They don't use it for nothing, only storage. There, with plenty blankets he will be comfortable, with a door which it goes right in the hall so he can come in and go out with his own key without bothering anybody. He can wash himself here in the store."

"A couple dollars less from the rent comes also from our poor pocket," Ida replied, pressing her clasped hands to her bosom. "But the most important is I don't want him here on account of Helen. I don't like the way he looks on her."

Morris gazed at her. "So you like maybe how Nat looks on her, or Louis Karp? That's the way they look, the boys. Tell me better, how does she look on him?"

She shrugged stiffly.

"This is what I thought. You know yourself Helen wouldn't be interested in such a boy. A grocery clerk don't interest her. Does she go out with the salesmen where she works, that they ask her? No. She wants better—so let her have better."

"Will be trouble," she murmured.

He belittled her fears, and when he came down on Saturday morning, spoke to Frank about stay-

ing on for a while. Frank had arisen before six
and was sitting dejectedly on the couch when the
grocer came in. He agreed at once to continue on
in the store under the conditions Morris offered.

More animated now, the clerk said he liked the
idea of living upstairs near Nick and Tessie; and
Morris that day arranged it, in spite of Ida's mis-
givings, by promising three dollars off their rent.
Tessie lugged out of the room a trunk, garment
bags and a few odds and ends of furniture; after,
she dusted and vacuumed. Between what she offered, and what Morris got out of his bin in the
cellar, they supplied a bed with a fairly good mattress, a usable chest of drawers, chair, small table,
electric heater and even an old radio Nick had
around. Although the room was cold, because it
had no radiator and was locked off from the Fusos' gas-heated bedroom, Frank was satisfied. Tessie worried about what would happen if he had to
go to the bathroom at night, and Nick talked the
matter over with Frank, saying apologetically that
she was ashamed to have him go through their
bedroom, but Frank said he never woke up at
night. Anyway, Nick had a key made to the front
door patent lock. He said if Frank ever had to get
up he could walk across the hall and let himself
in through the front without waking them. And
he could also use their bathtub, just so long as he
told them when he would want it.

This arrangement suited Tessie. Everyone was
satisfied but Ida, who was unhappy with herself
for having kept Frank on. She made the grocer
promise he would send the clerk away before the
summer. Business was always more active in the
summertime, so Morris agreed. She asked him to

tell Frank at once that he would be let go then, and when the grocer did, the clerk smiled amiably and said the summer was a long ways off but anyway it was all right with him.

The grocer felt his mood change. It was a better mood than he had expected. A few of his old customers had returned. One woman told him that Schmitz was not giving as good service as he once did; he was having trouble with his health and was thinking of selling the store. Let him sell, thought Morris. He thought, let him die, then severely struck his chest.

Ida stayed upstairs most of the day, reluctantly at first, less so as time went by. She came down to prepare lunch and supper—Frank still ate before Helen—or to make a salad when it was needed. She attended to little else in the store; Frank did the cleaning and mopping. Upstairs, Ida took care of the house, read a bit, listened to the Jewish programs on the radio and knitted. Helen bought some wool and Ida knitted her a sweater. In the night, after Frank had gone, Ida spent her time in the store, added up the accounts in her notebook and left with Morris when he closed up.

The grocer got along well with his assistant. They divided tasks and waited on alternate customers, though the waiting in between was still much too long. Morris went up for naps to forget the store. He too urged Frank to take some time off in the afternoon, to break the monotony of the day. Frank, somewhat restless, finally began to. Sometimes he went up to his room and lay on the bed, listening to the radio. Usually he put his coat on over his apron and visited one of the other stores on the block. He liked Giannola, the Italian barber across the street, an old man who had recently lost his wife and sat in the shop all day, even when it was long past time to go home; the old barber gave a fine haircut. Occasionally Frank dropped in on Louis Karp and gassed with him, but generally Louis bored him. Sometimes he went into the butcher store, next door to Morris, and talked in the back room with Artie, the butcher's son, a blond fellow with a bad complexion who was interested in riding horses. Frank said he might go riding with him sometime but he never did though Artie invited him. Once in a while he drank a beer in the bar on the corner, where he liked Earl, the bartender. Yet when the clerk got back to the grocery he was glad to go in.

When he and Morris were together in the back they spent a lot of time talking. Morris liked Frank's company; he liked to hear about strange places, and Frank told him about some of the cities he had been to, in his long wandering, and some of the different jobs he had worked at. He had passed part of his early life in Oakland, California, but most of it across the bay in a home in San Francisco. He told Morris stories about his hard times as a kid. In this second family the home had sent him to, the man used to work him hard in his machine shop. "I wasn't twelve," Frank said, "and he kept me out of school as long as he could get away with."

After staying with that family for three years, he took off. "Then began my long period of travels." The clerk fell silent, and the ticking clock, on the shelf above the sink, sounded flat and heavy. "I am mostly self-educated," he ended.

Morris told Frank about life in the old country. They were poor and there were pogroms. So when he was about to be conscripted into the czar's army his father said, "Run to America." A landsman, a friend of his father, had sent money for his passage. But he waited for the Russians to call him up, because if you left the district before they had conscripted you, then your father was arrested, fined and imprisoned. If the son got away after induction, then the father could not be blamed; it was the army's responsibility. Morris and his father, a peddler in butter and eggs, planned that he would try to get away on his first day in the barracks.

So on that day, Morris said, he told the sergeant, a peasant with red eyes and a bushy mustache which smelled of tobacco, that he wanted to buy some cigarettes in the town. He felt scared but was doing what his father had advised him to do. The half-drunk sergeant agreed he could go, but since Morris was not yet in uniform he would have to go along with him. It was a September day and had just rained. They walked along a muddy road till they reached the town. There, in an inn, Morris bought cigarettes for himself and the sergeant; then, as he had planned it with his father, he invited the soldier to drink some vodka with him. His stomach became rigid at the chance he was taking. He had never drunk in an inn before, and he had never before tried to deceive anybody to this extent. The sergeant, filling his glass often, told Morris the story of his life, crying when he came to the part where, through forgetfulness, he

had not attended his mother's funeral. Then he
blew his nose, and wagging a thick finger in Morris's face, warned him if he had any plans to skip,
he had better forget them if he expected to live.
A dead Jew was of less consequence than a live
one. Morris felt a heavy gloom descend on him.
In his heart he surrendered his freedom for years
to come. Yet once they had left the inn and were
trudging in the mud back to the barracks, his
hopes rose as the sergeant, in his stupor, kept
falling behind. Morris walked slowly on, then the
sergeant would cup his hands to his mouth, and
cursing, haloo for him to wait. Morris waited.
They would go on together, the sergeant muttering to himself, Morris uncertain what would happen next. Then the soldier stopped to urinate
into a ditch in the road. Morris pretended to wait
but he walked on, every minute expecting a bul-
let to crash through his shoulders and leave him
lying in the dirt, his future with the worms. But
then, as if seized by his fate, he began to run. The
halooing and cursing grew louder as the red-faced
sergeant, waving a revolver, stumbled after him;
but when he reached the bend of the tree-lined
road where he had last seen Morris, nobody was
there but a yellow-bearded peasant driving a nag
pulling a load of hay.

Telling this story excited the grocer. He lit a
cigarette and smoked without coughing. But
when he had finished, when there was no more to
say, a sadness settled on him. Sitting in his chair,
he seemed a small, lonely man. All the time he
had been upstairs his hair had grown bushier and
he wore a thick pelt of it at the back of his neck.
His face was thinner than before.

Frank thought about the story Morris had just told him. That was the big jig in his life but where had it got him? He had escaped out of the Russian Army to the U.S.A., but once in a store he was like a fish fried in deep fat.

"After I came here I wanted to be a druggist," Morris said. "I went for a year in night school. I took algebra, also German and English. ' "Come," said the wind to the leaves one day, "come over the meadow with me and play." ' This is a poem I learned. But I didn't have the patience to stay in night school, so when I met my wife I gave up my chances." Sighing, he said, "Without education you are lost."

Frank nodded.

"You're still young," Morris said. "A young man without a family is free. Don't do what I did."

"I won't," Frank said.

But the grocer didn't seem to believe him. It made the clerk uncomfortable to see the wet-eyed old bird brooding over him. His pity leaks out of his pants, he thought, but he would get used to it.

When they were behind the counter together, Morris kept an eye on Frank and tried to improve some of the things Ida had taught him. The clerk did very well what he was supposed to. As if ashamed somebody could learn the business so easily, Morris explained to him how different it had been to be a grocer only a few years ago. In those days one was more of a macher, a craftsman. Who was ever called on nowadays to slice up a loaf of bread for a customer, or ladle out a quart of milk?

"Now is everything in containers, jars, or pack-ages. Even hard cheeses that they cut them for hundreds of years by hand come now sliced up in cellophane packages. Nobody has to know any-thing any more."

"I remember the family milk cans," Frank said, "only my family sent me out to get beer in them."

But Morris said it was a good idea that milk wasn't sold loose any more. "I used to know gro-cers that they took out a quart or two cream from the top of the can, then they put in water. This water-milk they sold at the regular price."

He told Frank about some other tricks he had seen. "In some stores they bought two kinds loose coffee and two kinds tub butter. One was low grade, the other was medium, but the medium they put half in the medium bin and half in the best. So if you bought the best coffee or the best butter you got medium—nothing else."

Frank laughed. "I'll bet some of the customers came back saying that the best butter tasted better than the medium."

"It's easy to fool people," said Morris.

"Why don't you try a couple of those tricks yourself, Morris? Your amount of profit is small."

Morris looked at him in surprise. "Why should I steal from my customers? Do they steal from me?"

"They would if they could."

"When a man is honest he don't worry when he sleeps. This is more important than to steal a nickel."

Frank nodded.

But he continued to steal. He would stop for a few days then almost with relief go back to it.

There were times stealing made him feel good. It felt good to have some change in his pocket, and it felt good to pluck a buck from under the Jew's nose. He would slip it into his pants pocket so deftly that he had to keep himself from laughing. With this money, and what he earned, he bought a suit and hat, and got new tubes for Nick's radio. Now and then, through Sam Pearl, who telephoned it in for him, he laid a two-buck bet on a horse, but as a rule he was careful with the dough. He opened a small savings account in a bank near the library and hid the bankbook under his mattress. The money was for future use.

When he felt pepped up about stealing, it was also because he felt he had brought them luck. If he stopped stealing he bet business would fall off again. He was doing them a favor, at the same time making it a little worth his while to stay on and give them a hand. Taking this small cut was his way of showing himself he had something to give. Besides, he planned to return everything sometime or why would he be marking down the figure of what he took? He kept it on a small card in his shoe. He might someday plunk down a tenner or so on some longshot and then have enough to pay back every lousy cent of what he had taken.

For this reason he could not explain why, from one day to another, he should begin to feel bad about snitching the bucks from Morris, but he did. Sometimes he went around with a quiet grief in him, as if he had just buried a friend and was carrying the fresh grave within himself. This was an old feeling of his. He remembered having had something like it for years back. On days he felt this way he sometimes got headaches and went around muttering to himself. He was afraid to look into the mirror for fear it would split apart and drop into the sink. He was wound up so tight he would spin for a week if the spring snapped. He was full of sudden rages at himself. These were his worst days and he suffered trying to hide his feelings. Yet they had a curious way of ending. The rage he felt disappeared like a windstorm that quietly pooped out, and he felt a sort of gentleness creeping in. He felt gentle to the people who came into the store, especially the kids, whom he gave penny crackers to for nothing. He was gentle to Morris, and the Jew was gentle to him. And he was filled with a quiet gentleness for Helen and no longer climbed the air shaft to spy on her, naked in the bathroom.

And there were days when he was sick to death of everything. He had had it, up to here. Going downstairs in the morning he thought he would gladly help the store burn if it caught on fire. Thinking of Morris waiting on the same lousy customers day after day throughout the years, as they picked out with dirty fingers the same cheap items they ate every day of their flea-bitten lives, then when they were gone, waiting for them to come back again, he felt like leaning over the banister and throwing up. What kind of a man did you have to be born to shut yourself up in an overgrown coffin and never once during the day, so help you, outside of going for your Yiddish newspaper, poke your beak out of the door for a snootful of air? The answer wasn't hard to say— you had to be a Jew. They were born prisoners.

That was what Morris was, with his deadly patience, or endurance, or whatever the hell it was;
and it explained Al Marcus, the paper products
salesman, and that skinny rooster Breitbart, who
dragged from store to store his two heavy cartons
full of bulbs.

Al Marcus, who had once, with an apologetic
smile, warned the clerk not to trap himself in a
grocery, was a well-dressed man of forty-six, but
he looked, whenever you saw him, as if he had
just lapped up cyanide. His face was the whitest
Frank had ever seen, and what anybody saw in
his eyes if he took a good look, would not help his
appetite. The truth of it was, the grocer had con-
fided to Frank, that Al had cancer and was supposed to be dead in his grave a year ago, but he
fooled the doctors; he stayed alive if you could
call it that. Although he had a comfortable pile,
he wouldn't quit working and showed up regularly once a month to take orders for paper bags,
wrapping paper and containers. No matter how
bad business was, Morris tried to have some kind
of little order waiting for him. Al would suck on
an unlit cigar, scribble an item or two on a pink
page in his metal-covered salesbook, then stand
around a few minutes, making small talk, his eyes
far away from what he was saying; and after that,
tip his hat and take off for the next place. Everybody knew how sick he was, and a couple of the
storekeepers earnestly advised him to quit working, but Al, smiling apologetically, took his cigar
out of his mouth and said, "If I stay home, somebody in a high hat is gonna walk up the stairs and
put a knock on my door. This way let him at least
move his bony ass around and try and find me."

As for Breitbart, according to Morris, nine years ago he had owned a good business, but his brother ran it into the ground, gambling, then he took off with what was left of the bank account, persuading Breitbart's wife to come along and keep it company. That left him with a drawerful of bills and no credit; also a not too bright five-year-old boy. Breitbart went bankrupt; his creditors plucked every feather. For months he and the boy lived in a small, dirty furnished room, Breitbart not having the heart to go out to look for work. Times were bad. He went on relief and later took to peddling. He was now in his fifties but his hair had turned white and he acted like an old man. He bought electric bulbs at wholesale and carried two cartons of them slung, with clothesline rope, over his shoulder. Every day, in his crooked shoes, he walked miles, looking into stores and calling out in a mournful voice, "Lights for sale." At night he went home and cooked supper for his Hymie, who played hooky whenever he could from the vocational school where they were making him into a shoemaker.

When Breitbart first came to Morris's neighborhood and dropped into the store, the grocer, seeing his fatigue, offered him a glass of tea with lemon. The peddler eased the rope off his shoulder and set his boxes on the floor. In the back he gulped the hot tea in silence, warming both hands on the glass. And though he had, besides his other troubles, the seven-year itch, which kept him awake half the night, he never complained. After ten minutes he got up, thanked the grocer, fitted the rope onto his lean and itchy shoulder and left.

One day he told Morris the story of his life and
they both wept.

That's what they live for, Frank thought, to suffer. And the one that has got the biggest pain in
the gut and can hold onto it the longest without
running to the toilet is the best Jew. No wonder
they got on his nerves.

Winter tormented Helen. She ran from it, hid
in the house. In the house she revenged herself on
December by crossing off the calendar all its days.
If Nat would only call, she thought endlessly, but
the telephone was deaf and dumb. She dreamed
of him nightly, felt deeply in love, famished for
him; would gladly have danced into his warm
white bed if only he nodded, or she dared ask him
to ask her; but Nat never called. She hadn't for a
minute glimpsed him since running into him on
the subway early in November. He lived around
the corner but it might as well be Paradise. So
with a sharp-pointed pencil she scratched out each
dead day while it still lived.

Though Frank hungered for her company he
rarely spoke to her. Now and then he passed her
on the street. She murmured hello and walked on
with her books, conscious of his eyes following
her. Sometimes in the store, as if in defiance of her
mother, she stopped to talk for a minute with the
clerk. Once he startled her by abruptly mention-
ing this book he was reading. He longed to ask
her to go out with him, but never dared; the old
lady's eyes showed distrust of the goings on. So
he waited. Mostly he watched for her at the window. He studied her hidden face, sensed her

lacks, which deepened his own, but didn't know what to do about it.

December yielded nothing to spring. She awoke to each frozen, lonely day with dulled feeling. Then one Sunday afternoon winter leaned backward for an hour and she went walking. Suddenly she forgave everyone everything. A warmish breath of air was enough to inspire; she was again grateful for living. But the sun soon sank and it snowed pellets. She returned home, leaden. Frank was standing at Sam Pearl's deserted corner but she seemed not to see him though she brushed by. He felt very bad. He wanted her but the facts made a terrible construction. They were Jews and he was not. If he started going out with Helen her mother would throw a double fit and Morris another. And Helen made him feel, from the way she carried herself, even when she seemed most lonely, that she had plans for something big in her life—nobody like F. Alpine. He had nothing, a backbreaking past, had committed a crime against her old man, and in spite of his touchy conscience, was stealing from him too. How complicated could impossible get?

He saw only one way of squeezing through the stone knot; start by shoveling out the load he was carrying around in his mind by admitting to Morris that he was one of the guys that had held him up. It was a funny thing about that; he wasn't really sorry they had stuck up a Jew but he hadn't expected to be sorry that they had picked on this particular one, Bober; yet now he was. He had not minded, if by mind you meant in expectation, but what he hadn't minded no longer seemed to matter. The matter was how he now felt, and he now felt bad he had done it. And when Helen was around he felt worse.

So the confession had to come first—this stuck like a bone through the neck. From the minute he had tailed Ward Minogue into the grocery that night, he had got this sick feeling that he might someday have to vomit up in words, no matter how hard or disgusting it was to do, the thing he was then engaged in doing. He felt he had known this, in some frightful way, a long time before he went into the store, before he had met Minogue, or even come east; that he had really known all his life he would sometime, through throat blistered with shame, his eyes in the dirt, have to tell some poor son of a bitch that he was the one who had hurt or betrayed him. This thought had lived in him with claws; or like a thirst he could never spit out, a repulsive need to get out of his system all that had happened—for whatever had happened had happened wrong; to clean it out of his self and bring in a little peace, a little order; to change the beginning, beginning with the past that always stupendously stank up the now—to change his life before the smell of it suffocated him.

Yet when the chance came to say it, when he was alone with Morris that November morning in the back of the store, as they were drinking the coffee that the Jew had served him, and the impulse came on him to spill everything now, *now,* he had strained to heave it up, but it was like tearing up your whole life, with the broken roots and blood; and a fear burned in his gut that once he had got started saying the wrongs he had done he would never leave off until he had turned black;

so instead he had told him a few hurried things about how ass-backward his life had gone, which didn't even begin to say what he wanted. He had worked on Morris's pity and left halfway satisfied, but not for long, because soon the need to say it returned and he heard himself groaning, but groans weren't words.

He argued with himself that he was smart in not revealing to the grocer more than he had. Enough was enough; besides, how much of a confession was the Jew entitled to for the seven and a half bucks he had taken, then put back into his cash register drawer, and for the knock on the head he had got from Ward, whom he himself had come with unwillingly? Maybe willing, but not to do what had finally been done. That deserved some consideration, didn't it? Furthermore, he had begged the creep not to hurt anybody, and later turned him down when he cooked up another scheme of stickup against Karp, who they were out to get in the first place. That showed his good intentions for the future, didn't it? And who was it, after all was said and done, that had waited around shivering in his pants in the dark cold, to pull in Morris's milk boxes, and had worked his ass to a frazzle twelve hours a day while the Jew lay upstairs resting in his bed? And was even now keeping him from starvation in his little rat hole? All that added up to something too.

That was how he argued with himself, but it didn't help for long, and he was soon again fighting out how to jump free of what he had done. He would someday confess it all—he promised himself. If Morris accepted his explanation and solemn apology, it would clear the rocks out of the road for the next move. As for his present stealing from the cash register, he had decided that once he had told the grocer all there was to say about the holdup, he would at the same time start paying back into the drawer, out of his little salary and the few bucks he had put away in the bank, what he had taken, and that would fix that. It wouldn't necessarily mean that Helen Bober would then and there fall for him—the opposite could happen—but if she did, he wouldn't feel bad about it.

He knew by heart what he would say to the grocer once he got to say it. One day while they were talking in the back, he would begin, as he had once done, about how his life was mostly made up of lost chances, some so promising he could not stand to remember them. Well, after certain bad breaks through various causes, mostly his own mistakes—he was piled high with regrets —after many such failures, though he tried every which way to free himself from them, usually he failed; so after a time he gave up and let himself be a bum. He lived in gutters, cellars if he was lucky, slept in lots, ate what the dogs wouldn't, or couldn't, and what he scrounged out of garbage cans. He wore what he found, slept where he flopped and guzzled anything.

By rights this should have killed him, but he lived on, bearded, smelly, dragging himself through the seasons without a hope to go by. How many months he had existed this way he would never know. Nobody kept the score of it. But one day while he lay in some hole he had crawled into, he had this terrific idea that he was really an important guy, and was torn out of his reverie with the thought that he was living this kind of life only because he hadn't known he was meant for something a whole lot better—to do something big, different. He had not till that minute understood this. In the past he had usually thought of himself as an average guy, but there in this cellar it came to him he was wrong. That was why his luck had so often curdled, because he had the wrong idea of what he really was and had spent all his energy trying to do the wrong things. Then when he had asked himself what should he be doing, he had another powerful idea, that he was meant for crime. He had at times teased himself with this thought, but now it wouldn't let go of him. At crime he would change his luck, make adventure, live like a prince. He shivered with pleasure as he conceived robberies, assaults—murders if it had to be—each violent act helping to satisfy a craving that somebody suffer as his own fortune improved. He felt infinitely relieved, believing that if a person figured for himself something big, something different in his life, he had a better chance to get it than some poor jerk who couldn't think that high up.

So he gave up his outhouse existence. He began to work again, got himself a room, saved and bought a gun. Then he headed east, where he figured he could live the way he wanted—where there was money, nightclubs, babes. After a week of prowling around in Boston, not sure where he ought to start off, he hopped a freight to Brooklyn and a couple of days after he got there met Ward Minogue. As they were shooting pool one night, Ward cannily detected the gun on him and made him the proposition that they do a holdup together. Frank welcomed the idea of some kind of start but said he wanted to think about it more. He went to Coney Island, and while sitting on the boardwalk, worrying about what he ought to do, got this oppressive feeling he was being watched. When he turned around it was Ward Minogue. Ward sat down and told him that it was a Jew he planned to rob, so Frank agreed to go with him.

But on the night of the holdup he found himself nervous. In the car Ward sensed it and cursed him. Frank felt he had to stick it out, but the minute they were both in the grocery and tying handkerchiefs around their mouths, the whole idea seemed senseless. He could feel it poop out in his mind. His plans of crime lay down and died. He could hardly breathe in his unhappiness, wanted to rush out into the street and be swallowed up out of existence, but he couldn't let Ward stay there alone. In the back, nauseated by the sight of the Jew's bloodied head, he realized he had made the worst mistake yet, the hardest to wipe out. And that ended his short life of violent crime, another pipe dream, and he was trapped tighter in the tangle of his failures. All this he thought he would someday tell Morris. He knew the Jew well enough to feel sure of his mercy.

Yet there were times when he imagined himself, instead, telling it all to Helen. He wanted to do something that would open her eyes to his true self, but who could be a hero in a grocery store? Telling her would take guts and guts was something. He continued to feel he deserved a better fate, and he would find it if he only once— *once*—did the right thing—the thing to do at the right time. Maybe if they were ever together for any decent amount of time, he would ask her to listen. At first she might be embarrassed, but when he started telling her about his life, he knew she would hear him to the end. After that—who knew? With a dame all you needed was a beginning.

But when the clerk caught himself coldly and saw the sentimentality of his thinking—he was a sentimental wop at heart—he knew he was having another of his hopped-up dreams. What kind of a chance did he think he would have with her after he had admitted the stickup of her old man? So he figured the best thing was to keep quiet. At the same time a foreboding crept into him that if he said nothing now, he would someday soon have a dirtier past to reveal.

A few days after Christmas, on the night of a full moon, Frank, dressed in his new clothes, hurried to the library, about a dozen blocks from the grocery. The library was an enlarged store, well lit, with bulging shelves of books that smelled warm on winter nights. In the rear there were a few large reading tables. It was a pleasant place to come to out of the cold. His guess was good, soon Helen arrived. She wore a red woolen scarf on her head, one end thrown over her shoulder. He was at a table reading. She noticed him as she closed the door behind her; he knew it. They had met here, briefly, before. She had wondered what he read at the table, and once in passing, glanced quickly over his shoulder. She had guessed *Popular Mechanics,* but it was the life of somebody or other. Tonight, as usual, she was aware of his eyes on her as she moved about from shelf to shelf. When, after an hour, she left, he caught a tight hidden glance in his direction. Frank got up and checked out a book. She was halfway down the street before he caught up with her.

"Big moon." He reached up to tip his hat and awkwardly discovered he wasn't wearing any.

"It feels like snow," Helen answered.

He glanced at her to see if she was kidding, then at the sky. It was cloudless, flooded with moonlight.

"Maybe." As they approached the street corner, he remarked, "We could take a walk in the park if it's okay with you."

She shivered at the suggestion, yet turned with a nervous laugh at the corner, and walked by his side. She had said almost nothing to him since the night he had called her to answer the empty phone. Who it had been she would never know; the incident still puzzled her.

Helen felt for him, as they walked, an irritation bordering on something worse. She knew what caused it—her mother, in making every gentile, by definition, dangerous; therefore he and she, together, represented some potential evil. She was also annoyed that his eating eyes were always on her, for he saw, she felt, more than his occasionally trapped gaze revealed. She fought her dislike of him, reasoning it wasn't his fault if her mother had made him into an enemy; and if he was always looking at her, it meant at least he saw something attractive or why would he look? Considering her lonely life, for that she owed him gratitude.

The unpleasant feeling passed and she glanced guardedly up at him. He was walking unmarked in moonlight, innocent of her reaction to him. She felt then—this thought had come to her before—that there might be more to him than she had imagined. She felt ashamed she had never thanked him for the help he had given her father.

In the park the moon was smaller, a wanderer in the white sky. He was talking about winter.

"It's funny you mentioned snow before," Frank said. "I was reading about the life of St. Francis in the library, and when you mentioned the snow it made me think about this story where he wakes up one winter night, asking himself did he do the right thing to be a monk. My God, he thought, supposing I met some nice young girl and got married to her and by now I had a wife and a family? That made him feel bad so he couldn't sleep. He got out of his straw bed and went outside of the church or monastery or wherever he was staying. The ground was all covered with snow. Out of it he made this snow woman, and he said, 'There, that's my wife.' Then he made two or three kids out of the snow. After, he kissed them all and went inside and laid down in the straw. He felt a whole lot better and fell asleep."

The story surprised and touched her.

"Did you just read that?"

"No. I remember it from the time I was a kid. My head is full of those stories, don't ask me why. A priest used to read them to the orphans in this home I was in, and I guess I never forgot them. They come into my thoughts for no reason at all."

He had had a haircut and in his new clothes was hardly recognizable as her father's baggypants assistant who had slept a week in their cellar. Tonight he looked like somebody she had never seen before. His clothes showed taste, and he was, in his way, interesting looking. Without an apron on he seemed younger.

They passed an empty bench. "What do you say if we sit down?" Frank said.

"I'd rather walk."

"Smoke?"

"No."

He lit a cigarette, then caught up with her.

"Sure is some night."

"I want to say thanks for helping my father," Helen said, "You've been very kind. I should have mentioned it before."

"Nobody has to thank me. Your father did me some good favors." He felt uncomfortable.

"Anyway, don't make a career of a grocery," she said. "There's no future in it."

He puffed with a smile on his lips. "Everybody warns me. Don't worry, my imagination is too big for me to get stuck in a grocery. It's only temporary work."

"It isn't what you usually do?"

"No." He set himself to be honest. "I'm just taking a breather, you could call it. I started out wrong and have to change my direction where I am going. The way it happened I landed up in your father's store, but I'm only staying there till I figure out what's my next move."

He remembered the confession he had considered making to her, but the time wasn't ready yet. You could confess as a stranger, and you could confess as a friend.

"I've tried about everything," he said, "now I

got to choose one thing and stick with it. I'm tired of being on the move all the time."

"Isn't it a little late for you to be getting started?"

"I'm twenty-five. There are plenty of guys who start that late and some I have read about started later. Age don't mean a thing. It doesn't make you less than anybody else."

"I never said so." At the next empty bench she paused. "We could sit here for a few minutes if you like."

"Sure." Frank wiped the seat with his handkerchief before she sat down. He offered her his cigarettes.

"I said I don't smoke."

"Sorry, I thought you didn't want to smoke while you were walking. Some girls don't like to." He put his pack away.

She noticed the book he was carrying. "What are you reading?"

He showed it to her.

"*The Life of Napoleon*"?

"That's right."

"Why him?"

"Why not—he was great, wasn't he?"

"Others were in better ways."

"I'll read about them too," Frank said.

"Do you read a lot?"

"Sure. I am a curious guy. I like to know why people tick. I like to know the reason they do the things they do, if you know what I mean."

She said she did.

He asked her what book she was reading.

"*The Idiot*. Do you know it?"

"No. What's it about?"

"It's a novel."

"I'd rather read the truth," he said.

"It is the truth."

Helen asked, "Are you a high school graduate?"

He laughed. "Sure I am. Education is free in this country."

She blushed. "It was a silly question."

"I didn't mean any wisecrack," he said quickly.

"I didn't take it as such."

"I went to high school in three different states and finally got finished up at night—in a night school. I planned on going to college but this job came along that I couldn't turn down, so I changed my mind, but it was a mistake."

"I had to help my mother and father out," Helen said, "so I couldn't go either. I've taken courses in NYU at night—mostly lit courses—and I've added up about a year's credit, but it's very hard at night. My work doesn't satisfy me. I would still like to go full time in the day."

He flipped his butt away. "I've been thinking about starting in college lately, even if I am this age. I know a guy who did it."

"Would you go at night?" she asked.

"Maybe, maybe in the day if I could get the right kind of a job—in an all-night cafeteria or something like that, for instance. This guy I just mentioned did that—assistant manager or something. After five or six years he graduated an engineer. Now he's making his pile, working all over the country."

"It's hard doing it that way—very hard."

"The hours are rough but you get used to it.

When you got something good to do, sleep is a waste of time."

"It takes years at night."

"Time don't mean anything to me."

"It does to me."

"The way I figure, anything is possible. I always think about the different kinds of chances I have. This has stuck in my mind—don't get yourself trapped in one thing, because maybe you can do something else a whole lot better. That's why I guess I never settled down so far. I've been exploring conditions. I still have some very good ambitions which I would like to see come true. The first step to that, I know for sure now, is to get a good education. I didn't use to think like that, but the more I live the more I do. Now it's always on my mind."

"I've always felt that way," Helen said.

He lit another cigarette, throwing the burnt match away. "What kind of work do you do?"

"I'm a secretary."

"You like it?" He smoked with half-closed eyes. She sensed he knew she didn't care for her job and suspected he had heard her father or mother say so.

After a while, she answered, "No, I don't. The job never changes. And I could live happily without seeing some of those characters I have to deal with all day long, the salesmen, I mean."

"They get fresh?"

"They talk a lot. I'd like to be doing something that feels useful—some kind of social work or maybe teaching. I have no sense of accomplishment in what I'm doing now. Five o'clock comes

and at last I go home. That's about all I live for,
I guess."

She spoke of her daily routine, but after a minute saw he was only half-listening. He was staring
at the moon-drenched trees in the distance, his
face drawn, his lit eyes elsewhere.

Helen sneezed, unwound her scarf and
wrapped it tightly around her head.

"Shall we go now?"

"Just till I finish my cigarette."

Some fat nerve, she thought.

Yet his face, even with the broken nose, was
sensitive in the dark light. What makes me so irritable? She had had the wrong idea of him but it
was her own fault, the result of staying so long
apart from people.

He drew a long jagged breath.

"Is something the matter?" she asked.

Frank cleared his throat but his voice was
hoarse. "No, just something popped into my
mind when I was looking at the moon. You know
how your thoughts are."

"Nature sets you thinking?"

"I like scenery."

"I walk a lot for that reason."

"I like the sky at night, but you see more of it
in the West. Out here the sky is too high, there
are too many big buildings."

He squashed his cigarette with his heel and
wearily rose, looking now like someone who had
parted with his youth.

She got up and walked with him, curious about
him. The moon moved above them in the home-
less sky.

After a long silence, he said as they were walking, "I like to tell you what I was thinking about."

"Please, you don't have to."

"I feel like talking," he said. "I got to thinking about this carnie outfit I worked for one time when I was about twenty-one. Right after I got the job I fell for a girl in an acrobatic act. She was built something like you—on the slim side, I would say. At first I don't think I rated with her. I think she thought I wasn't a serious type of guy. She was kind of a complicated girl, you know, moody, with lots of problems in her mind that she kept to herself. Well, one day we got to talking and she told me she wanted to be a nun. I said, 'I don't think it will suit you.' 'What do you know about me?' she said. I didn't tell her, although I know people pretty well, don't ask me why, I guess you are born with certain things. Anyway, the whole summer long I was nuts about her but she wouldn't give me another look though there was nobody else around that I saw she went with. 'Is it my age?' I asked her. 'No, but you haven't lived,' she answered me. 'If you only could see in my heart all I have lived through,' I said, but I have my doubts if she believed me. All we ever did was talk like that. Once in a while I would ask her for a date, not thinking I would ever get one, and I never did. 'Give up,' I said to myself, 'all she is interested in is herself.'

"Then one morning, when it was getting to be around fall and you could smell the season changing, I said to her I was taking off when the show closed. 'Where are you going?' she asked me. I said I was going to look for a better life. She didn't answer anything to that. I said, 'Do you still want to be a nun?' She got red and looked away, then she answered she wasn't sure about that any more. I could see she had changed but I wasn't fool enough to think it was account of me. But I guess it really was, because by accident our hands sort of touched, and when I saw the way she looked at me, it was hard to breathe. My God, I thought, we are both in love. I said to her, 'Honey, meet me here after the show tonight and let's go where we will be alone.' She said yes. Before she left she gave me a quick kiss.

"Anyway, that same afternoon she took off in her old man's jalopy to buy a blouse she had seen in some store window in the last town, but on the way back it started to rain. Exactly what happened I don't know. I guess she misjudged a curve or something and went flying off the road. The jalopy bounced down the hill, and her neck was broken. . . . That's how it ended."

They walked in silence. Helen was moved. But why, she thought, all the sad music?

"I'm awfully sorry."

"It was years ago."

"It was a tragic thing to happen."

"I couldn't expect better," he said.

"Life renews itself."

"My luck stays the same."

"Go on with your plans for an education."

"That's about it," Frank said. "That's what I got to do."

Their eyes met, she felt her scalp prickle.

Then they left the park and went home.

Outside the dark grocery store she quickly said good night.

"I'll stay out a little longer," Frank said. "I like to see the moon."

She went upstairs.

In bed she thought of their walk, wondering how much to believe of what he had told her about his ambitions and plans for college. He could not have said anything to make a better impression on her. And what was the purpose of the sad tale of the carnival girl "built something like you"? Who was he mixing up with his carnival girls? Yet he had told the story simply, without any visible attempt to work on her sympathy. Probably it was a true memory, recalled because he happened to be feeling lonely. She had had her own moonlit memories to contend with. Thinking about Frank, she tried to see him straight but came up with a confusing image: the grocery clerk with the greedy eyes, on top of the ex-carnival hand and future serious college student, a man of possibilities.

On the verge of sleep she sensed a desire on his part to involve her in his life. The aversion she felt for him before returned but she succeeded without too much effort in dispelling it. Thoroughly awake now, she regretted she could not see the sky from her window in the wall, or look down into the street. Who was he making into a wife out of snowy moonlight?

Earnings in the grocery, especially around Christmas and New Year's, continued to rise. For the last two weeks in December Morris averaged an unusual one hundred and ninety. Ida had a new theory to explain the spurt of business: an apartment house had opened for rentals a few blocks away; furthermore, she had heard that Schmitz was not so attentive to his store as he was before. An unmarried storekeeper was sometimes erratic. Morris didn't deny these things but he still attributed their good fortune mostly to his clerk. For reasons that were clear to him the customers liked Frank, so they brought in their friends. As a result, the grocer could once more meet his running expenses, and with pinching and scrimping, even pay off some outstanding bills. Grateful to Frank—who seemed to take for granted the upswing of business—he planned to pay him more than the measly five dollars they shamefacedly gave him, but cautiously decided to see if the added income would continue in January, when business usually slackened off. Even if he regularly took in two hundred a week, with the slight profit he made he could hardly afford a clerk. Before things were easier they had to take in a minimum of two-fifty or three hundred, an impossibility.

Since, though, the situation was better, Morris told Helen that he wanted her to keep more of her hard-earned twenty-five dollars; he said she must now keep fifteen, and if business stayed as it was maybe he would not need her assistance any more. He hoped so. Helen was overwhelmed at having fifteen a week to spend on herself. She needed shoes badly and could use a new coat—hers was little better than a rag—and a dress or two. And she wanted to put away a few dollars for future tuition at NYU. She felt like her father about Frank—he had changed their luck. Remembering what he had said in the park that night about his ambitions and desire for education, she felt he someday would get what he wanted because he was obviously more than just an ordinary person.

He was often at the library. Almost every time Helen went there she saw him sitting over an open book at one of the tables; she wondered if all he did in his spare time was come here and read. She respected him for it. She herself averaged two weekly visits, each time checking out only a book or two, because it was one of her few pleasures to return for another. Even at her loneliest she liked being among books, although she was sometimes depressed to see how much there was to read that she hadn't. Meeting Frank so often, she was at first uneasy: he haunted the place, for what? But, a library was a library; he came here, as she did, to satisfy certain needs. Like her he read a lot because he was lonely, Helen thought. She thought this after he had told her about the carnival girl. Gradually her uneasiness left her.

Although he left, as a rule, when she did, if she wanted to walk home alone, he did not intrude. Sometimes he rode back on the trolley while she walked. Sometimes she was on the trolley and saw him walking. But generally, so long as the weather was not too bad, they went home together, a couple of times turning off into the park. He told her more about himself. He had lived a different life from most people she had known, and she envied him all the places he had been to. Her own life, she thought, was much like her father's, restricted by his store, his habits, hers. Morris hardly ever journeyed past the corner, except on rare occasions, usually to return something a customer had left on the counter. When Ephraim was alive, when they were kids, her father liked to go bathing Sunday afternoons at Coney Island; and on Jewish holidays they would sometimes see a Yiddish play, or ride on the subway to the Bronx to call on landsleit. But after Ephraim died Morris had for years gone nowhere. Neither had she, for other reasons. Where could she go without a cent? She read with eagerness of far-off places but spent her life close to home. She would have given much to visit Charleston, New Orleans, San Francisco, cities she had heard so much about, but she hardly ever got beyond the borough of Manhattan. Hearing Frank talk of Mexico, Texas, California, other such places, she realized anew the meagerness of her movements: every day but Sunday on the BMT to Thirty-fourth Street and back. Add to that a twice-weekly visit to the library at night. In summer,

the same as before, except a few times—usually
during her vacation—to Manhattan Beach; also,
if she were lucky, to a concert or two at Lewisohn
Stadium. Once when she was twenty and worn
out, her mother had insisted she go for a week to
an inexpensive adult camp in New Jersey. Before
that, while in high school, she had traveled to
Washington, D.C., with her American history
class for a week end of visiting government buildings. So far and no further in the open world. To
stick so close to where she had lived her whole
life was a crime. His stories made her impatient—
she wanted to travel, experience, live.

One night as they were sitting on a bench in an
enclosed part of the park beyond the tree-lined
plaza, Frank said he had definitely made up his
mind to start college in the fall. This excited her,
and for hours afterward Helen couldn't stop
thinking about it. She imagined all the interesting
courses he could take, envied him the worthwhile
people he'd meet in his classes, the fun he'd have
studying. She pictured him in nice clothes, his
hair cut shorter, maybe his nose straightened,
speaking a more careful English, interested in mu
sic and literature, learning about politics, psy-
chology, philosophy; wanting to know more the
more he knew, in this way growing in value to
himself and others. She imagined herself invited
by him to a campus concert or play, where she
would meet his college friends, people of promise. Afterward as they crossed the campus in the
dark, Frank would point out the buildings his
classes met in, classes taught by distinguished pro-
fessors. And maybe if she closed her eyes she
could see a time—miracle of miracles—when

Helen Bober was enrolled here, not just a stranger on the run, pecking at a course or two at night, and tomorrow morning back at Levenspiel's Louisville Panties and Bras. At least he made her dream.

To help him prepare for college Helen said he ought to read some good novels, some of the great ones. She wanted Frank to like novels, to enjoy in them what she did. So she checked out *Madame Bovary, Anna Karenina* and *Crime and Punishment,* all by writers he had barely heard of, but they were very satisfying books, she said. He noticed she handled each yellow-paged volume as though she were holding in her respectful hands the works of God Almighty. As if—according to her—you could read in them everything you couldn't afford not to know—the Truth about Life. Frank carried the three books up to his room, and huddled in a blanket to escape the cold that seeped in through the loose window frames, had rough going. The stories were hard to get into because the people and places were strange to him, their crazy names difficult to hold in his mind and some of the sentences were so godawful complicated he forgot the beginning before he got to the end. The opening pages irritated him as he pushed through forests of odd facts and actions. Though he stared for hours at the words, starting one book, then another, then the third—in the end, in exasperation, he flung them aside.

But because Helen had read and respected these books, it shamed him that he hadn't, so he picked one up from the floor and went back to it. As he dragged himself through the first chapters, gradually the reading became easier and he got interested in the people—their lives in one way or another wounded—some to death. Frank read, at the start, in snatches, then in bursts of strange hunger, and before too long he had managed to finish the books. He had started *Madame Bovary* with some curiosity, but in the end he felt disgusted, wearied, left cold. He did not know why people would want to write about that kind of a dame. Yet he felt a little sorry for her and the way things had happened, till there was no way out of it but her death. *Anna Karenina* was better; she was more interesting and better in bed. He didn't want her to kill herself under the train in the end. Still, although Frank felt he could also take the book or leave it, he was moved at the deep change that came over Levin in the woods just after he had thought of hanging himself. At least he wanted to live. *Crime and Punishment* repelled yet fascinated him, with everybody in the joint confessing to something every time he opened his yap—to some weakness, or sickness, or crime. Raskolnikov, the student, gave him a pain, with all his miseries. Frank first had the idea he must be a Jew and was surprised when he found he wasn't. He felt, in places in the book, even when it excited him, as if his face had been shoved into dirty water in the gutter; in other places, as if he had been on a drunk for a month. He was glad when he finished with the book, although he liked Sonia, the prostitute, and thought of her for days after he had read it.

Afterward Helen suggested other novels by the same writers, so he would know them better, but Frank balked, saying he wasn't sure that he had understood those he had read. "I'm sure you have," she answered, "if you got to know the people." "I know them," he muttered. But to please her he worked through two more thick books, sometimes tasting nausea on his tongue, his face strained as he read, eyes bright black, frowning, although he usually felt some relief at the end of the book. He wondered what Helen found so satisfying in all this goddamned human misery, and suspected her of knowing he had spied on her in the bathroom and was using the books to punish him for it. But then he thought it was an unlikely idea. Anyway, he could not get out of his thoughts how quick some people's lives went to pot when they couldn't make up their minds what to do when they had to do it; and he was troubled by the thought of how easy it was for a man to wreck his whole life in a single wrong act. After that the guy suffered forever, no matter what he did to make up for the wrong. At times, as the clerk had sat in his room late at night, a book held stiffly in his reddened hands, his head numb although he wore a hat, he felt a strange falling away from the printed page and had this crazy sensation that he was reading about himself. At first this picked him up but then it deeply depressed him.

One rainy night, as Helen was about to go up to Frank's room to ask him to take back something he had given her that she didn't want, before she could go the phone rang, and Ida hastened out into the hall to call her. Frank, lying on his bed in his room, watching the rainy window, heard her go downstairs. Morris was in the store waiting on someone as Helen came in, but her mother sat in the back over a cup of tea.

"It's Nat," Ida whispered, not moving.

She'll tell herself she isn't listening, thought Helen.

Her first feeling was that she didn't want to talk to the law student, but his voice was warm, which for him meant extended effort, and a warm voice on a wet night was a warm voice. She could easily picture what he looked like as he spoke into the phone. Yet she wished he had called her in December, when she had so desperately wanted him, for now she was again aware of a detachment in herself that she couldn't account for.

"Nobody sees you any more, Helen," Nat began. "Where've you disappeared to?"

"Oh, I've been around," she said, trying to hide a slight tremble in her voice. "And you?"

"Is somebody there where you're talking that you sound so restrained?"

"That's right."

"I thought so. So let me make it quick and clean. Helen, it's been a long time. I want to see you. What do you say if we take in a play this Saturday night? I can stop off for tickets on my way uptown tomorrow."

"Thanks, Nat. I don't think so." She heard her mother sigh.

Nat cleared his throat. "Helen, I honestly want to know how somebody's supposed to defend himself when he hasn't any idea what's in the indictment against him? What kind of a crime have I committed? Yield the details."

"I'm not a lawyer—I don't make indictments."

"So call it a cause—what's the cause? One day we're close to each other, the next I'm alone on an island, holding my hat. What did I do, please tell me?"

"Let's drop this subject."

Here Ida rose and went into the store, softly closing the door behind her. Thanks, thought Helen. She kept her voice low so they wouldn't hear her through the window in the wall.

"You're a funny kid," Nat was saying. "You've got some old-fashioned values about some things. I always told you you punish yourself too much. Why should anybody have such a hot and heavy conscience in these times? People are freer in the twentieth century. Pardon me for saying it but it's true."

She blushed. His insight was to his credit. "My values are my values," she replied.

"What," Nat argued, "would people's lives be like if everybody regretted every beautiful minute of all that happened? Where's the poetry of living?"

"I hope you're alone," she said angrily, "where you're so blithely discussing this subject."

He sounded weary, hurt. "Of course I'm alone. My God, Helen, how low have I fallen in your opinion?"

"I told you what was going on at this end. Up to a minute ago my mother was still in the room."

"I'm sorry, I forgot."

"It's all right now."

"Look, girl," he said affectionately, "the telephone is no place to hash out our personal relations. What do you say if I run upstairs and see you right away? We got to come to some kind of a sensible understanding. I'm not exactly a pig, Helen. What you don't want is your privilege, if

I may be so frank. So you don't want, but at least
let's be friends and go out once in a while. Let
me come up and talk to you."

"Some other time, Nat, I have to do something
now."

"For instance?"

"Some other time," she said.

"Why not?" Nat answered amiably.

When he had hung up, Helen stood at the
phone, wondering if she had done right. She felt
she hadn't.

Ida entered the kitchen. "What did he want—
Nat?"

"Just to talk."

"He asked you to go out?"

She admitted it.

"What did you answer him?"

"I said I would some other time."

"What do you mean 'some other time?' " Ida
said sharply. "What are you already, Helen, an
old lady? What good is it to sit so many nights
alone upstairs? Who gets rich from reading?
What's the matter with you?"

"Nothing's the matter, Mama." She left the
store and went into the hall.

"Don't forget you're twenty-three years old,"
Ida called after her.

"I won't."

Upstairs her nervousness grew. When she
thought what she had to do she didn't want to, yet
felt she must.

They had met, she and Frank, last night at the
library, the third time in eight days. Helen noticed as they were leaving that he clumsily carried
a package she took to contain some shirts or under-

wear, but on the way home Frank flung away his cigarette, and under a street lamp handed it to her. "Here, this is for you."

"For me? What is it?"

"You'll find out."

She took it half-willingly, and thanked him. Helen carried it awkwardly the rest of the way home, neither of them saying much. She had been caught by surprise. If she had given herself a minute to think, she would have refused it on grounds that it was wise just to stay friends; because, she thought, neither of them really knew the other. But once she had the thing in her hands she hadn't the nerve to ask him to take it back. It was a medium-sized box of some sort with something heavy in it—she guessed a book; yet it seemed too big for a book. As she held it against her breast, she felt a throb of desire for Frank and this disturbed her. About a block from the grocery, nervously saying good night, she went on ahead. This was how they parted when the store window was still lit.

Ida was downstairs with Morris when Helen came into the house, so no questions were asked. She shivered a little as she unwrapped the box on her bed, ready to hide it the minute she heard a footstep on the stairs. Lifting the carton lid, she found two packages in it, each wrapped in white tissue paper and tied with red ribbons with uneven bows, obviously by Frank. When she had untied the first present, Helen gasped at the sight of a long, hand-woven scarf—rich black wool interlaced with gold thread. She was startled to discover that the second present was a red leather copy of Shakespeare's plays. There was no card.

She sat weakly down on the bed. I can't, she told herself. They were expensive things, probably had cost him every penny of the hard-earned money he was saving for college. Even supposing he had enough for that, she still couldn't take his gifts. It wasn't right, and coming from him, it was, somehow, less than not right.

She wanted then and there to go up to his room and leave them at the door with a note, but hadn't the heart to the very night he had given them to her.

The next evening, after a day of worry, she felt she must return them; and now she wished she had done it before Nat had called, then she might have been more relaxed on the phone.

Helen got down on her hands and knees and reached under the bed for the carton with Frank's scarf and book in it. It touched her that he had given her such lovely things—so much nicer than anyone else ever had. Nat, at his best, had produced a half-dozen small pink roses.

For gifts you pay, Helen thought. She drew a deep breath, and taking the box went quietly up the stairs. She tapped hesitantly on Frank's door. He had recognized her step and was waiting behind the door. His fists were clenched, the nails cutting his palms.

When he opened the door and his glance fell on what she was carrying, he frowned as though struck in the face.

Helen stepped awkwardly into the little room, quickly shutting the door behind her. She suppressed a shudder at the smallness and barrenness of the place. On his unmade bed lay a sock he had been trying to mend.

"Are the Fusos home?" she asked in a low voice.

"They went out." He spoke dully, his eyes hopelessly stuck to the things he had given her.

Helen handed him the box with the presents. "Thanks so much, Frank," she said, trying to smile, "but I really don't think I ought to take them. You'll need every cent for your college tuition in the fall."

"That's not the reason you mean," he said.

Her face reddened. She was about to explain that her mother would surely make a scene if she saw his gifts, but instead said, "I can't keep them."

"Why not?"

It wasn't easy to answer and he didn't make it easier, just held the rejected presents in his big hands as if they were living things that had suddenly died.

"I can't," she got out. "Your taste is so nice, I'm sorry."

"Okay," he said wearily. He tossed the box on the bed and the Shakespeare fell to the floor. She stooped quickly to pick it up and was unnerved to see it had opened to "Romeo and Juliet."

"Good night." She left his room and went hastily downstairs. In her room she thought she heard the distant sound of a man crying. She listened tensely, her hand on her throbbing throat, but no longer heard it.

Helen took a shower to relax, then got into a nightgown and housecoat. She picked up a book but couldn't read. She had noticed before signs he might be in love with her, but now she was almost sure of it. Carrying his package as he had walked with her last night, he had been somebody different, though the hat and overcoat were the same. There seemed to be about him a size and potentiality she had not seen before. He did not say love but love was in him. When the insight came to her, at almost the minute he was handing her the package, she had reacted with gooseflesh. That it had gone this far was her own fault. She had warned herself not to get mixed up with him but hadn't obeyed her warning. Out of loneliness she had encouraged him. What else, going so often to the library, knowing he would be there? And she had stopped off with him, on their walks, for pizzas and coffee; had listened to his stories, discussed with him plans for college, talked at length about books he was reading; at the same time she had been concealing these meetings from her father and mother. He knew it, no wonder he had built up hopes.

The strange thing was there were times she felt she liked him very much. He was, in many ways, a worthwhile person, and where a man gave off honest feeling, was she a machine to shut off her own? Yet she knew she mustn't become seriously attracted to him because there would be trouble in buckets. Trouble, thank you, she had had enough of. She wanted now a peaceful life without worry —any more worries. Friends they could be, in a minor key; she might on a moonlit night even hold hands with him, but beyond that nothing. She should have said something of the sort; he would have saved his presents for a better prospect and she would not now be feeling guilt at having hurt him. Yet in a way he had surprised her by his apparent depth of affection. She had not expected anything to happen so quickly, be-

cause, for her, things had happened in reverse
order. Usually she fell in love first, then the man,
if he wasn't Nat Pearl, responded. So the other
way around was nice for a change, and she wished
it would happen more often, but with the right
one. She must go, she decided, less to the library;
he would then understand, if he didn't already,
and give up any idea of having her love. When
he realized what was what he would get over his
pain, if he really felt any. But her thoughts gave
her no peace, and though she tried often, she
could still not concentrate on her books. When
Morris and Ida trudged through her room, her
light was out and she seemed to be sleeping.

As she left the house for work the next morning, to her dismay she spied the carton containing
his presents on top of some greasy garbage bags in
the stuffed rubbish can at the curb. The cover of
the can apparently had been squeezed down on
the box but had fallen off and now lay on the sidewalk. Lifting the carton cover, Helen saw the two
gifts, loosely covered with the tissue paper. Angered by the waste, she plucked the scarf and book
out of the crushed cardboard box and went quickly into the hall with them. If she took them upstairs Ida would want to know what she had, so
she decided to hide them in the cellar. She turned
on the light and went quietly down, trying to keep
her high heels from clicking on the stairs. Then
she removed the tissue paper and hid the presents, neither of which had been harmed, in the
bottom drawer of a broken chiffonier in their bin.
The dirty tissue paper and red ribbons she rolled
up in a sheet of old newspaper, then went upstairs and pressed it into the garbage can. Helen

noticed her father at the window, idly watching her. She passed into the store, said good morning, washed her hands and left for work. On the subway she felt despondent.

After supper that night, while Ida was washing dishes, Helen sneaked down into the cellar, got the scarf and book and carried them up to Frank's room. She knocked and nobody answered. She considered leaving them at the door but felt he would throw them away again unless she spoke to him first.

Tessie opened her door. "I heard him go out a while before, Helen." Her eyes were on the things in her hands.

Helen blushed. "Thanks, Tessie."

"Any message?"

"No." She returned to her floor and once more pushed the gifts under her bed. Changing her mind, she put the book and scarf in different bureau drawers, hiding them under her underwear. When her mother came up she was listening to the radio.

"You going someplace tonight, Helen?"

"Maybe, I don't know. Maybe to the library."

"Why so much to the library? You went a couple days ago."

"I go to meet Clark Gable, Mama."

"Helen, don't get fresh."

Sighing, she said she was sorry.

Ida sighed too. "Some people want their children to read more. I want you to read less."

"That won't get me married any faster."

Ida knitted but soon grew restless and went down to the store again. Helen got out Frank's things, packed them in heavy paper she had bought on her way home, tied the bundle with cord, and took the trolley to the library. He wasn't there.

The next night she tried first his room, then when she was able to slip out of the house, again the library, but found him in neither place.

"Does Frank still work here?" she asked Morris in the morning.

"Of course he works."

"I haven't seen him for a while," she said. "I thought he might be gone."

"In the summer he leaves."

"Did he say that?"

"Mama says."

"Does he know?"

"He knows. Why you ask me?"

She said she was just curious.

As Helen came into the hall that evening she heard the clerk descending the stairs and waited for him at the landing. Lifting his hat, he was about to pass when she spoke.

"Frank, why did you throw your two presents into the garbage?"

"What good were they to me?"

"It was a terrible waste. You should have got your money back."

He smiled in the corners of his mouth. "Easy come, easy go."

"Don't joke. I took them out of the rubbish and have them in my room for you. They weren't damaged."

"Thanks."

"Please give them back and get your money. You'll need every penny for the fall."

"Since I was a kid I hate to go back with stuff I bought."

"Then let me have the sales checks and I'll return them during my lunch hour."

"I lost them," he answered.

She said gently, "Frank, sometimes things turn out other than we plan. Don't feel hurt."

"When I don't feel hurt, I hope they bury me."

He left the house, she walked up the stairs.

Over the week end Helen went back to crossing off the days on the calendar. She found she had crossed nothing since New Year's. She fixed that. On Sunday the weather turned fair and she grew restless. She wished again for Nat to call her; instead his sister did and they walked, in the early afternoon, on the Parkway.

Betty was twenty-seven and resembled Sam Pearl. She was large-boned and on the plain side but made good use of reddish hair and a nice nature. She was in her ideas, Helen thought, somewhat dull. They had not too much in common and saw each other infrequently, but liked to talk once in a while, or go to a movie together. Recently Betty had become engaged to a CPA in her office and was with him most of the time. Now she sported a prosperous diamond ring on her stylish finger. Helen, for once, envied her, and Betty, as if she had guessed, wished her the same good luck.

"And it should happen soon," she said.

"Many thanks, Betty."

After they had gone a few blocks, Betty said, "Helen, I don't like to butt in somebody else's private business but for a long time I wanted to ask you what happened between you and my brother Nat. I once asked him and he gave me double talk."

"You know how such things go."

"I thought you liked him?"

"I did."

"Then why don't you see him any more? Did you have some kind of a fight?"

"No fights. We didn't have the same things in mind."

Betty asked no more. Later, she remarked, "Sometime give him another chance, Helen. Nat really has the makings of a good person. Shep, my boy friend, thinks so too. His worst fault is he thinks his brains entitle him to certain privileges. You'll see, in time he'll get over it."

"I may," Helen said. "We'll see sometime."

They returned to the candy store, where Shep Hirsch, Betty's stout, eyeglassed, future husband was waiting to take her for a drive in his Pontiac.

"Come along, Helen," said Betty.

"With pleasure." Shep tipped his hat.

"Go, Helen," advised Goldie Pearl.

"Thanks, all, from the bottom of my heart," said Helen, "but I have some of my underthings to iron."

Upstairs, she stood at the window, looking out at the back yards. The remnants of last week's dirty snow. No single blade of green, or flower to light the eye or lift the heart. She felt as if she were made of knots and in desperation got on her coat, tied a yellow kerchief around her head and left the house again, not knowing which way to go. She wandered toward the leafless park.

At the approach to the park's main entrance there was a small island in the street, a concrete

triangle formed by intersecting avenues. Here
people sat on benches during the day and tossed
peanuts or pieces of bread to the noisy pigeons
that haunted the place. Coming up the block,
Helen saw a man squatting by one of the benches,
feeding the birds. Otherwise, the island was deserted. When the man rose, the pigeons fluttered
up with him, a few landing on his arms and shoulders, one perched on his fingers, pecking peanuts
from his cupped palm. Another fat bird sat on his
hat. The man clapped his hands when the peanuts
were gone and the birds, beating their wings,
scattered.

When she recognized Frank Alpine, Helen
hesitated. She felt in no mood to see him, but remembering the package hidden in her bureau
drawer, determined once and for all to get rid of
it. Reaching the corner, she crossed over to the
island.

Frank saw her coming and wasn't sure he cared
one way or the other. The return of his presents
had collapsed his hopes. He had thought that if
she ever fell for him it would change his life in the
way he wanted it to happen, although at times
the very thought of another change, even in this
sense of it, made him miserable. Yet what was the
payoff, for instance, of marrying a dame like her
and having to do with Jews the rest of his life? So
he told himself he didn't care one way or the
other.

"Hi," Helen said.

He touched his hat. His face looked tired but
his eyes were clear and his gaze steady, as if he had
been through something and had beat it. She felt
sorry if she had caused him any trouble.

"I had a cold," Frank remarked.

"You should get more sun."

Helen sat down on the edge of the bench, as if she were afraid, he thought, she would be asked to take a lease on it; and he sat a little apart from her. One of the pigeons began to chase another running in circles and landed on its back. Helen looked away but Frank idly watched the birds until they flew off.

"Frank," she said, "I hate to sound like a pest on this subject, but if there's anything I can't stand it's waste. I know you're not Rockefeller, so would you mind giving me the names of the stores where you bought your kind presents so that I can return them? I think I can without the sales checks."

Her eyes, he noticed, were a hard blue, and though he thought it ridiculous, he was a little scared of her, as if she were far too determined, too dead serious for him. At the same time he felt he still liked her. He had not thought so, but with them sitting together like this he thought again that he did. It was in a way a hopeless feeling, yet it was more than that because he did not exactly feel hopeless. He felt, as he sat next to her and saw her worn, unhappy face, that he still had a chance.

Frank cracked his knuckles one by one. He turned to her. "Look, Helen, maybe I try to work too fast. If so, I am sorry. I am the type of a person, who if he likes somebody, has to show it. I like to give her things, if you understand that, though I do know that not everybody likes to take. That's their business. My nature is to give and I couldn't change it even if I wanted. So okay. I am also sorry I got sore and dumped your presents in the can and you had to take them out. But what I want to say is this. Why don't you just go ahead and keep one of those things that I got for you? Let it be a little memory of a guy you once knew that wants to thank you for the good books you told him to read. You don't have to worry that I expect anything for what I give you."

"Frank . . ." she said, reddening.

"Just let me finish. How's this for a deal? If you keep one of those things, I will take the other back to the store and get what I paid for it. What do you say?"

She was not sure what to say, but since she wanted to be finished with it, nodded at his proposal.

"Fine," Frank said. "Now what do you want the most?"

"Well, the scarf is awfully nice, but I'd rather keep the book."

"So keep the book then," he said. "You can give me the scarf anytime you want and I promise I will bring it back."

He lit a cigarette and inhaled deeply.

She considered whether to say good-by, now that the matter had been settled, and go on with her walk.

"You busy now?" he asked.

She guessed a short stroll. "No."

"How about a movie?"

It took her a minute to reply. Was he starting up once more? She felt she must quickly set limits to keep him from again creeping too close. Yet out of respect for his already hurt feelings, she thought it best that she think out exactly what to say and tactfully say it, later on.

"I'll have to be back early."

"So let's go," he said, getting up.

Helen slowly untied her kerchief, then knotted it, and they went off together.

As they walked she kept wondering if she hadn't made a mistake in accepting the book. In spite of what he had said about expecting nothing she felt a gift was a claim, and she wanted none on her. Yet, when, almost without noticing, she once more asked herself if she liked him at all, she had to admit she did a little. But not enough to get worried about; she liked him but not with an eye to the possibility of any deeper feeling. He was not the kind of man she wanted to be in love with. She made that very clear to herself, for among his other disadvantages there was something about him, evasive, hidden. He sometimes appeared to be more than he was, sometimes less. His aspirations, she sensed, were somehow apart from the self he presented normally when he wasn't trying, though he was always more or less trying; therefore when he was trying less. She could not quite explain this to herself, for if he could make himself seem better, broader, wiser when he tried, then he had these things in him because you couldn't make them out of nothing. There was more to him than his appearance. Still, he hid what he had and he hid what he hadn't. With one hand the magician showed his cards, with the other he turned them into smoke. At the very minute he was revealing himself, saying who he was, he made you wonder if it was true. You looked into mirrors and saw mirrors and didn't know

what was right or real or important. She had gradually got the feeling that he only pretended to be
frank about himself, that in telling so much about
his experiences, his trick was to hide his true self.
Maybe not purposely—maybe he had no idea he
was doing it. She asked herself whether he might
have been married already. He had once said he
never was. And was there more to the story of the
once-kissed, tragic carnival girl? He had said no.
If not, what made her feel he had done something
—committed himself in a way she couldn't guess?

As they were approaching the movie theater, a
thought of her mother crossed her mind and she
heard herself say, "Don't forget I'm Jewish."

"So what?" Frank said.

Inside in the dark, recalling what he had answered her, he felt this elated feeling, as if he had
crashed head on through a brick wall but hadn't
bruised himself.

She had bitten her tongue but made no reply.

Anyway, by summer he'd be gone.

Ida was very unhappy that she had kept Frank
on when she could have got rid of him so easily.
She was to blame and she actively worried.
Though she had no evidence, she suspected Helen
was interested in the clerk. *Something* was going
on between them. She did not ask her daughter
what, because a denial would shame her. And
though she had tried she felt she could not really
trust Frank. Yes, he had helped the business, but
how much would they have to pay for it? Sometimes when she came upon him alone in the store,
his expression, she told herself, was sneaky. He
sighed often, muttered to himself, and if he saw he
was observed, pretended he hadn't. Whatever he

did there was more in it than he was doing. He was like a man with two minds. With one he was here, with the other someplace else. Even while he read he was doing more than reading. And his silence spoke a language she couldn't understand. Something bothered him and Ida suspected it was her daughter. Only when Helen happened to come into the store or the back while he was there, did he seem to relax, become one person. Ida was troubled, although she could not discover in Helen any response to him. Helen was quiet in his presence, detached, almost cold to the clerk. She gave him for his restless eyes, nothing—her back. Yet for this reason, too, Ida worried.

One night after Helen had left the house, when her mother heard the clerk's footsteps going down the stairs, she quickly got into a coat, wrapped a shawl around her head and trudged through a sprinkle of snow after him. He walked to the movie house several blocks away, paid his money, and passed in. Ida was almost certain that Helen was inside, waiting for him. She returned home with nails in her heart and found her daughter upstairs, ironing. Another night she followed Helen to the library. Ida waited across the street, shivering for almost an hour in the cold, until Helen emerged, then followed her home. She chided herself for her suspicions but they would not fly from her mind. Once, listening from the back, she heard her daughter and the clerk talking about a book. This annoyed her. And when Helen later happened to mention that Frank had plans to begin college in the autumn, Ida felt he was saying that only to get her interested in him.

She spoke to Morris and cautiously asked if he

had noticed anything developing between Helen
and the clerk.

"Don't be foolish," the grocer replied. He had
thought about the possibility, at times felt concerned, but after pondering how different they
were, had put the idea out of his head.

"Morris, I am afraid."

"You are afraid of everything, even which it
don't exist."

"Tell him to leave now—business is better."

"So is better," he muttered, "but who knows
how will be next week. We decided he will stay till
summer."

"Morris, he will make trouble."

"What kind trouble will he make?"

"Wait," she said, clasping her hands, "a tragedy
will happen."

Her remark at first annoyed, then worried him.

The next morning the grocer and his clerk
were sitting at the table, peeling hot potatoes. The
pot had been drained of water and dumped on its
side; they sat close to the steaming pile of potatoes, hunched over, ripping off the salt-stained
skins with small knives. Frank seemed ill at ease.
He hadn't shaved and had dark blobs under his
eyes. Morris wondered if he had been drinking
but there was never any smell of liquor about him.
They worked without speaking, each lost in his
thoughts.

After a half-hour, Frank squirming restlessly in
his chair, remarked, "Say, Morris, suppose somebody asked you what do the Jews believe in, what
would you tell them?"

The grocer stopped peeling, unable at once to reply.

"What I like to know is what is a Jew anyway?"

Because he was ashamed of his meager education Morris was never comfortable with such questions, yet he felt he must answer.

"My father used to say to be a Jew all you need is a good heart."

"What do you say?"

"The important thing is the Torah. This is the Law—a Jew must believe in the Law."

"Let me ask you this," Frank went on. "Do you consider yourself a real Jew?"

Morris was startled, "What do you mean if I am a real Jew?"

"Don't get sore about this," Frank said, "But I can give you an argument that you aren't. First thing, you don't go to the synagogue—not that I have ever seen. You don't keep your kitchen kosher and you don't eat kosher. You don't even wear one of those little black hats like this tailor I knew in South Chicago. He prayed three times a day. I even hear the Mrs say you kept the store open on Jewish holidays, it makes no difference if she yells her head off."

"Sometimes," Morris answered, flushing, "to have to eat, you must keep open on holidays. On Yom Kippur I don't keep open. But I don't worry about kosher, which is to me old-fashioned. What I worry is to follow the Jewish Law."

"But all those things are the Law, aren't they? And don't the Law say you can't eat any pig, but I have seen you taste ham."

"This is not important to me if I taste pig or if I don't. To some Jews is this important but not to me. Nobody will tell me that I am not Jewish because I put in my mouth once in a while, when my tongue is dry, a piece ham. But they will tell me, and I will believe them, if I forget the Law. This means to do what is right, to be honest, to be good. This means to other people. Our life is hard enough. Why should we hurt somebody else? For everybody should be the best, not only for you or me. We ain't animals. This is why we need the Law. This is what a Jew believes."

"I think other religions have those ideas too," Frank said. "But tell me why it is that the Jews suffer so damn much, Morris? It seems to me that they like to suffer, don't they?"

"Do you like to suffer? They suffer because they are Jews."

"That's what I mean, they suffer more than they have to."

"If you live, you suffer. Some people suffer more, but not because they want. But I think if a Jew don't suffer for the Law, he will suffer for nothing."

"What do you suffer for, Morris?" Frank said.

"I suffer for you," Morris said calmly.

Frank laid his knife down on the table. His mouth ached. "What do you mean?"

"I mean you suffer for me."

The clerk let it go at that.

"If a Jew forgets the Law," Morris ended, "he is not a good Jew, and not a good man."

Frank picked up his knife and began to tear the skins off the potatoes. The grocer peeled his pile in silence. The clerk asked nothing more.

When the potatoes were cooling, Morris, troubled by their talk, asked himself why Frank had brought up this subject. A thought of Helen, for some reason, crossed his mind.

"Tell me the truth," he said, "why did you ask me such questions?"

Frank shifted in his chair. He answered slowly, "To be truthful to you, Morris, once I didn't have much use for the Jews."

Morris looked at him without moving.

"But that was long ago," said Frank, "before I got to know what they were like. I don't think I understood much about them."

His brow was covered with sweat.

"Happens like this many times," Morris said.

But his confession had not made the clerk any happier.

One afternoon, shortly after lunch, happening to glance at himself in the mirror, Morris saw how bushy his hair was and how thick the pelt on his neck; he felt ashamed. So he said to Frank he was going across the street to the barber. The clerk, studying the racing page of the *Mirror,* nodded. Morris hung up his apron and went into the store to get some change from the cash register. After he took a few quarters out of the drawer, he checked the receipts for the day and was pleased. He left the grocery and crossed the car tracks to the barber shop.

The chair was empty and he didn't have to wait. As Mr. Giannola, who smelled of olive oil, worked on him and they talked, Morris, though embarrassed at all the hair that had to be cut by the barber, found himself thinking mostly of his store. If it would only stay like this—no Karp's paradise, but at least livable, not the terrible mis-

ery of only a few months ago—he would be satisfied. Ida had again been nagging him to sell, but
what was the use of selling until things all over
got better and he could find a place he would
have confidence in? Al Marcus, Breitbart, all the
drivers he talked to, still complained about business. The best thing was not to look for trouble
but stay where he was. Maybe in the summer,
after Frank left, he would sell out and search for
a new place.

As he rested in the barber's chair, the grocer,
watching through the window his own store, saw
with satisfaction that at least three customers had
been in since he had sat down. One man left with
a large lumpy bag, in which Morris imagined at
least six bottles of beer. Also, two women had
come out with heavy packages, one carrying a
loaded market bag. Figuring, let's say, at least two
dollars apiece for the women, he estimated he had
taken in a nice fiver and earned his haircut. When
the barber unpinned the sheet around him and
Morris returned to the grocery, he struck a match
over the cash register and peered with anticipation at the figures. To his great surprise he saw
that only a little more than three dollars had been
added to the sum he had noted on leaving the
store. He was stunned. How could it be only three
if the bags had been packed tight with groceries?
Could it be they contained maybe a couple of
boxes of some large item like cornflakes, that came
to nothing? He could hardly believe this and felt
upset to the point of illness.

In the back he hung up his overcoat, and with
fumbling fingers tied his apron strings.

Frank glanced up from the racing page with a

smile. "You look different without all the kelp on you, Morris. You look like a sheep that had the wool clipped off it."

The grocer, ashen, nodded.

"What's the matter your face is so pale?"

"I don't feel so good."

"Whyn't you go up then and take your snooze?"

"After."

He shakily poured himself a cup of coffee.

"How's business?" he asked, his back to the clerk.

"So-so," said Frank.

"How many customers you had since I went to the barber?"

"Two or three."

Unable to meet Frank's eye, Morris went into the store and stood at the window, staring at the barber shop, his thoughts in a turmoil, tormented by anxiety. Was the Italyener stealing from the cash register? The customers had come out with stuffed bags, what was there to show for it? Could he have given things on credit? They had told him never to. So what then?

A man entered and Morris waited on him. The man spent forty-one cents. When Morris rang up the sale, he saw it added correctly to the previous total. So the register was not broken. He was now almost certain that Frank had been stealing, and when he asked himself how long, he was numbed.

Frank went into the store and saw the dazed grocer at the window.

"Don't you feel any better, Morris?"

"It will go away."

"Take care of yourself. You don't want to get sick any more."

Morris wet his lips but made no reply. All day
he went around, dragging his heart. He had said
nothing to Ida, he didn't dare.

For the next few days he carefully watched the
clerk. He had decided to give him the benefit of
doubt yet not rest till he knew the truth. Sometimes he sat at the table inside, pretending to be
reading, but he was carefully listening to each
item the customer ordered. He jotted down the
prices and when Frank packed the groceries,
quickly calculated the approximate sum. After
the customer had gone he went idly to the register
and secretly examined the amount the clerk had
rung up. Always it was near the figure he had figured, a few pennies more or less. So Morris said he
would go upstairs for a few minutes, but instead
stationed himself in the hall, behind the back
door. Peering through a crack in the wood, he
could see into the store. Standing here, he added
in his head the prices of the items ordered, and
later, about fifteen minutes, casually checked the
receipts and found totaled there the sum he had
estimated. He began to doubt his suspicions. He
may have wrongly guessed the contents of the
customers' bags when he was at the barber's. Yet
he could still not believe they had spent only three
dollars; maybe Frank had caught on and was being wary.

Morris then thought, yes, the clerk could have
been stealing, but if so it was more his fault than
Frank's. He was a grown man with a man's
needs and all he was paying him, including his
meager commission, was about six or seven dollars a week. True, he got his room and meals free,
plus cigarettes, but what was six or seven dollars

to anybody in times like these, when a decent pair of shoes cost eight to ten? The fault was therefore his for paying slave wages for a workman's services, including the extra things Frank did, like last week cleaning out the stopped sewer pipe in the cellar with a long wire and so saving five or ten dollars that would surely have gone to the plumber, not to mention how his presence alone had improved the store.

So although he worked on a slim markup, one late afternoon when he and Frank were packing out some cartons of goods that had just been delivered, Morris said to his assistant standing on the stepladder, "Frank, I think from now on till it comes summer I will raise you your wages to straight fifteen dollars without any commission. I would like to pay you more, but you know how much we do here business."

Frank looked down at the grocer. "What for, Morris? The store can't afford to pay me any more than I am getting. If I take fifteen your profit will be shot. Let it go the way it is now. I am satisfied."

"A young man needs more and he spends more."

"I got all I want."

"Let it be like I said."

"I don't want it," said the clerk, annoyed.

"Take," insisted the grocer.

Frank finished his packing then got down, saying he was going to Sam Pearl's. His eyes were averted as he went past the grocer.

Morris continued to pack the cans on the shelves. Rather than admit Frank's raise to Ida and start a fuss, he decided to withhold from the register the money he would need to pay him, a

little every day so it would not be noticed. He
would privately give it to the clerk sometime on
Saturday, before Ida handed him his regular
wages.

Helen felt herself, despite the strongest doubts, falling in love with Frank. It was a dizzying dance, she didn't want to. The month was cold—it often snowed—she had a rough time, fighting hesitancies, fears of a disastrous mistake. One night she dreamed their house had burned down and her poor parents had nowhere to go. They stood on the sidewalk, wailing in their underwear. Waking, she fought an old distrust of the broken-faced stranger, without success. The stranger had changed, grown unstrange. That was the clue to what was happening to her. One day he seemed unknown, lurking at the far end of an unlit cellar; the next he was standing in sunlight, a smile on his face, as if all she knew of him and all she didn't, had fused into a healed and easily remembered whole. If he was hiding anything, she thought, it was his past pain, his orphanhood and consequent suffering. His eyes were quieter, wiser. His crooked nose fitted his face and his face fitted him. It stayed on straight. He was gentle, waiting for whatever he awaited with a grace she respected. She felt she had changed him and this affected her. That she had willed to stay free of him made little difference now. She felt tender to him, wanted him close by. She had, she thought, changed in changing him.

After she had accepted his gift of a book their relationship had subtly altered. What else, if whenever she read in her Shakespeare, she thought of Frank Alpine, even heard his voice in the plays? Whatever she read, he crept into her thoughts; in every book he haunted the words, a character in a plot somebody else had invented, as if all associations had only one end. He was, to begin with, everywhere. So, without speaking of it, they met again in the library. That they were meeting among books relieved her doubt, as if she believed, what possible wrong can I do among books, what possible harm can come to me here?

In the library he too seemed surer of himself— though once they were on their way home he became almost remote, strangely watchful, looking back from time to time as though they were being followed, but who or what would follow them? He never took her as far as the store; as before, by mutual consent, she went on ahead, then he walked around the block and entered the hall from the other way so he wouldn't have to go past the grocery window and possibly be seen coming from the direction she had come from. Helen interpreted his caution to mean he sensed victory and didn't want to endanger it. It meant he valued her more than she was altogether sure she wanted to be.

Then one night they walked across a field in the park and turned to one another. She tried to awaken in herself a feeling of danger, but danger was dulled, beyond her, in his arms. Pressed against him, responsive to his touch, she felt the

cold ebb out of the night, and a warmth come
over her. Her lips parted—she drew from his
impassioned kiss all she had long desired. Yet at
the moment of sweetest joy she felt again the presence of doubt, almost a touch of illness. This made
her sad. The fault was her. It meant she still could
not fully accept him. There were still signals
signaling no. She had only to think of them and
they would work in her, pinching the nerves. On
their way home she could not forget the first happiness of their kiss. But why should a kiss become
anxiety? Then she saw that his eyes were sad, and
she wept when he wasn't looking. Would it never
come spring?

She stalled love with arguments, only to be surprised at their swift dissolution; found it difficult
to keep her reasons securely nailed down, as they
were before. They flew up in the mind, shifted,
changed, as if something had altered familiar
weights, values, even experience. He wasn't, for
instance, Jewish. Not too long ago this was the
greatest barrier, her protection against ever taking
him seriously; now it no longer seemed such an
urgently important thing—how could it in times
like these? How could anything be important but
love and fulfillment? It had lately come to her
that her worry he was a gentile was less for her
own sake than for her mother and father. Although she had only loosely been brought up as
Jewish she felt loyal to the Jews, more for what
they had gone through than what she knew of
their history or theology—loved them as a people,
thought with pride of herself as one of them; she
had never imagined she would marry anybody but
a Jew. But she had recently come to think that in

such unhappy times—when the odds were so high against personal happiness—to find love was miraculous, and to fulfill it as best two people could was what really mattered. Was it more important to insist a man's religious beliefs be exactly hers (if it was a question of religion) , or that the two of them have in common ideals, a desire to keep love in their lives, and to preserve in every possible way what was best in themselves? The less difference among people, the better; thus she settled it for herself yet was dissatisfied for those for whom she hadn't settled it.

But her logic, if it was logic, wouldn't decide a thing for her unhappy parents once they found out what was going on. With Frank enrolled in college maybe some of Ida's doubts of his worth as a person might wither away, but college was not the synagogue, a B.A. not a bar mitzvah; and her mother and even her father with his liberal ideas would insist that Frank had to be what he wasn't. Helen wasn't at all sure she could handle them if it ever came to a showdown. She dreaded the arguments, their tear-stained please and her own misery for taking from the small sum of peace they had in the world, adding to the portion of their unhappiness. God knows they had had enough of that. Still, there was just so much time to live, so little of youth among the years; one had to make certain heartbreaking choices. She foresaw the necessity of upholding her own, enduring pain yet keeping to her decisions. Morris and Ida would be greviously hurt, but before too long their pain would grow less and perhaps leave them; yet she could not help but hope her own children would someday marry Jews.

And if she married Frank, her first job would be to help him realize his wish to be somebody. Nat Pearl wanted to be "somebody," but to him this meant making money to lead the life of some of his well-to-do friends at law school. Frank, on the other hand, was struggling to realize himself as a person, a more worthwhile ambition. Though Nat had an excellent formal education, Frank knew more about life and gave the impression of greater potential depth. She wanted him to become what he might, and conceived a plan to support him through college. Maybe she could even see him through a master's degree, once he knew what he wanted to do. She realized this would mean the end of her own vague plans for going to day college, but that was really lost long ago, and she thought she would at last accept the fact once Frank had got what she hadn't. Maybe after he was working, perhaps as an engineer or chemist, she could take a year of college just to slake her thirst. By then she would be almost thirty, but it would be worth postponing having a family to give him a good start and herself a taste of what she had always wanted. She also hoped they would be able to leave New York. She wanted to see more of the country. And if things eventually worked out, maybe Ida and Morris would someday sell the store and come to live near them. They might all live in California, her parents in a little house of their own where they could take life easy and be near their grandchildren. The future offered more in the way of realizable possibilities, Helen thought, if a person dared take a chance with it. The question was, did she?

She postponed making any important decision.

She feared most of all the great compromise—she had seen so many of the people she knew settle for so much less than they had always wanted. She feared to be forced to choose beyond a certain point, to accept less of the good life than she had hungered for, appreciably less—to tie up with a fate far short of her ideals. That she mustn't do, whether it meant taking Frank or letting him go. Her constant fear, underlying all others, was that her life would not turn out as she had hoped, or would turn out vastly different. She was willing to change, make substitutions, but she would not part with the substance of her dreams. Well, she would know by summertime what to do. In the meantime Frank went every third night to the library and there she was. But when the old-maid librarian smiled knowingly upon them, Helen felt embarrassed, so they met elsewhere. They met in cafeterias, movie houses, the pizza place—where it was impossible to say much, or hold him or be held. To talk they walked, to kiss they hid.

Frank said he was getting the college bulletins he had written for, and around May he would have a transcript of his high school record sent to whichever place they picked for him to go. He showed he knew she had plans for him. He didn't say much more, for he was always afraid the old jinx would grab hold of him if he opened his mouth a little too wide.

At first he waited patiently. What else was there to do? He had waited and was still waiting. He had been born waiting. But before long, though he tried not to show it, he was beginning to be fed up with his physical loneliness. He grew tired of the frustrations of kissing in doorways, a cold feel on a bench in the park. He thought of her as he had seen her in the bathroom, and the memory became a burden. He was the victim of the sharp edge of his hunger. So he wanted her to the point where he thought up schemes for getting her into his room and in bed. He wanted satisfaction, relief, a stake in the future. She's not yours till she gives it to you, he thought. That's the way they all are. It wasn't always true, but it was true enough. He wanted an end to the torment of coming to a boil, then thank you, no more. He wanted to take her completely.

They met more often now. At a bench on the Parkway, on street corners—in the wide windy world. When it rained or snowed, they stepped into doorways, or went home.

He complained one night, "What a joke. We leave the same warm house to meet out in the cold here."

She said nothing.

"Forget it," Frank said, looking into her troubled eyes, "we will take it the way it is."

"This is our youth," she said bitterly.

He wanted then to ask her to come to his room but felt she wouldn't, so he didn't ask.

One cold, starry night she led him through the trees in the park near where they usually sat, onto a broad meadow where on summer nights lovers lay in the grass.

"Come on and sit down on the ground for a minute," Frank urged, "there's nobody here now."

But Helen wouldn't.

"Why not?" he asked.

"Not now," she said.

She realized, though he later denied it, that the situation had made him impatient. Sometimes he was moody for hours. She worried, wondering what rusty wound their homelessness had opened in him.

One evening they sat alone on a bench on the Parkway, Frank with his arm around her; but because they were so close to home Helen was jumpy and moved away whenever somebody passed by.

After the third time Frank said, "Listen, Helen, this is no good. Some night we will have to go where we can be inside."

"Where?" she asked.

"Where do you say?"

"I can't say anything, Frank. I don't know."

"How long is this going to keep up like this?"

"As long as we like," she said, smiling faintly, "or as long as we like each other."

"I don't mean it that way. What I am talking about is not having any place private to go to."

She answered nothing.

"Maybe some night we ought to sneak up to my room," he suggested. "We could do it easy enough —I don't mean tonight but maybe Friday, after Nick and Tessie go to the show and your mother is down in the store. I bought a new heater and the room keeps warm. Nobody will know you are there. We would be alone for once. We have never been alone that way."

"I couldn't," Helen said.

"Why?"

"Frank, I can't."

"When will I get a chance to put my arms around you without being an acrobat?"

"Frank," said Helen, "there's one thing I wish

to make clear to you. I won't sleep with you now, if that's what you mean. It'll have to wait till I am really sure I love you, maybe till we're married, if we ever are."

"I never asked you to," Frank said. "All I said was for you to come up to my room so we could spend the time more comfortable, not you bucking away from me every time a shadow passes."

He lit a cigarette and smoked in silence.

"I'm sorry." After a minute she said, "I thought I ought to tell you how I feel on this subject. I was going to sometime anyway."

They got up and walked, Frank gnawing his wound.

A cold rain washed the yellow slush out of the gutters. It rained drearily for two days. Helen had promised to see Frank on Friday night but she didn't like the thought of going out in the wet. When she came home from work, and got the chance, she slipped a note under his door, then went down. The note said that if Nick and Tessie did go to the movies, she would try to come up to his room for a while.

At half past seven Nick knocked on Frank's door and asked him if he wanted to go to the pictures. Frank said no, he thought he had seen the picture that was playing. Nick said good-by and he and Tessie, bundled in raincoats and carrying umbrellas, left the house. Helen waited for her mother to go down to Morris, but Ida complained that her feet hurt, and said she would rest. Helen then went down herself, knowing Frank would hear her on the stairs and figure something had gone wrong. He would understand she could not go up to see him so long as anyone might hear her.

But a few minutes later, Ida came down, saying she felt restless upstairs. Helen then said she intended to drop in on Betty Pearl and might go along with her to the dressmaker who was making her wedding things.

"It's raining," said Ida.

"I know, Mama," Helen answered, hating her deceit.

She went up to her room, got her hat and coat, rubbers and an umbrella; then walked down, letting the door bang, as if she had just left the house. She quietly opened it and went on tiptoe up the stairs.

Frank had guessed what was going on and opened his door to her quick tap. She was pale, obviously troubled, but very lovely. He held her hard and could feel her heartbeat against his chest.

She will let me tonight, he told himself.

Helen was still uneasy. It took her a while to quiet her conscience for having lied to her mother. Frank had put out the light and tuned in the radio to soft dance music; now he lay on the bed, smoking. For a time she sat awkwardly in his chair, watching the glow of his cigarette, and when not that, the drops of lit rain on the window, reflecting the street light. But after he had rubbed his butt into an ash tray on the floor, Helen stepped out of her shoes and lay down beside him on the narrow bed, Frank moving over to the wall.

"This is more like it," he sighed.

She lay with closed eyes in his arms, feeling the

warmth of the heater like a hand on her back. For a minute she half-dozed, then woke to his kisses. She lay motionless, a little tense, but when he stopped kissing her, relaxed. She listened to the quiet sound of the rain in the street, making it in her mind into spring rain, though spring was weeks away; and within the rain grew all sorts of flowers; and amid the spring flowers, in this flowering dark—a sweet spring night—she lay with him in the open under new stars and a cry rose to her throat. When he kissed her again, she responded with passion.

"Darling."

"I love you, Helen, you are my girl."

They kissed breathlessly, then he undid the buttons of her blouse. She sat up to unhook her brassière but as she was doing it, felt his fingers under her skirt.

Helen grabbed his hand. "Please, Frank. Let's not get that hot and bothered."

"What are we waiting for, honey?" He tried to move his hand but her legs tightened and she swung her feet off the bed.

He pulled her back, pressing her shoulders down. She felt his body trembling on hers and for a fleeting minute thought he might hurt her; but he didn't.

She lay stiff, unresponsive on the bed. When he kissed her again she didn't move. It took a while before he lay back. She saw by the reflected glow of the heater how unhappy he looked.

Helen sat on the edge of the bed, buttoning her blouse.

His hands covered his face. He said nothing but she could feel his body shivering on the bed.

"Christ," he muttered.

"I'm sorry," she said softly. "I told you I wouldn't."

Five minutes passed. Frank slowly sat up. "Are you a virgin, is that what's eating you?"

"I'm not," she said.

"I thought you were," he said, surprised. "You act like one."

"I said I wasn't."

"Then why do you act like one? Don't you know what it does to people?"

"I'm people."

"Then why do you do it for?"

"Because I believe in what I'm doing."

"I thought you said you weren't a virgin?"

"You don't have to be a virgin to have ideals in sex."

"What I don't understand is if you did it before, what's the difference if we do it now?"

"We can't, just because I did," she said, brushing her hair back. "That's the point. I did it and that's why I can't with you now. I said I wouldn't, that night on the Parkway."

"I don't get it," Frank said.

"Loving should come with love."

"I said I love you, Helen, you heard me say it."

"I mean I have to love you too. I think I do but sometimes I'm not sure."

He fell again into silence. She listened absent-mindedly to the radio but nobody was dancing now.

"Don't be hurt, Frank."

"I'm tired of that," he said harshly.

"Frank," said Helen, "I said I slept with some-body before and the truth of it is, if you want to know, I'm sorry I did. I admit I had some pleasure, but after, I thought it wasn't worth it, only I didn't know at the time I would feel that way, because at the time I didn't know what I wanted. I suppose I felt I wanted to be free, so I settled for sex. But if you're not in love sex isn't being free, so I made a promise to myself that I never would any more unless I really fell in love with somebody. I don't want to dislike myself. I want to be disciplined, and you have to be too if I ask it. I ask it so I might someday love you without reservations."

"Crap," Frank said, but then, to his surprise, the idea seized him. He thought of himself as disciplined, then wished he were. This seemed to him like an old and faraway thought, and he remembered with regret and strange sadness how often he had wished for better control over himself, and how little of it he had achieved.

He said, "I didn't mean to say what I just now did, Helen."

"I know," she answered.

"Helen," he said huskily, "I want you to know I am a very good guy in my heart."

"I don't think otherwise."

"Even when I am bad I am good."

She said she thought she knew what he meant.

They kissed, again and again. He thought there were a whole lot worse things than waiting for something that was going to be good once he got it.

Helen lay back on the bed and dozed, awaking when Nick and Tessie came into their bedroom, talking about the movie they had seen. It was a love story and Tessie had liked it very much. After they undressed and got into bed their double bed creaked. Helen felt bad for Frank but Frank did not seem to feel bad. Nick and Tessie soon fell asleep. Helen, breathing lightly, listened to their heavy breathing, worrying how she was going to get down to her floor, because if Ida was awake she would hear her on the stairs. But Frank said in a low voice that he would carry her to the vestibule, then she could go up after a few minutes, as if she had just come home from some place.

She put on her coat, hat and rubbers, and was careful to remember her umbrella. Frank carried her down the stairs. There were only his slow, heavy steps going down. And not long after they had kissed good night and he had gone for a walk in the rain, Helen opened the hall door and went up.

Then Ida fell asleep.

Thereafter Helen and Frank met outside the house.

It was snowing in the afternoon, when the front door opened and in came Detective Minogue, pushing before him this stocky handcuffed guy, unshaven, and wearing a faded green wind-breaker and denim slacks. He was about twenty-seven, with tired eyes and no hat. In the store, he lifted his manacled hands to wipe the snow off his wet hair.

"Where's Morris?" the detective asked the clerk.

"In the back."

"Go on in," said Detective Minogue to the handcuffed man.

They went into the back. Morris was sitting on the couch, stealing a smoke. He hurriedly put out the butt and dropped it into the garbage pail.

"Morris," said the detective, "I think I have got the one who hit you on the head."

The grocer's face turned white as flour. He stared at the man but didn't approach him.

After a minute he muttered, "I don't know if it's him. He had his face covered with a handkerchief."

"He's a big son of a bitch," the detective said. "The one that hit you was big, wasn't he?"

"Heavy," said Morris. "The other was big."

Frank was standing in the doorway, watching.

Detective Minogue turned to him. "Who're you?"

"He's my clerk," explained Morris.

The detective unbuttoned his overcoat and took a clean handkerchief out of his suit pocket. "Do me a favor," he said to Frank. "Tie this around his puss."

"I would rather not," Frank answered.

"As a favor. To save me the trouble of getting hit on the head with his cuffs."

Frank took the handkerchief, and though not liking to, tied it around the man's face, the suspect holding himself stiffly erect.

"How about it now, Morris?"

"I can't tell you," Morris said, embarrassed. He had to sit down.

"You want some water, Morris?" Frank asked.

"No."

"Take your time," said Detective Minogue, "look him over good."

"I don't recognize him. The other acted more rough. He had a rough voice—not nice."

"Say something, son," the detective said.

"I didn't hold this guy up," said the suspect in a dead voice.

"Is that the voice, Morris?"

"No."

"Does he look like the other one—the heavy guy's partner?"

"No, this is a different man."

"How are you so sure?"

"The helper was a nervous man. He was bigger than this one. Also this one has got small hands. The helper had big heavy hands."

"Are you positive? We grabbed him on a job last night. He held up a grocery with another guy who got away."

The detective pulled the handkerchief off the man's face.

"I don't know him," Morris said with finality.

Detective Minogue folded the handkerchief and tucked it into his pocket. He slipped his eyeglasses into a leather case. "Morris, I think I asked you already if you saw my son Ward Minogue around here. Have you yet?"

"No," said the grocer.

Frank went over to the sink and rinsed his mouth with a cup of water.

"Maybe you know him?" the detective asked him.

"No," said the clerk.

"O.K., then." The detective unbuttoned his overcoat. "By the way, Morris, did you ever find out who was stealing your milk that time?"

"Nobody steals any more," said Morris.

"Come on, son," said the detective to the suspect.

The handcuffed man went out of the store into the snow, the detective following him.

Frank watched them get into the police car, sorry for the guy. What if they arrested me now, he thought, although I am not the same guy I once was?

Morris, thinking of the stolen milk bottles, gazed guiltily at his assistant.

Frank happened to notice the size of his hands, then had to go to the toilet.

As he was lying in his bed after supper, thinking about his life, Frank heard footsteps coming up the stairs and someone banged on his door. For a minute his head hammered with fear, but he got up and forced himself to open the door. Grinning at him from under his fuzzy hat stood Ward Minogue, his eyes small and smeary. He had lost weight and looked worse.

Frank let him in and turned on the radio. Ward sat on the bed, his shoes dripping from the snow.

"Who told you I lived here?" Frank asked.

"I watched you go in the hall, opened the door and heard you go up the stairs," Ward said.

How am I ever going to get rid of this bastard, Frank thought.

"You better stay away from here," he said with a heavy heart. "If Morris recognizes you in that goddamned hat, we will both go to jail."

"I came to visit my popeyed friend, Louis Karp," said Ward. "I wanted a bottle but he wouldn't give it to me because I am short on cash, so I thought my good-looking friend Frank Alpine will lend me some. He's an honest, hard-working bastard."

"You picked the wrong guy. I am poor."

Ward eyed him craftily. "I was sure you'd have saved up a pile by now, stealing from the Jew."

Frank stared at him but didn't answer.

Ward's glance shifted. "Even if you are stealing his chicken feed, it ain't any skin off me. Why I came is this. I got a new job that we can do without any trouble."

"I told you I am not interested in your jobs, Ward."

"I thought you would like to get your gun back, otherwise it might accidentally get lost with your name on it."

Frank rubbed his hands.

"All you got to do is drive," Ward said amiably. "The job is a cinch, a big liquor joint in Bay Ridge. After nine o'clock they only keep one man on. The take will be over three hundred."

"Ward, you don't look to me in any kind of condition to do a stickup. You look more like you need to be in a hospital."

"All I got is a bad heartburn."

"You better take care of yourself."

"You are making me cry."

"Why don't you start going straight?"

"Why don't you?"

"I am trying to."

"Your Jew girl must be some inspiration."

"Don't talk about her, Ward."

"I tailed you last week when you took her in the park. She's a nice piece. How often do you get it?"

"Get the hell out of here."

Ward got up unsteadily. "Hand over fifty bucks or I will fix you good with your Jew boss and your

Jew girl. I will write them a letter who did the stickup last November."

Frank rose, his face hard. Taking his wallet out of his pocket, he emptied it on the bed. There were eight single dollar bills. "That's all I have got."

Ward snatched up the money. "I'll be back for more."

"Ward," Frank said through tight teeth, "if you drag your ass up here any more to make trouble, or if you ever follow me and my girl again, or tell Morris anything, the first thing I will do is telephone your old man at the police station and tell him under which rock he can find you. He was in the grocery asking about you today, and if he ever meets up with you, he looks like he will bust your head off."

Ward with a moan spat at the clerk and missed, the gob of spit trickling down the wall.

"You stinking kike," he snarled. Rushing out into the hall, he all but fell down two flights of stairs.

The grocer and Ida ran out to see who was making the racket, but by then Ward was gone.

Frank lay in bed, his eyes closed.

One dark and windy night when Helen left the house late, Ida followed her through the cold streets and across the plaza into the interior of the deserted park, and saw her meet Frank Alpine. There, in an opening between a semicircle of tall lilac shrubs and a grove of dark maples, were a few benches, dimly lit and private, where they liked to come to be alone. Ida watched them sitting together on one of the benches, kissing. She dragged herself home and went upstairs, half-dead. Morris was asleep and she didn't want to wake him, so she sat in the kitchen, sobbing.

When Helen returned and saw her mother weeping at the kitchen table, she knew Ida knew, and Helen was both moved and frightened.

Out of pity she asked, "Mama, why are you crying?"

Ida at last raised her tear-stained face and said in despair, "Why do I cry? I cry for the world. I cry for my life that it went away wasted. I cry for you."

"What have I done?"

"You have killed me in my heart."

"I've done nothing that's wrong, nothing I'm ashamed of."

"You are not ashamed that you kissed a goy?"

Helen gasped. "Did you follow me, Mama?"

"Yes," Ida wept.

"How could you?"

"How could you kiss a goy?"

"I'm not ashamed that we kissed."

She still hoped to avoid an argument. Everything was unsettled, premature.

Ida said, "If you marry such a man your whole life will be poisoned."

"Mama, you'll have to be satisfied with what I now say. I have no plans to marry anybody."

"What kind plans you got then with a man that he kisses you alone in a place where nobody can find you in the park?"

"I've been kissed before."

"But a goy, Helen, an Italyener."

"A man, a human being like us."

"A man is not good enough. For a Jewish girl must be a Jew."

"Mama, it's very late. I don't wish to argue. Let's not wake Papa."

"Frank is not for you. I don't like him. His eyes don't look at a person when he talks to them."

"His eyes are sad. He's had a hard life."

"Let him go and find someplace a shikse that he likes, not a Jewish girl."

"I have to work in the morning. I'm going to bed."

Ida quieted down. When Helen was undressing she came into her room. "Helen," she said, holding back her tears, "the only thing I want for you is the best. Don't make my mistake. Don't make worse and spoil your whole life, with a poor man that he is only a grocery clerk which we don't know about him nothing. Marry somebody who can give you a better life, a nice professional boy with a college education. Don't mix up now with a stranger. Helen, I know what I'm talking. Believe me, I know." She was crying again.

"I'll try my best," Helen said.

Ida dabbed at her eyes with a handkerchief. "Helen, darling, do me one favor."

"What is it? I am very tired."

"Please call up Nat tomorrow. Just to speak to him. Say hello, and if he asks you to go out with him, tell him yes. Give him a chance."

"I gave him one."

"Last summer you enjoyed so much with him. You went to the beach, to concerts. What happened?"

"Our tastes are different," Helen said wearily.

"In the summer you said your tastes were the same."

"I learned otherwise."

"He is a Jewish boy, Helen, a college graduate. Give him another chance."

"All right," said Helen, "now will you go to sleep?"

"Also don't go no more with Frank. Don't let him kiss you, it's not nice."

"I can't promise."

"Please, Helen."

"I said I'd call Nat. Let that be an end of it now. Good night, Mama."

"Good night," Ida said sadly.

Though her mother's suggestion depressed her, Helen called Nat from her office the next day. He was cordial, said he had bought a secondhand car from his future brother-in-law and invited her to go for a drive.

She said she would sometime.

"How about Friday night?" Nat asked.

She was seeing Frank on Friday. "Could you make it Saturday?"

"I happen to have an engagement Saturday, also Thursday—something doing at the law school."

"Then Friday is all right." She agreed reluctantly, thinking it would be best to change the date with Frank, to satisfy her mother.

When Morris came up for his nap that afternoon Ida desperately begged him to send Frank away at once.

"Leave me alone on this subject ten minutes."

"Morris," she said, "last night I went out when Helen went, and I saw she met Frank in the park, and they kissed each the other."

Morris frowned. "He kissed her?"

"Yes."

"She kissed him?"

"I saw with my eyes."

But the grocer, after thinking about it, said wearily, "So what is a kiss? A kiss is nothing."

Ida said furiously, "Are you crazy?"

"He will go away soon," he reminded her. "In the summer."

Tears sprang into her eyes. "By summer could happen here ten times a tragedy."

"What kind tragedy you expecting—murder?"

"Worse," she cried.

His heart turned cold, he lost his temper. "Leave me alone on this subject, for God's sakes."

"Wait," Ida bitterly warned.

On Thursday of that week Julius Karp left Louis in the liquor store and stepped outside to peek through the grocery window to see if Morris was alone. Karp had not set foot in Morris's store since the night of the holdup, and he uneasily considered the reception he might meet if he were to go in now. Usually, after a time of not speaking to one another, it was Morris Bober, by nature unable to hold a grudge, who gave in and spoke to Karp; but this time he had put out of his mind the possibility of seeking out the liquor dealer and re-establishing their fruitless relationship. While in bed during his last convalescence he had thought much of Karp—an unwilling and distasteful thinking—and had discovered he disliked him more than he had imagined. He resented him as a crass and stupid person who had fallen through luck into flowing prosperity. His every good for-

tune spattered others with misfortune, as if there
was just so much luck in the world and what Karp
left over wasn't fit to eat. Morris was incensed by
thoughts of the long years he had toiled without
just reward. Though this was not Karp's fault, it
was that a delicatessen had moved in across the
street to make a poor man poorer. Nor could the
grocer forgive him the blow he had taken on the
head in his place, who could in health and wealth
better afford it. Therefore it gave him a certain
satisfaction not to have anything to do with the
liquor dealer, though he was every day next door.

Karp, on the other hand, had been content to
wait for Morris to loosen up first. He pictured the
grocer yielding his aloof silence while he enjoyed
the signs of its dissolution, meanwhile pitying the
poor Jew his hard luck life—in capital letters.
Some were born that way. Whereas Karp in whatever he touched now coined pure gold, if Morris
Bober found a rotten egg in the street, it was already cracked and leaking. Such a one needed
someone with experience to advise him when to
stay out of the rain. But Morris, whether he knew
how Karp felt, or not, remained rigidly uncom-
municative—offering not so much as a flicker of
recognition when on his way to the corner for his
daily *Forward,* he passed the liquor dealer standing in front of his store or caught his eye peeking
into his front window. As a month passed, now,
quickly, almost four, Karp came to the uncomfortable conclusion that although Ida was still friendly to him, he would this time get nothing for free
from Morris; he wasn't going to give in. He reacted
coldly to this insight, would give back what he got
—so let it be indifference. But indifference was

not a commodity he was pleased to exchange. For
some reason that was not clear to him Karp liked
Morris to like him, and it soon rankled that his
down-at-the-heels neighbor continued to remain
distant. So he had been hit on the head in a holdup, but was the fault Karp's? *He* had taken care
—why hadn't Morris, the shlimozel? Why, when he
had warned him there were two holdupniks across
the street, hadn't he like a sensible person gone first
to lock his door, then telephoned the police? Why?
—because he was inept, unfortunate.

And because he was, his troubles grew like bananas in bunches. First, in another accident to his
hard head, then through employing Frank Alpine.
Karp, no fool, knew the makings of a bad situation
when he saw it. Frank, whom he had got acquainted with and considered a fly-by-night rolling
stone, would soon make trouble—of that he was
certain. Morris's fly-specked, worm-eaten shop did
not earn half enough to pay for a full-time helper,
and it was idiotic extravagance for the grocer, after he was better, to keep the clerk working for
him. Karp soon learned from Louis that his esti-
mate of a bad situation was correct. He found out
that Frank every so often invested in a bottle of
the best stuff, paying, naturally, cash—but whose?
Furthermore Sam Pearl, another waster, had mentioned that the clerk would now and then paste a
two-dollar bill on some nag's useless nose, from
which it blew off in the breeze. This done by a
man who was no doubt paid in peanuts added
up to only one thing—he stole. Who did he steal
from? Naturally from M. Bober, who had anyway
nothing—who else? Rockefeller knew how to take
care of his millions, but if Morris earned a dime he

lost it before he could put it into his torn pocket.
It was the nature of clerks to steal from those they
were working for. Karp had, as a young man, privately peculated from his employer, a half-blind
shoe wholesaler; and Louis, he knew, snitched
from him, but by Louis he was not bothered. He
was, after all, a son; he worked in the business
and would someday—it shouldn't be too soon—
own it. Also, by strict warnings and occasional surprise inventories he held Louis down to a bare
minimum—beans. A stranger stealing money was
another matter—slimy. It gave Karp gooseflesh to
think of the Italian working for him.

And since misfortune was the grocer's lot, the
stranger would shovel on more, not less, for it was
always dangerous to have a young goy around
where there was a Jewish girl. This worked out
by an unchangeable law that Karp would gladly
have explained to Morris had they been speaking,
and saved him serious trouble. That *this* trouble,
too, existed he had confirmed twice in the last
week. Once he saw Helen and Frank walking on
the Parkway under the trees, and another time
while driving home past the local movie house, he
had glimpsed them coming out after a show,
holding hands. Since then he had often thought
about them, indeed with anxiety, and felt he
would in some way like to assist the luckless Bober.

Without doubt Morris kept Frank on to make
his life easier, and probably, being Bober, he had
no idea what was happening behind his back.
Well, Julius Karp would warn him of his daughter's
danger. Tactfully he would explain him what was
what. After, he would put in a plug for Louis,
who, Karp was aware, had long liked Helen but

was not sure enough of himself to be successful with her. Swat Louis down and he retreated to tenderize his fingernails with his teeth. In some things he needed a push. Karp felt he could ease his son's way to Helen by making Morris a proposition he had had in the back of his head for almost a year. He would describe Louis' prospects after marriage in terms of cold cash and other advantages, and suggest that Morris speak to Helen on the subject of going with him seriously. If they went together a couple of months—Louis would give her an extravagant good time—and the combination worked out, it would benefit not only the daughter, but the grocer as well, for then Karp would take over Morris's sad gesheft and renovate and enlarge it into a self-service market with the latest fixtures and goods. His tenant around the corner he would eliminate when his lease expired—a sacrifice, but worthwhile. After that, with himself as the silent partner giving practical advice, it would take a marvelous catastrophe to keep the grocer from earning a decent living in his old age.

Karp foresaw that the main problem of this matter would be Helen, whom he knew as a strictly independent yet not unworthy girl, even if she had pretensions to marriage with a professional—although she had got no place with Nat Pearl. To be successful, Nat needed what Louis Karp would have plenty of, not a poor girl. So he had acted in his best interests in gently shooing Helen away when her thoughts got too warm—a fact Karp had picked up from Sam Pearl. Louis, on the other hand, could afford a girl like Helen, and Helen, independent and intelligent, would be good for

Louis. The liquor store owner decided that when the opportunity came he would talk turkey to her like a Dutch uncle. He would patiently explain that her only future with Frank would be as an outcast, poorer even than her father and sharing his foolish fate; whereas with Louis she could have what she wanted and more—leave it to her father-in-law. Karp felt that once Frank had gone she would listen to reason and appreciate the good life he was offering her. Twenty-three or -four was a dangerous age for a single girl. At that age she would not get younger; at that age even a goy looked good.

Having observed that Frank had gone into Sam Pearl's place, and that Morris was for the moment alone in the back of his store, Karp coughed clear his throat and stepped inside the grocery. When Morris, emerging from the rear, saw who it after all was, he experienced a moment of vindictive triumph, but this was followed by annoyance that the pest was once more present, and at the same time by an uncomfortable remembrance that Karp never entered unaccompanied by bad news. Therefore he stayed silent, waiting for the liquor dealer, in prosperous sport jacket and gabardine slacks which could not camouflage his protrusive belly nor subtract from the foolishness of his face, to speak; but for once Karp's active tongue lay flat on its back as, embarrassed in recalling the results of his very last visit here, he stared at the visible scar on Morris's head.

In pity for him, the grocer spoke, his tone friendlier than he would have guessed. "So how are you, Karp?"

"Thanks. What have I got to complain?" Beaming, he thrust a pudgy hand across the counter and Morris found himself unwillingly weighing the heavy diamond ring that pressed his fingers.

Since it did not seem sensible to Karp, one minute after their reconciliation, to blurt out news of a calamity concerning Morris's daughter, he fiddled around for words to say and came up with, "How's business?"

Morris had hoped he would ask. "Fine, and every day gets better."

Karp contracted his brows; yet it occurred to him that Morris's business might have improved more than he had guessed, when peering at odd moments through the grocery window, he had discovered a customer or two instead of the usual dense emptiness. Now on the inside after several months, he noticed the store seemed better taken care of, the shelves solidly packed with stock. But if business was better he at once knew why.

Yet he casually asked, "How is this possible? You are maybe advertising in the paper?"

Morris smiled at the sad joke. Where there was no wit money couldn't buy it. "By word of mouth," he remarked, "is the best advertising."

"This is according to what the mouth says."

"It says," Morris answered without shame, "that I got a fine clerk who has pepped me up the business. Instead going down in the winter, every day goes up."

"Your clerk did this?" Karp said, thoughtfully scratching under one buttock.

"The customers like him. A goy brings in goyim."

"New customers?"

"New, old."

"Something else helps you also?"

"Also helps a little the new apartment house that it opened in December."

"Hmm," said Karp, "nothing more?"

Morris shrugged. "I don't think so. I hear your Schmitz don't feel so good and he don't give service like he used to give. Came back a few customers from him, but the most important help to me is Frank."

Karp was astonished. Could it be that the man didn't know what had happened practically under his nose? He then and there saw a God-given opportunity to boot the clerk out of the place forever. "That wasn't Frank Alpine who improved you your business," he said decisively. "That was something else."

Morris smiled slightly. As usual the sage knew every reason for every happening.

But Karp persisted. "How long does he work here?"

"You know when he came—in November."

"And right away the business started to pick up?"

"Little by little."

"This happened," Karp announced with excitement, "not because this goy came here. What did he know about the grocery business? Nothing. Your store improved because my tenant Schmitz got sick and had to close his store part of the day. Didn't you know that?"

"I heard he was sick," Morris answered, his throat tightening, "but the drivers said his old father came to give him a help."

"That's right," Karp said, "but in the middle December he went every morning to the hospital for treatments. First the father stayed in the store, then he got too tired so Schmitz didn't open till maybe nine, ten o'clock, instead of seven. And instead of closing ten o'clock at night, he closed eight. This went on like this till last month, then he couldn't open till eleven o'clock in the morning, and so he lost half a day's business. He tried to sell the store but nobody would buy then. Yesterday he closed up altogether. Didn't somebody mention that to you?"

"One of the customers said," Morris answered, distressed, "but I thought it was temporary."

"He's very sick," said Karp solemnly. "He won't open again."

My God, thought Morris. For months he had watched the store when it was empty and while it was being altered, but never since its opening had he gone past Sam Pearl's corner to look at it. He hadn't the heart to. But why had no one told him that the place had been closing part of the day for more than two months—Ida, Helen? Probably they had gone past it without noticing the door was sometimes closed. In their minds, as in his, it was always open for *his* business.

"I don't say," Karp was saying, "that your clerk didn't help your income, but the real reason things got better is when Schmitz couldn't stay open, some of his customers came here. Naturally, Frank wouldn't tell you that."

Filled with foreboding, Morris reflected on what the liquor dealer had said. "What happened to Schmitz?"

"He has a bad blood disease and lays now in the hospital."

"Poor man," the grocer sighed. Hope wrestled

shame as he asked, "Will he give the store in auction?"

Karp was devastating. "What do you mean give in auction? It's a good store. He sold it Wednesday to two up-to-date Norwegian partners and they will open next week a modern fancy grocery and delicatessen. You will see where your business will go."

Morris, with clouded eyes, died slowly.

Karp, to his horror, realized he had shot at the clerk and wounded the grocer. He remarked hastily, "What could I do? I couldn't tell him to go in auction if he had a chance to sell."

The grocer wasn't listening. He was thinking of Frank with a violent sense of outrage, of having been deceived.

"Listen, Morris," Karp said quickly, "I got a proposition for you about your gesheft. Throw out first on his ass this Italyener that he fooled you, then tell Helen that my Louis—"

But when the ghost behind the counter cursed him in a strange tongue for the tidings he had brought, Karp backed out of the store and was swallowed in his own.

After a perilous night at the hands of ancient enemies, Morris escaped from his bed and appeared in the store at five A.M. There he faced the burdensome day alone. The grocer had struggled all night with Karp's terrible news—had tossed around like a red coal why nobody had told him before how sick the German was—maybe one of the salesmen, or Breitbart, or a customer. Probably no one had thought it too important, seeing that Schmitz's store was until yesterday open daily.

Sure he was sick, but somebody had already mentioned that, and why should they tell him again if they figured that people got sick but then they got better? Hadn't he himself been sick, but who had talked of it in the neighborhood? Probably nobody. People had their own worries to worry about. As for the news that Schmitz had sold his store, the grocer felt that here he had nothing to complain of—he had been informed at once, like a rock dropped on his skull.

As for what he would do with Frank, after long pondering the situation, thinking how the clerk had acted concerning their increase in business— as if he alone had created their better times—Morris at length decided that Frank had not—as he had assumed when Karp told him the news— tried to trick him into believing that he was responsible for the store's change for the better. The grocer supposed that the clerk, like himself, was probably ignorant of the true reason for their change of luck. Maybe he shouldn't have been, since he at least got out during the day, visited other places on the block, heard news, gossip— maybe he should have known, but Morris felt he didn't, possibly because he wanted to believe he was their benefactor. Maybe that was why he had been too blind to see what he should have seen, too deaf to have heard what he had heard. It was possible.

After his first confusion and fright, Morris had decided he must sell the store—he had by eight o'clock already told a couple of drivers to pass the word around—but he must under no circumstances part with Frank and must keep him here to do all he could to prevent the Norwegian partners, after they had reopened the store, from quickly calling back the customers of Schmitz who were with him now. He couldn't believe that Frank hadn't helped. It had not been proved in the Supreme Court that the German's sickness was the only source of their recent good fortune. Karp said so but since when did Karp speak the word of God? Of course Frank had helped the business— only not so much as they had thought. Ida was not so wrong about that. But maybe Frank could hold onto a few people; the grocer doubted he himself could. He hadn't the energy, the nerve to be alone in the store during another time of change for the worse. The years had eaten away his strength.

When Frank came down he at once noticed that the grocer was not himself, but the clerk was too concerned with his own problems to ask Morris what ailed him. Often since the time Helen had been in his room he had recalled her remark that he must discipline himself and wondered why he had been so moved by the word, why it should now bang around in his head like a stick against a drum. With the idea of self-control came the feeling of the beauty of it—the beauty of a person being able to do things the way he wanted to, to do good if he wanted; and this feeling was followed by regret—of the slow dribbling away, starting long ago, of his character, without him lifting a finger to stop it. But today, as he scraped at his hard beard with a safety razor, he made up his mind to return, bit by bit until all paid up, the hundred and forty-odd bucks he had filched from Morris in the months he had worked for him, the figure of which he had kept for this very purpose written on a card hidden in his shoe.

To clean up the slate in a single swipe, he thought again of telling Morris about his part in the holdup. A week ago he was on the point of getting it past his teeth, had even spoken aloud the grocer's name, but when Morris looked up Frank felt it was useless and said never mind. He was born he thought, with a worrisome conscience that had never done him too much good, although at times he had liked having the acid weight of it in him because it had made him feel he was at least that different from other people. It made him want to set himself straight so he could build his love for Helen right, so it would stay right.

But when he pictured himself confessing, the Jew listening with a fat ear, he still could not stand the thought of it. Why should he make more trouble for himself than he could now handle, and end by defeating his purpose to fix things up and have a better life? The past was the past and the hell with it. He had unwillingly taken part in a holdup, but he was, like Morris, more of a victim of Ward Minogue. If alone, he wouldn't have done it. That didn't excuse him that he did, but it at least showed his true feelings. So what was there to confess if the whole thing had been sort of an accident? Let bygones be gone. He had no control over the past—could only shine it up here and there and shut up as to the rest. From now on he would keep his mind on tomorrow, and tomorrow take up the kind of life that he saw he valued more than how he had been living. He would change and live in a worthwhile way.

Impatient to begin, he waited to empty the contents of his wallet into the cash drawer. He thought he could try it when Morris was napping;

but then for some cockeyed reason, although there was nothing for her to do in the store today, Ida came down and sat in the back with him. She was heavy-faced, dispirited; she sighed often but said nothing, although she acted as if she couldn't stand the sight of him. He knew why, Helen had told him, and he felt uncomfortable, as if he were wearing wet clothes she wouldn't let him take off; but the best thing was to keep his trap shut and let Helen handle her end of it.

Ida wouldn't leave, so he couldn't put the dough back although his itch to do so had grown into impatience. Whenever somebody went into the store Ida insisted on waiting on them, but this last time after she came back she said to Frank, stretched out on the couch with a butt in his mouth, that she wasn't feeling so well and was going up.

"Feel better," he said sitting up, but she didn't reply and at last left. He went quickly into the store, once he was sure she was upstairs. His wallet contained a five-dollar bill and a single, and he planned to put it all back in the register, which would leave him only with a few coins in his pocket but tomorrow was payday anyway. After ringing up the six bucks, to erase the evidence of an unlikely sale he rang up "no sale." Frank then felt a surge of joy at what he had done and his eyes misted. In the back he drew off his shoe, got out the card, and subtracted six dollars from the total amount he owed, He figured he could pay it all up in a couple-three months, by taking out of the bank the money—about eighty bucks—that was left there, returning it bit by bit, and when that was all used up, giving back part of his weekly salary till he had the debt squared. The trick was to get the money back without arousing anybody's suspicion he was putting in the drawer more than the business was earning.

While he was still in a good mood over what he had done, Helen called up.

"Frank," she said, "are you alone? If not say wrong number and hang up."

"I am alone."

"Have you seen how nice it is today? I went for a walk at lunchtime and it feels like spring has arrived."

"It's still in February. Don't take your coat off too soon."

"After Washington's Birthday winter loses its heart. Do you smell the wonderful air?"

"Not right now."

"Get outside in the sun," she said, "it's warm and wonderful."

"Why did you call me for?" he asked.

"Must I have an excuse to call?" she said softly.

"You never do."

"I called because I wished I were seeing you tonight instead of Nat."

"You don't have to go out with him if you don't want to."

"I'd better, because of my mother."

"Change it to some other time."

She thought a minute then said she had better to get it over with.

"Do it any way you like."

"Frank, do you think we could meet after I see Nat—maybe at half past eleven, or twelve at the latest? Would you like to meet me then?"

"Sure, but what's it all about?"

"I'll tell you when I see you," she said with a

little laugh. "Should we meet on the Parkway or our regular place in front of the lilac trees?"

"Wherever you say. The park is okay."

"I really hate to go there since my mother followed us."

"Don't worry about that, honey." He said, "Have you got something nice to tell me?"

"Very nice," Helen said.

He thought he knew what it was. He thought he would carry her like a bride up to his room, then when it was over carry her down so she could go up alone without fear her mother suspected where she had been.

Just then Morris came into the store so he hung up.

The grocer inspected the figure in the cash register and the satisfying sum there set him sighing. By Saturday they would surely have two-forty or fifty, but it wouldn't be that high any more once the Norwegians opened up.

Noticing Morris peering at the register under the yellow flame of his match, Frank remembered that all he had left on him was about seventy cents. He wished Helen had called him before he had put back the six bucks in the drawer. If it rained tonight they might need a cab to get home from the park, or maybe if they went up in his room she would be hungry after and want a pizza or something. Anyway, he could borrow a buck from her if he needed it. He also thought of asking Louis Karp for a little loan but didn't like to.

Morris went out for his *Forward* and spread it before him on the table, but he wasn't reading. He was thinking how distracted he was about the future. While he was upstairs, he had lain in bed trying to think of ways to cut down his expenses. He had thought of the fifteen dollars weekly he paid Frank and had worried over how large the sum was. He had also thought of Helen being kissed by the clerk, and of Ida's warnings, and all this had worked on his nerves. He seriously considered telling Frank to go but couldn't make the decision to. He wished he had let him go long ago.

Frank had decided he didn't like to ask Helen for any money—it wasn't a nice thing to do with a girl you liked. He thought it was better to take a buck out of the register drawer, out of the amount he had just put back. He wished he had paid back the five and kept himself the one-buck bill.

Morris sneaked a glance at his clerk sitting on the couch. Recalling the time he had sat in the barber's chair, watching the customers coming out of the grocery with big bags, he felt uneasy. I wonder if he steals from me, he thought. The question filled him with dread because he had asked it of himself many times yet had never answered it with certainty.

He saw through the window in the wall that a woman had come into the store. Frank got up from the couch. "I'll take this one, Morris."

Morris spoke to his newspaper. "I got anyway something to clean up in the cellar."

"What have you got there?"

"Something."

When Frank walked behind the counter, Morris went down into the cellar but didn't stay there. He stole up the stairs and stationed himself behind the hall door. Peering through a crack in the wood, he clearly saw the woman and heard her ordering. He added up the prices of the items as she ordered them.

The bill came to $1.81. When Frank rang up the money, the grocer held his breath for a painful second, then stepped inside the store.

The customer, hugging her bag of groceries, was on her way out of the front door. Frank had his hand under his apron, in his pants pocket. He gazed at the grocer with a startled expression. The amount rung up on the cash register was eighty-one cents.

Morris groaned within himself.

Frank, though tense with shame, pretended nothing was wrong. This enraged Morris. "The bill was a dollar more, why did you ring a dollar less?"

The clerk, after a time of long agony, heard himself say, "It's just a mistake, Morris."

"No," thundered the grocer. "I heard behind the hall door how much you sold her. Don't think I don't know you did many times the same thing before."

Frank could say nothing.

"Give it here the dollar," Morris ordered, extending his trembling hand.

Anguished, the clerk tried lying. "You're making a mistake. The register owes me a buck. I ran short on nickels so I got twenty from Sam Pearl with my own dough. After, I accidentally rang up one buck instead of 'no sale.' That's why I took it back this way. No harm done, I tell you."

"This is a lie," cried Morris. "I left inside a roll of nickels in case anybody needed." He strode behind the counter, rang "no sale" and held up the roll of nickels. "Tell the truth."

Frank thought. This shouldn't be happening to me. for I am a different person now.

"I was short, Morris," he admitted, "that's the truth of it. I figured I would pay you back tomorrow after I got my pay." He took the crumpled dollar out of his pants pocket and Morris snatched it from his hand.

"Why didn't you ask me to lend you a dollar instead to steal it?"

The clerk realized it hadn't occurred to him to borrow from the grocer. The reason was simple—he had never borrowed, he had always stolen.

"I didn't think about it. I made a mistake."

"Always mistakes," the grocer said wrathfully.

"All my life," sighed Frank.

"You stole from me since the day I saw you."

"I confess to it," Frank said, "but for God's sake, Morris, I swear I was paying it back to you. Even today I put back six bucks. That's why you got so much in the drawer from the time you went up to snooze until now. Ask the Mrs if we took in more than two bucks while you were upstairs. The rest I put in."

He thought of taking off his shoe and showing Morris how carefully he had kept track of the money he had taken, but he didn't want to do that because the amount was so large it might anger the grocer more.

"You put it in," Morris cried, "but it belongs to me. I don't want a thief here." He counted fifteen dollars out of the register. "Here's your week's pay —the last. Please leave now the store."

His anger was gone. He spoke in sadness and fear of tomorrow.

"Give me one last chance," Frank begged,

"Morris, please." His face was gaunt, his eyes haunted, his beard like night.

Morris, though moved by the man, thought of Helen.

"No."

Frank stared at the gray and broken Jew and seeing, despite tears in his eyes, that he would not yield, hung up his apron on a hook and left.

The night's new beauty struck Helen with the anguish of loss as she hurried into the lamplit park a half-hour after midnight. That morning as she had stepped into the street, wearing a new dress under her old coat, the fragrant day had moved her to tears and she felt then she was truly in love with Frank. Whatever the future held it couldn't deny her the sense of release and fulfillment she had felt then. Hours later, when she was with Nat Pearl, as they stopped off for a drink at a roadside tavern, then at his insistence drove into Long Island, her thoughts were still on Frank and she was impatient to be with him.

Nat was Nat. He exerted himself tonight, giving out with charm. He talked with charm and was hurt with charm. Unchanged after all the months she hadn't been with him, as they were parked on the dark shore overlooking the starlit Sound, after a few charming preliminaries he had put his arms around her. "Helen, how can we forget what pleasure we had in the past?"

She pushed him away, angered. "It's gone, I've forgotten. If you're so much of a gentleman, Nat, you ought to forget it too. Was a couple of times in bed a mortgage on my future?"

"Helen, don't talk like a stranger. For Pete's sake, be human."

"I *am* human, please remember."

"We were once good friends. My plea is for friendship again."

"Why don't you admit by friendship you mean something different?"

"Helen . . ."

"No."

He sat back at the wheel. "Christ, you have become a suspicious character."

She said, "Things have changed—you must realize."

"Who have they changed for," he asked sullenly, "that dago I hear you go with?"

Her answer was ice.

On the way home he tried to unsay what he had said, but Helen yielded him only a quick good-by. She left him with relief and a poignant sense of all she had wasted of the night.

Worried that Frank had had to wait so long, she hurried across the lit plaza and along a gravel path bordered by tall lilac shrubs, toward their meeting place. As she approached their bench, although she was troubled by a foreboding he would not be there, she couldn't believe it, then was painfully disappointed to find that though others were present—it was true, he wasn't.

Could he have been and gone already? It didn't seem possible; he had always waited before, no matter how late she was. And since she had told him she had something important to say, nothing less than that she now knew she loved him, surely he would want to hear what. She sat down, fearing he had had an accident.

Usually they were alone at this spot, but the almost warmish late-February night had brought out company. On a bench diagonally opposite Helen, in the dark under budding branches, sat two young lovers locked in a long kiss. The bench at her left was empty, but on the one beyond that a man was sleeping under a dim lamp. A cat nosed at his shadow and departed. The man woke with a grunt, squinted at Helen, yawned and went back to sleep. The lovers at last broke apart and left in silence, the boy awkwardly trailing the happy girl. Helen deeply envied her, an awful feeling to end the day with.

Glancing at her watch she saw it was already past one. Shivering, she rose, then sat down to wait five last minutes. She felt the stars clustered like a distant weight above her head. Utterly lonely, she regretted the spring-like loveliness of the night; it had gone, in her hands, to waste. She was tired of anticipation, of waiting for nothing.

A man was standing unsteadily before her, heavy, dirty, stinking of whiskey. Helen half-rose, struck with fright.

He flipped off his hat and said huskily, "Don't be afraid of me, Helen. I'm personally a fine guy—son of a cop. You remember me, don't you—Ward Minogue that went to your school? My old man beat me up once in the girls' yard."

Though it was years since she had seen him she recognized Ward, at once recalling the incident of his following a girl into a lavatory. Instinctively Helen raised her arm to protect herself. She kept herself from screaming, or he might grab her. How stupid, she thought, to wait for this.

"I remember you, Ward."

"Could I sit down?"

She hesitated. "All right."

Helen edged as far away from him as she could. He looked half-stupefied. If he made a move she would run, screaming.

"How did you recognize me in the dark?" she asked, pretending to be casual as she glanced stealthily around to see how best to escape. If she could get past the trees, it was then another twenty feet along the shrub-lined path before she could be out in the open. Once on the plaza there would be people around she could appeal to.

God only help me, she thought.

"I saw you a couple of times lately," Ward answered, rubbing his hand slowly across his chest.

"Where?"

"Around. Once I saw you come out of your old man's grocery and I figured it was you. You have still kept your looks," he grinned.

"Thanks. Don't you feel so well?"

"I got gas pains in my chest and a goddam headache."

"In case you want one I have a box of aspirins in my purse."

"No, they make me puke." She noticed that he was glancing toward the trees. She grew more anxious, thought of offering him her purse if he only wouldn't touch her.

"How's your boy friend, Frank Alpine?" Ward asked, with a wet wink.

She said in surprise, "Do you know Frank?"

"He's an old friend of mine," he answered. "He was here lookin' for you."

"Is—he all right?"

"Not so hot," said Ward. "He had to go home."

She got up. "I have to leave now."

But he was standing.

"Good night." Helen walked away from him.

"He told me to give you this paper." Ward thrust his hand into his coat pocket.

She didn't believe him but paused long enough for him to move forward. He grabbed her with astonishing swiftness, smothering her scream with his smelly hand, as he dragged her toward the trees.

"All I want is what you give that wop," Ward grunted.

She kicked, clawed, bit his hand, broke loose. He caught her by her coat collar, ripped it off. She screamed again and ran forward but he pounced upon her and got his arm over her mouth. Ward shoved her hard against a tree, knocking the breath out of her. He held her tightly by the throat as with his other hand he ripped open her coat and tore her dress off the shoulder, exposing her brassière.

Struggling, kicking wildly, she caught him between the legs with her knee. He cried out and cracked her across the face. She felt the strength go out of her and fought not to faint. She screamed but heard no sound.

Helen felt his body shuddering against her. I am disgraced, she thought, yet felt curiously freed of his stinking presence, as if he had dissolved into a can of filth and she had kicked it away. Her legs buckled and she slid to the ground. I've fainted, went through her mind, although she felt she was still fighting him.

Dimly she realized that a struggle was going on near her. She heard the noise of a blow, and Ward

Minogue cried out in great pain and staggered away.

Frank, she thought with tremulous joy. Helen felt herself gently lifted and knew she was in his arms. She sobbed in relief. He kissed her eyes and lips and he kissed her half-naked breast. She held him tightly with both arms, weeping, laughing, murmuring she had come to tell him she loved him.

He put her down and they kissed under the dark trees. She tasted whiskey on his tongue and was momentarily afraid.

"I love you, Helen," he murmured, attempting clumsily to cover her breast with the torn dress as he drew her deeper into the dark, and from under the trees onto the star-dark field.

They sank to their knees on the winter earth, Helen urgently whispering, "Please not now, darling," but he spoke of his starved and passionate love, and all the endless heartbreaking waiting. Even as he spoke he thought of her as beyond his reach, forever in the bathroom as he spied, so he stopped her pleas with kisses. . . .

Afterward, she cried, "Dog—uncircumcised dog!"

While Morris was sitting alone in the back the next morning, a boy brought in a pink handbill and left it on the counter. When the grocer picked it up he saw it announced the change of management and reopening on Monday, by Taast and Pederson, of the grocery and fancy delicatessen around the corner. There followed, in large print, a list of specials they were offering during their first week, bargains Morris could never hope to match, because he couldn't afford the loss the Norwegians were planning to take. The grocer felt he was standing in an icy draft blowing from some hidden hole in the store. In the kitchen, though he stood with his legs and buttocks pressed against the gas radiator, it took an age to diminish the chill that had penetrated his bones.

All morning he scanned the crumpled handbill, muttering to himself; he sipped cold coffee, thinking of the future, and off and on, of Frank Alpine. The clerk had left last night without taking his fifteen dollars' wages. Morris thought he would come in for it this morning but, as the hours passed, knew he wouldn't, maybe having left it to make up some of the money he had stolen; yet maybe not. For the thousandth time the grocer wondered if he had done right in ordering Frank to go. True, he had stolen from him, but also true, he was paying it back. His story that he had put six dollars into the register and then found he had left himself without a penny in his pocket was probably the truth, because the sum in the register, when Morris counted it, was more than they usually took in during the dead part of the afternoon when he napped. The clerk was an unfortunate man; yet the grocer was alternately glad and sorry the incident had occurred. He was glad he had finally let him go. For Helen's sake it had had to be done, and for Ida's peace of mind, as well as his own. Still, he felt unhappy to lose his assistant and be by himself when the Norwegians opened up.

Ida came down, puffy-eyed from poor sleep. She felt a hopeless rage against the world. What will become of Helen? she asked herself, and cracked her knuckles against her chest. But when Morris looked up to listen to her complaints, she was afraid to say anything. A half-hour later, aware that something had changed in the store, she thought of the clerk.

"Where is he?" she asked.

"He left," Morris answered.

"Where did he leave?" she said in astonishment.

"He left for good."

She gazed at him. "Morris, what happened, tell me?"

"Nothing," he said, embarrassed. "I told him to leave."

"Why, all of a sudden?"

"Didn't you say you didn't want him here no more?"

"From the first day I saw him, but you always said no."

"Now I said yes."

"A stone falls off my heart." But she was not satisfied. "Did he move out of the house yet?"

"I don't know."

"I will go and ask the upstairske."

"Leave her alone. We will know when he moves."

"When did you tell him to leave?"

"Last night."

"So why didn't you tell me last night?" she said angrily. "Why you told me he went early to the movies?"

"I was nervous."

"Morris," she asked in fright. "Did something else happen? Did Helen—"

"Nothing happened."

"Does she know he left?"

"I didn't tell her. Why she went so early to work this morning?"

"She went early?"

"Yes."

"I don't know," Ida said uneasily.

He produced the handbill. "This is why I feel bad."

She glanced at it, not comprehending.

"The German," he explained. "They bought him out, two Norwegians."

She gasped. "When?"

"This week. Schmitz is sick. He lays now in the hospital."

"I told you," Ida said.

"You told me?"

"Vey is mir. I told you after Christmas—when

improved more the business. I told you the drivers
said the German was losing customers. You said
Frank improved the business. A goy brings in
goyim, you said. How much strength I had to argue with you?"

"Did you tell me he kept closed in the morning
his store?"

"Who said? I didn't know this."

"Karp told me."

"Karp was here?"

"He came on Thursday to tell me the good
news."

"What good news?"

"That Schmitz sold out."

"Is this good news?" she asked.

"Maybe to him but not to me."

"You didn't tell me he came."

"I tell you now," he said irritably. "Schmitz sold
out. Monday will open two Norwegians. Our business will go to hell again. We will starve here."

"Some helper you had," she said with bitterness.
"Why didn't you listen to me when I said let him
go?"

"I listened," he said wearily.

She was silent, then asked, "So when Karp told
you Schmitz sold his store you told Frank to
leave?"

"The next day."

"Thank God."

"See if you say next week 'Thank God.' "

"What is this got to do with Frank? Did he help
us?"

"I don't know."

"You don't know," she said shrilly. "You just

told me you said he should leave when you found out where came our business."

"I don't know," he said miserably, "I don't know where it came."

"It didn't come from him."

"Where it came I don't worry any more. Where will it come next week I worry." He read aloud the specials the Norwegians were offering.

She squeezed her hands white. "Morris, we must sell the store."

"So sell." Sighing, Morris removed his apron. "I will take my rest."

"It's only half past eleven."

"I feel cold." He looked depressed.

"Eat something first—your soup."

"Who can eat?"

"Drink a hot glass tea."

"No."

"Morris." she said quietly, "don't worry so much. Something will happen. We will always have to eat."

He made no reply, folded the handbill into a small square and took it upstairs with him.

The rooms were cold. Ida always shut off the radiators when she went down and lit them again in the late afternoon about an hour before Helen returned. Now the house was too cold. Morris turned on the stopcock of the bedroom radiator, then found he had no match in his pocket. He got one in the kitchen.

Under the covers he felt shivery. He lay under two blankets and a quilt yet shivered. He wondered if he was sick but soon fell asleep. He was glad when he felt sleep come over him, although it brought night too quickly. But if you slept it was night, that's how things were. Looking, that same night, from the street into his store, he beheld Taast and Pederson—one with a small blond mustache, the other half-bald, a light shining on his head—standing behind *his* counter, poking into *his* cash register. The grocer rushed in but they were gabbing in German and paid no attention to his gibbering Yiddish. At that moment Frank came out of the back with Helen. Though the clerk spoke a musical Italian, Morris recognized a dirty word. He struck his assistant across the face and they wrestled furiously on the floor, Helen screaming mutely. Frank dumped him heavily on his back and sat on his poor chest. He thought his lungs would burst. He tried hard to cry out but his voice cracked his throat and no one would help. He considered the possibility of dying and would have liked to.

Tessie Fuso dreamed of a tree hit by thunder and knocked over; she dreamed she heard someone groan terribly and awoke in fright, listened, then went back to sleep. Frank Alpine, at the dirty end of a long night, awoke groaning. He awoke with a shout—awake, he thought, forever. His impulse was to leap out of bed and rush down to the store; then he remembered that Morris had thrown him out. It was a gray, dreary winter morning. Nick had gone to work and Tessie, in her bathrobe, was sitting in the kitchen, drinking coffee. She heard Frank cry out again but had just discovered that she was pregnant, so did nothing more than wonder at his nightmare.

He lay in bed with the blankets pulled over his head, trying to smother his thoughts but they es-

caped and stank. The more he smothered them
the more they stank. He smelled garbage in the
bed and couldn't move out of it. He couldn't because he was it—the stink in his own broken nose.
What you did was how bad you smelled. Unable
to stand it he flung the covers ʳside and struggled
to dress but couldn't make it. The sight of his bare
feet utterly disgusted him. He thirsted for a
cigarette but couldn't light one for fear of seeing
his hand. He shut his eyes and lit a match. The
match burned his nose. He stepped on the lit
match with his bare feet and danced in pain.

Oh my God, why did I do it? Why did I ever do
it? Why did I do it?

His thoughts were killing him. He couldn't
stand them. He sat on the edge of the twisted bed,
his thoughtful head ready to bust in his hands. He
wanted to run. Part of him was already in flight,
he didn't know where. He just wanted to run. But
while he was running, he wanted to be back. He
wanted to be back with Helen, to be forgiven. It
wasn't asking too much. People forgave people—
who else? He could explain if she would listen.
Explaining was a way of getting close to somebody
you had hurt; as if in hurting them you were giving them a reason to love you. He had come, he
would say, to the park to wait for her, to hear what
she had to tell him. He felt he knew she would
say she loved him; it meant they would soon sleep
together. This stayed in his mind and he sat there
waiting to hear her say it, at the same time in an
agony that she never would, that he would lose
her the minute she found out why her father had
kicked him out of the grocery. What could he tell
her about that? He sat for hours trying to think

what to say, at last growing famished. At midnight he left to get a pizza but stopped instead in a bar. Then when he saw his face in the mirror he felt a nose-thumbing revulsion. Where have you ever been, he asked the one in the glass, except on the inside of a circle? What have you ever done but always the wrong thing? When he returned to the park, there was Ward Minogue hurting her. He just about killed Ward. Then when he had Helen in his arms, crying, saying at last that she loved him, he had this hopeless feeling it was the end and now he would never see her again. He thought he must love her before she was lost to him. She said no, not to, but he couldn't believe it the same minute she was saying she loved him. He thought, Once I start she will come along with me. So then he did it. He loved her with his love. She should have known that. She should not have gone wild, beat his face with her fists, called him dirty names, run from him, his apologies, pleadings, sorrow.

Oh, Jesus, what did I do?

He moaned; had got instead of a happy ending, a bad smell. If he could root out what he had done, smash and destroy it; but it was done, beyond him to undo. It was where he could never lay hands on it any more—in his stinking mind. His thoughts would forever suffocate him. He had failed once too often. He should somewhere have stopped and changed the way he was going, his luck, himself, stopped hating the world, got a decent education, a job, a nice girl. He had lived without will, betrayed every good intention. Had he ever confessed the holdup to Morris? Hadn't he stolen from the cash register till the minute he was canned? In a single terrible act in the park hadn't he murdered the last of his good hopes, the love he had so long waited for—his chance at a future? His goddamned life had pushed him wherever it went; he had led it nowhere. He was blown around in any breath that blew, owned nothing, not even experience to show for the years he had lived. If you had experience you knew at least when to start and where to quit; all he knew was how to mangle himself more. The self he had secretly considered valuable, for all he could make of it, a dead rat. He stank.

This time his shout frightened Tessie. Frank got up on the run but he had run everywhere. There was no place left to escape to. The room shrank. The bed was flying up at him. He felt trapped—sick, wanted to cry but couldn't. He planned to kill himself, at the same minute had a terrifying insight: that all the while he was acting like he wasn't, he was really a man of stern morality.

Ida had awakened in the night and heard her daughter crying. Nat did something to her, she thought wildly, but was ashamed to go to Helen and beg her to say what. She guessed he had acted like a lout—it was no wonder Helen had stopped seeing him. All night she blamed herself for having urged her to go out with the law student. She fell into an unhappy sleep.

It was growing light when Morris left the flat. Helen dragged herself out of bed and sat with reddened eyes in the bathroom, sewing on her coat collar. Once near the office she would give it to a tailor to fix so the tear couldn't be seen. With her

new dress she could do nothing. Rolling it into a
hopeless ball, she hid it under some things in her
bottom bureau drawer. Monday she would buy
one exactly like it and hang it in her closet. Undressing for a shower—her third in hours—she
burst into tears at the sight of her body. Every man
she drew to her dirtied her. How could she have
encouraged him? She felt a violent self-hatred
for trusting him, when from the very beginning
she had sensed he was untrustable. How could she
have allowed herself to fall in love with anybody
like him? She was filled with loathing at the fan-
tasy she had created, of making him into what he
couldn't be—educable, promising, kind and good,
when he was no more than a bum. Where were
her wits, her sense of elemental self-preservation?

Under the shower she soaped herself heavily,
crying as she washed. At seven, before her mother
awakened, she dressed and left the house, too sick-
ened to eat. She would gladly have forgotten her
life, in sleep, but dared not stay home, dared not
be questioned. When she returned from her half-
day of work, if he was still there, she would order
him to leave or would scream him out of the
house.

Coming home from the garage, Nick smelled
gas in the hall. He inspected the radiators in his
flat, saw they were both lit, then knocked on
Frank's door.

After a minute the door opened a crack.

"Do you smell anything?" Nick said, staring at
the eye in the crack.

"Mind your goddamned business."

"Are you nuts? I smell gas in the house, it's dangerous."

"Gas?" Frank flung open the door. He was in pajamas, haggard.

"What's the matter, you sick?"

"Where do you smell the gas?"

"Don't tell me you can't smell it."

"I got a bad cold," Frank said hoarsely.

"Maybe it's comin' from the cellar," said Nick.

They ran down a flight and then the odor hit Frank, an acrid stench thick enough to wade through.

"It's coming from this floor," Nick said.

Frank pounded on the door. "Helen, there's gas here, let me in, Helen," he cried.

"Shove it," said Nick.

Frank pushed his shoulder against the door. It was unlocked and he fell in. Nick quickly opened the kitchen window while Frank, in his bare feet, roamed through the house. Helen was not there but he found Morris in bed.

The clerk, coughing, dragged the grocer out of bed and carrying him to the living room, laid him on the floor. Nick closed the stopcock of the bedroom radiator and threw open every window. Frank got down on his knees, bent over Morris, clamped his hands to his sides and pumped.

Tessie ran in in fright, and Nick shouted to her to call Ida.

Ida came stumbling up the stairs, moaning, "Oh, my God, oh, my God."

Seeing Morris lying on the floor, his underwear soaked, his face the color of a cooked beet, flecks of foam in the corners of his mouth, she let out a piercing shriek.

Helen, coming dully into the hall, heard her mother's cry. She smelled the gas and ran in terror up the stairs, expecting death.

When she saw Frank in his pajamas bent over her father's back, her throat thickened in disgust. She screamed in fear and hatred.

Frank couldn't look at her, frightened to.

"His eyes just moved," Nick said.

Morris awoke with a massive ache in his chest. His head felt like corroded metal, his mouth horribly dry, his stomach crawling with pain. He was ashamed to find himself stretched out in his long underwear on the floor.

"Morris," cried Ida.

Frank got up, embarrassed at his bare feet and pajamas.

"Papa, Papa." Helen was on her knees.

"Why did you do it for?" Ida yelled in the grocer's ear.

"What happened?" he gasped.

"Why did you do it for?" she wept.

"Are you crazy?" he muttered. "I forgot to light the gas. A mistake."

Helen broke into sobbing, her lips twisted. Frank had to turn his head.

"The only thing that saved him was he got some air," Nick said. "You're lucky this flat ain't windproof, Morris."

Tessie shivered. "It's cold. Cover him, he's sweating."

"Put him in bed," Ida said.

Frank and Nick lifted the grocer and carried him in to his bed. Ida and Helen covered him with blankets and quilt.

"Thanks," Morris said to them. He stared at Frank. Frank looked at the floor.

"Shut the windows," Tessie said. "The smell is gone."

"Wait a little longer," said Frank. He glanced at Helen but her back was to him. She was still crying.

"Why did he do it?" Ida moaned.

Morris gazed long at her, then shut his eyes.

"Leave him rest," Nick advised.

"Don't light any matches for another hour," Frank told Ida.

Tessie closed all but one window and they left. Ida and Helen remained with Morris in the bedroom.

Frank lingered in Helen's room but nothing welcomed him there.

Later he dressed and went down to the store. Business was brisk. Ida came down, and though he begged her not to, shut the store.

That afternoon Morris developed a fever and the doctor said he had to go to the hospital. An ambulance came and took the grocer away, his wife and daughter riding with him.

From his window upstairs, Frank watched them go.

Sunday morning the store was still shut tight. Though he feared to, Frank considered knocking on Ida's door and asking for the key. But Helen might open the door, and since he would not know what to say to her over the doorsill, he went instead down the cellar, and mounting the dumbwaiter, wriggled through the little window in the air shaft, into the store toilet. Once in the back, the clerk shaved and had his coffee. He thought he would stay in the store till somebody told him to scram; and even if they did, he would try in some way to stay longer. That was his only hope left, if there was any. Turning the front door lock, he carried in the milk and rolls and was ready for business. The register was empty, so he borrowed five dollars in change from Sam Pearl, saying he would pay it back from what he took in. Sam wanted to know how Morris was and Frank said he didn't know.

Shortly after half past eight, the clerk was standing at the front window when Ida and her daughter left the house. Helen looked like last year's flower. Observing her, he felt a pang of loss, shame, regret. He felt an unbearable depriva-tion—that yesterday he had almost had some won-derful thing but today it was gone, all but the misery of remembering it was. Whenever he thought of what he had almost had it made him frantic. He felt like rushing outside, drawing her into a doorway, and declaring the stupendous value of his love for her. But he did nothing. He didn't exactly hide but he didn't show him-self, and they soon went away to the subway.

Later he thought he would also go and see Mor-ris in the hospital, as soon as he knew which one he was in—after they got home; but they didn't return till midnight. The store was closed and he saw them from his room, two dark figures getting out of a cab. Monday, the day the Norwegians opened their store, Ida came down at seven A.M. to paste a piece of paper on the door saying Mor-ris Bober was sick and the grocery would be closed till Tuesday or Wednesday. To her amazement,

Frank Alpine was standing, in his apron, behind the counter. She entered in anger.

Frank was miserably nervous that Morris or Helen, either or both, had told her all the wrong he had done them, because if they had, he was finished.

"How did you get in here?" Ida asked wrathfully.

He said through the air shaft window. "Thinking of your trouble, I didn't want to bother you about the key, Mrs."

She vigorously forbade him ever to come in that way again. Her face was deeply lined, her eyes weary, mouth bitter, but he could tell that for some miraculous reason she didn't know what he had done.

Frank pulled a handful of dollar bills out of his pants pocket and a little bag of change, laying it all on the counter. "I took in forty-one bucks yesterday."

"You were here yesterday?"

"I got in how I explained you. There was a nice rush around four till about six. We are all out of potato salad."

Her eyes grew tears. He asked how Morris felt.

She touched her wet lids with a handkerchief. "Morris has pneumonia."

"Ah, too bad. Give him my sorrow if you can. How's he coming along out of it?"

"He's a very sick man, he has weak lungs."

"I think I'll go to see him in the hospital."

"Not now," Ida said.

"When he's better. How long do you think he'll be there?"

"I don't know. The doctor will telephone to-day."

"Look, Mrs," Frank said. "Why don't you stop worrying about the store while Morris is sick and let me take care of it? You know I make no demands."

"My husband told you to go out from the store."

He furtively studied her face but there was no sign of accusation.

"I won't stay very long," he answered. "You don't have to worry about that. I'll stay here till Morris gets better. You'll need every cent for the hospital bills. I don't ask a thing for myself."

"Did Morris tell you why you must leave?"

His heart galloped. Did she or didn't she know? If yes, he would say it was a mistake—deny he had touched a red cent in the register. Wasn't the proof of that in the pile of dough that lay right in front of her eyes on the counter? But he answered, "Sure, he didn't want me to hang around Helen any more."

"Yes, she is a Jewish girl. You should look for somebody else. But he also found out that Schmitz was sick since December and kept closed his store in the mornings, also earlier in the night. This was what improved our income, not you."

She then told Frank that the German had sold out and two Norwegians were opening up today.

Frank flushed. "I knew that Schmitz was sick and kept his store closed sometimes, but that isn't what made your business get better. What did that was how hard I worked building up the trade. And I bet I can keep this place in the shape it is, even with two Norwegians around the corner or three Greeks. What's more, I bet I can raise the take-in higher."

Though she was half-inclined to believe him, she couldn't.

"Wait, you'll see how smart you are."

"Then let me have a chance to show you. Don't pay me anything, the room and meals are enough."

"What," she asked in desperation, "do you want from us?"

"Just to help out. I have my debt to Morris."

"You have no debt. He has a debt to you that you saved him from the gas."

"Nick smelled it first. Anyway I feel I have a debt to him for all the things he has done for me. That's my nature, when I'm thankful, I'm thankful."

"Please don't bother Helen. She is not for you."

"I won't."

She let him stay. If you were so poor where was your choice?

Taast and Pederson opened up with a horseshoe of spring flowers in their window. Their pink handbills brought them steady business and Frank had plenty of time on his hands. During the day only a few of the regulars came into the grocery. At night, after the Norwegians had closed, the grocery had a spurt of activity, but when Frank pulled the strings of the window lights around eleven, he had only fifteen dollars in the register. He didn't worry too much. Monday was a slow day anyway, and besides, people were entitled to grab off a few specials while they could get them. He figured nobody could tell what difference the Norwegians would make to the business until a couple of weeks had gone by, when the neighborhood was used to them and things settled back to normal. Nobody was going to give specials away that cheap every day. A store wasn't a charity, and when they stopped giving something for nothing, he would match them in service and also prices and get his customers back.

Tuesday was slow, also as usual. Wednesday picked up a little, but Thursday was slow again. Friday was better. Saturday was the best day of the week, although not so good as Saturdays lately. At the end of the week the grocery was close to a hundred short of its recent weekly average. Expecting something like this, Frank had closed up for a half hour on Thursday and taken the trolley to the bank. He withdrew twenty-five dollars from his savings account and put the money into the register, five on Thursday, ten on Friday and ten on Saturday, so that when Ida wrote the figures down in her book each night she wouldn't feel too bad. Seventy-five less for the week wasn't as bad as a hundred.

Morris, better after ten days in the hospital, was brought home in a cab by Ida and Helen and laid to bed to convalesce. Frank, gripping his courage, thought of going up to see him and this time starting out right, right off. He thought of bringing him some freshed baked goods to eat, maybe a piece of cheese cake that he knew the grocer liked, or some apple strudel; but the clerk was afraid it was still too soon and Morris might ask him where he had got the money to buy the cake. He might yell, "You thief, you, the only reason you stay here still is because I am sick upstairs." Yet if Morris

felt this way he would already have told Ida what
Frank had done. The clerk now was sure he hadn't
mentioned it, because she wouldn't have waited this long to pitch him out on his ear. He
thought a lot about the way Morris kept things to
himself. It was a way a person had if he figured he
could be wrong about how he sized up a situation. It could be that he might take a different
view of Frank in time. The clerk tried to invent
reasons why it might be worth the grocer's while,
after he got on his feet again, to keep him on in
the grocery. Frank felt he would promise anything
to stay there. "Don't worry that I ever will steal
from you or anybody else any more, Morris. If I
do, I hope I drop dead on the spot." He hoped
that this promise, and the favor he was doing him
by keeping the store open, would convince Morris of his sincerity. Yet he thought he would wait a
while longer before going up to see him.

Helen hadn't said anything to anybody about
him either and it wasn't hard to understand why.
The wrong he had done her was never out of his
mind. He hadn't intended wrong but he had
done it; now he intended right. He would do anything she wanted, and if she wanted nothing he
would do something, what he should do; and he
would do it all on his own will, nobody pushing
him but himself. He would do it with discipline
and with love.

All this time he had snatched only glimpses of
her, though his heart was heavy with all he hoped
to say. He saw her through the plate glass window
—she on the undersea side. Through the green
glass she looked drowned, yet never, God help him,
lovelier. He felt a tender pity for her, mixed with

shame for having made her pitiable. Once, as she
came home from work, her eyes happened to look
into his and showed disgust. Now I am finished, he
thought, she will come in here and tell me to go
die some place; but when she looked away she was
never there. He was agonized to be so completely
apart from her, left apologizing to her shadow, to
the floral fragrance she left in the air. To himself he confessed his deed, but not to her. That
was the curse of it, to have it to make but who
would listen? At times he felt like crying but it
made him feel too much like a kid to cry. He
didn't like to, did it badly.

Once he met her in the hall. She was gone before he could move his lips. He felt for her a rush
of love. He felt, after she had left, that hopeless-
ness was his punishment. He had expected that
punishment to be drastic, swift; instead it came
slowly—it never came, yet was there.

There was no approach to her. What had happened had put her in another world, no way in.

Early one morning, he stood in the hall till she
came down the stairs.

"Helen," he said, snatching off the cloth cap he
now wore in the store, "my heart is sorrowful. I
want to apologize."

Her lips quivered. "Don't speak to me," she
said, in a voice choked with contempt. "I don't
want your apologies. I don't want to see you, and
I don't want to know you. As soon as my father is
better, please leave. You've helped him and my
mother and I thank you for that, but you're no
help to me. You make me sick."

The door banged behind her.

That night he dreamed he was standing in the

snow outside her window. His feet were bare yet
not cold. He had waited a long time in the falling
snow, and some of it lay on his head and had all
but frozen his face; but he waited longer until,
moved by pity, she opened the window and flung
something out. It floated down; he thought it
was a piece of paper with writing on it but saw
that it was a white flower, surprising to see in wintertime. Frank caught it in his hand. As she had
tossed the flower out through the partly opened
window he had glimpsed her fingers only, yet he
saw the light of her room and even felt the warmth
of it. Then when he looked again the window was
shut tight, sealed with ice. Even as he dreamed,
he knew it had never been open. There was no
such window. He gazed down at his hand for the
flower and before he could see it wasn't there, felt
himself wake.

The next day he waited for her at the foot of
the stairs, bareheaded in the light that fell on his
head from the lamp.

She came down, her frozen face averted.

"Helen, nothing can kill the love I feel for you."

"In your mouth it's a dirty word."

"If a guy did wrong, must he suffer forever?"

"I personally don't care what happens to you."

Whenever he waited at the stairs, she passed
without a word, as if he didn't exist. He didn't.

If the store blows away some dark night I might
as well be dead, Frank thought. He tried every
way to hang on. Business was terrible. He wasn't
sure how long the grocery could last or how long
the grocer and his wife would let him try to keep
it alive. If the store collapsed everything would be

gone. But if he kept it going there was always the chance that something might change, and if it did, maybe something else might. If he kept the grocery on its feet till Morris came down, at least he would have a couple of weeks to change how things were. Weeks were nothing but it might as well be nothing because to do what he had to do he needed years.

Taast and Pederson had the specials going week after week. They thought of one come-on after another to keep the customers buying. Frank's customers were disappearing. Some of them now passed him in the street without saying hello. One or two crossed the trolley tracks and walked on the other side of the street, not to have to see his stricken face at the window. He withdrew all he had left in the bank and each week padded the income a little, but Ida saw how bad things were. She was despondent and talked of giving the place over to the auctioneer. This made him frantic. He felt he had to try harder.

He tried out all sorts of schemes. He got specials on credit and sold half the stuff, but then the Norwegians began to sell it cheaper, and the rest remained on his shelves. He stayed open all night for a couple of nights but did not take in enough to pay for the light. Having nothing much to do, he thought he would fix up the store. With all but the last five dollars from the bank account, he bought a few gallons of cheap paint. Then removing the goods from one section of the shelves, he scraped away the mildewed paper on the walls and painted them a nice light yellow. When one section was painted he went to work on the next. After he had finished the walls he borrowed a tall ladder, scraped the ceiling bit by bit and painted it white. He also replaced a few shelves and neatly finished them in dime store varnish. In the end he had to admit that all his work hadn't brought back a single customer.

Though it seemed impossible the store got worse.

"What are you telling Morris about the business?" Frank asked Ida.

"He don't ask me so I don't tell him," she said dully.

"How is he now?"

"Weak yet. The doctor says his lungs are like paper. He reads or he sleeps. Sometimes he listens to the radio."

"Let him rest. It's good for him."

She said again, "Why do you work so hard for nothing? What do you stay here for?"

For love, he wanted to say, but hadn't the nerve. "For Morris."

But he didn't fool her. She would even then have told him to pack and go, although he kept them for the moment off the street, had she not known for a fact that Helen no longer bothered with him. He had probably through some stupidity fallen out of her good graces. Possibly her father's illness had made her more considerate of them. She had been a fool to worry. Yet she now worried because Helen, at her age, showed so little interest in men. Nat had called but she wouldn't go near the phone.

Frank scraped down on expenses. With Ida's permission he had the telephone removed. He hated to do it because he thought Helen might sometime come down to answer it. He also reduced the gas bill by lighting only one of the two radiators downstairs. He kept the one in the front lit so the customers wouldn't feel the cold, but he no longer used the one in the kitchen. He wore a heavy sweater, a vest and a flannel shirt under his apron, and his cap on his head. But Ida, even with her coat on, when she could no longer stand the emptiness of the front, or the freezing back, escaped upstairs. One day she came into the kitchen, and seeing him salting a soup plate of boiled potatoes for lunch, began to cry.

He thought always of Helen. How could she know what was going on in him? If she ever looked at him again she would see the same guy on the outside. He could see out but nobody could see in.

When Betty Pearl got married Helen didn't go to the wedding. The day before she apologized embarrassedly, said she wasn't feeling too well— blamed her father's illness. Betty said she understood, thinking it had something to do with her brother. "Next time," she remarked with a little laugh, but Helen, seeing she was hurt, felt bad. She reconsidered facing the ceremony, rigmarole, relatives, Nat or no Nat—maybe she could still go; but couldn't bring herself to. She was no fixture for a wedding. They might say to her, "With such a face, go better to a funeral." Though she had many a night wept herself out, her memories kept a hard hold in her mind. Crazy woman, how could she have brought herself to love such a man? How could she have considered marrying someone not Jewish? A total, worthless stranger. Only

God had saved her from a disastrous mistake. With such thoughts she lost all feeling for weddings.

Her sleep suffered. Every day she dreaded every night. From bedtime to dawn she eked out only a few wearisome unconscious hours. She dreamed she would soon awake and soon awoke. Awake, she felt sorry for herself, and sorrow, no soporific, induced sorrow. Her mind stamped out endless worries: her father's health, for instance; he showed little interest in recovery. The store, as ever. Ida wept in whispers in the kitchen. "Don't tell Papa." But they would sometime soon have to. She cursed all grocery stores. And worried at seeing nobody, planning no future. Each morning she crossed off the calendar the sleepless day to be. God forbid such days.

Though Helen turned over all but four dollars of her check to her mother and it went into the register, they were always hard up for cash to meet expenses. One day Frank got an idea about how he might lay hold of some dough. He thought he would collect an old bill from Carl, the Swedish painter. He knew the painter owed Morris over seventy bucks. He looked for the housepainter every day but Carl did not come in.

One morning Frank was standing at the window when he saw him leave Karp's with a wrapped bottle in his pocket.

Frank ran out and reminded Carl of his old bill. He asked him to pay something on the account.

"This is all fixed up with me and Morris," the painter answered. "Don't stick your dirty nose in."

"Morris is sick, he needs the dough," Frank said.

Carl shoved the clerk aside and went on his way.

Frank was sore. "I'll collect from that drunk bastard."

Ida was in the store, so Frank said he would be back soon. He hung up his apron, got his overcoat and followed Carl to his house. After getting the address, he returned to the grocery. He was still angered at the painter for the way he had acted when he had asked him to pay his bill.

That evening he returned to the shabby four-story tenement and climbed the creaking staircase to the top floor. A thin, dark-haired woman came wearily to the door. She was old until his eyes got used to her face, then he realized she was young but looked old.

"Are you Carl the painter's wife?"

"That's right."

"Could I talk to him?"

"On a job?" she said hopefully.

"No. Something different."

She looked old again. "He hasn't worked for months."

"I just want to talk to him."

She let him into a large room which was a kitchen and living room combined, the two halves separated by an undrawn curtain. In the middle of the living room part stood a kerosene heater that stank. This smell mixed with the sour smell of cabbage cooking. The four kids, a boy about twelve and three younger girls, were in the room, drawing on paper, cutting and pasting. They stared at Frank but silently went on with what they were doing. The clerk didn't feel comfortable. He stood at the window, looking down on the dreary lamplit street. He now figured he would cut the bill in half if the painter would pay up the rest.

The painter's wife covered the sizzling frying pan with a pot lid and went into the bedroom. She came back and said her husband was sleeping.

"I'll wait a while," said Frank.

She went back to her frying. The oldest girl set the table, and they all sat down to eat. He noticed they had left a place for their old man. He would soon have to crawl out of his hole. The mother didn't sit down. Paying no attention to Frank, she poured skim milk out of a container into the kids' glasses, then served each one a frankfurter fried in dough. She also gave everybody a forkful of hot sauerkraut.

The kids ate hungrily, not talking. The oldest girl glanced at Frank then stared at her plate when he looked at her.

When the plates were empty she said, "Is there any more, Mama?"

"Go to bed," said the painter's wife.

Frank had a bad headache from the stink of the heater.

"I'll see Carl some other time," he said. His spit tasted like brass.

"I'm sorry he didn't wake up."

He ran back to the store. Under the mattress of his bed he had his last three bucks hidden. He took the bills and ran back to Carl's house. But on the way he met Ward Minogue. His face was yellow and shrunken, as if he had escaped out of a morgue.

"I been looking for you," said Ward. He pulled

Frank's revolver out of a paper bag. "How much is this worth to you?"

"Shit."

"I'm sick," sobbed Ward.

Frank gave the three bucks to him and later dropped the gun into a sewer.

He read a book about the Jews, a short history. He had many times seen this book on one of the library shelves and had never taken it down, but one day he checked it out to satisfy his curiosity. He read the first part with interest, but after the Crusades and the Inquisition, when the Jews were having it tough, he had to force himself to keep reading. He skimmed the bloody chapters but read slowly the ones about their civilization and accomplishments. He also read about the ghettos, where the half-starved, bearded prisoners spent their lives trying to figure it out why they were the Chosen People. He tried to figure out why but couldn't. He couldn't finish the book and brought it back to the library.

Some nights he spied on the Norwegians. He would go around the corner without his apron and stand on the step of Sam Pearl's hallway, looking across the street at the grocery and fancy delicatessen. The window was loaded with all kinds of shiny cans. Inside, the store was lit as bright as day. The shelves were tightly packed with appetizing goods that made him feel hungry. And there were always customers inside, although his place was generally empty. Sometimes after the partners locked up and went home, Frank crossed to their side of the street and peered through the window into the dark store, as if he might learn from what he saw in it the secret of all good fortune and so change his luck and his life.

One night after he had closed the store, he took a long walk and stepped into the Coffee Pot, an all-night joint he had been in once or twice.

Frank asked the owner if he needed a man for night work.

"I need a counterman for coffee, short orders, and to wash the few dishes," the owner answered.

"I am your boy," said Frank.

The work was from ten to six A.M. and paid thirty-five dollars. When he got home in the morning, Frank opened the grocery. At the end of a week's working, without ringing it up, he put the thirty-five into the cash register. This, and Helen's wages, kept them from going under.

The clerk slept on the couch in the back of the store during the day. He had rigged up a buzzer that waked him when somebody opened the front door. He did not suffer from lack of sleep.

He lived in his prison in a climate of regret that he had turned a good thing into a bad, and this thought, though ancient, renewed the pain in his heart. His dreams were bad, taking place in the park at night. The garbage smell stank in his nose. He groaned his life away, his mouth crammed with words he couldn't speak. Mornings, standing at the store window, he watched Helen go off to work. He was there when she came home. She walked, slightly bowlegged, toward the door, her eyes cast down, blind to his presence. A million things to say, some extraordinary, welled up in him, choked his throat; daily they died. He thought endlessly of escape, but that would be what he always did last—beat it. This time he would stay. They would carry him out in a box. When the walls caved in they could dig for him with shovels.

Once he found a two-by-four pine board in the cellar, sawed off a hunk, and with his jackknife began to carve it into something. To his surprise it turned into a bird flying. It was shaped off balance but with a certain beauty. He thought of offering it to Helen but it seemed too rough a thing —the first he had ever made. So he tried his hand at something else. He set out to carve her a flower and it came out a rose starting to bloom. When it was done it was delicate in the way its petals were opening yet firm as a real flower. He thought about painting it red and giving it to her but decided to leave off the paint. He wrapped the wooden flower in store paper, printed Helen's name on the outside, and a few minutes before she came home from work, taped the package onto the outside of the mailbox in the vestibule. He saw her enter, then heard her go up the stairs. Looking into the vestibule, he saw she had taken his flower.

The wooden flower reminded Helen of her unhappiness. She lived in hatred of herself for having loved the clerk against her better judgment. She had fallen in love, she thought, to escape her predicament. More than ever she felt herself a victim of circumstance—in a bad dream symbolized by the nightmarish store below, and the relentless, scheming presence in it of the clerk, whom she should have shouted out of the house but had selfishly spared.

In the morning, as he aimed a pail of garbage into the can at the curb, Frank saw at the bottom of it his wooden flower.

On the day he had returned from the hospital Morris felt the urge to jump into his pants and run down to the store, but the doctor, after listening to his lungs, then tapping his hairy knuckles across the grocer's chest, said, "You're coming along fine, so what's your big hurry?" To Ida he privately said, "He has to rest, I don't mean maybe." Seeing her fright he explained, "Sixty isn't sixteen." Morris, after arguing a bit, lay back in bed and after that didn't care if he ever stepped into the store again. His recovery was slow.

With reservations, spring was on its way. There was at least more light in the day; it burst through the bedroom windows. But a cold wind roared in the streets, giving him goose pimples in bed; and sometimes, after half a day of pure sunshine, the sky darkened and some rags of snow fell. He was filled with melancholy and spent hours dreaming of his boyhood. He remembered the green fields. Where a boy runs he never forgets. His father, his mother, his only sister whom he hadn't seen in years, gottenyu. The wailing wind cried to him. . . .

The awning flapping below in the street awoke his dread of the grocery. He had not for a long time asked Ida what went on downstairs but he

knew without thinking. He knew in his blood.
When he consciously thought of it he remembered that the register rang rarely, so he knew
again. He heard heavy silence below. What else
can you hear from a graveyard whose noiseless
tombstones hold down the sick earth? The smell
of death seeped up through the cracks in the
floor. He understood why Ida did not dare go
downstairs but sought anything to do here. Who
could stay in such a place but a goy whose heart
was stone? The fate of his store floated like a
black-feathered bird dimly in his mind; but as
soon as he began to feel stronger, the thing grew
lit eyes, worrying him no end. One morning as he
sat up against a pillow, scanning yesterday's *Forward,* his thoughts grew so wretched that he broke
into sweat and his heart beat erratically. Morris
heaved aside his covers, strode crookedly out of
bed and began hurriedly to dress.

Ida hastened into the bedroom. "What are you
doing, Morris—a sick man?"

"I must go down."

"Who needs you? There is nothing there. Go
rest some more."

He fought a greedy desire to get back into bed
and live there but could not quiet his anxiety.

"I must go."

She begged him not to but he wouldn't listen.

"How much he takes in now?" Morris asked as
he belted his trousers.

"Nothing. Maybe seventy-five."

"A week?"

"What else?"

It was terrible but he had feared worse. His
head buzzed with schemes for saving the store.

Once he was downstairs he felt he could make things better. His fear came from being here, not where he was needed.

"He keeps open all day?"

"From morning till night—why I don't know."

"Why he stays here?" he asked with sudden irritation."

"He stays," she shrugged.

"What do you pay him?"

"Nothing—he says he don't want."

"So what he wants—my bitter blood?"

"He says he wants to help you."

He muttered something to himself. "You watch him sometimes?"

"Why should I watch him?" she said, worried. "He took something from you?"

"I don't want him here no more. I don't want him near Helen."

"Helen don't talk to him."

He gazed at Ida. "What happened?"

"Go ask her. What happened with Nat? She's like you, she don't tell me anything."

"He's got to leave today. I don't want him here."

"Morris," she said hesitantly, "he gave you good help, believe me. Keep him one more week till you feel stronger."

"No." He buttoned his sweater and despite her pleading went shakily down the stairs.

Frank heard him coming and grew cold.

The clerk had for weeks feared the time the grocer would leave his bed, although in a curious way he had also looked forward to it. He had spent many fruitless hours trying to construct a

story that would make Morris relent and keep him
on. He had planned to say, "Didn't I starve rather
than to spend the money from the holdup, so I
could put it back in the register—which I did,
though I admit I took a couple of rolls and some
milk to keep myself alive?" But he had no confidence in that. He could also proclaim his long
service to the grocer, his long patient labor in the
store; but the fact that he had stolen from him
during all this time spoiled his claim. He might
mention that he had saved Morris after he had
swallowed a bellyful of gas, but it was Nick who
had saved him as much as he. The clerk felt he
was without any good appeal to the grocer—that
he had used up all his credit with him, but then
he was struck by a strange and exciting idea, a
possible if impossible ace in the hole. He figured
that if he finally sincerely revealed his part in the
holdup, he might in the telling of it arouse in
Morris a true understanding of his nature, and a
sympathy for his great struggle to overcome his
past. Understanding his clerk's plight—the meaning of his long service to him—might make the
grocer keep him on, so he would again have the
chance to square everything with all concerned.
As he pondered this idea, Frank realized it was a
wild chance that might doom rather than redeem
him. Yet he felt he would try it if Morris insisted
he had to leave. What could he lose after that? But
when the clerk pictured himself saying what he
had done and had been forgiven by the grocer, and
he tried to imagine the relief he would feel, he
couldn't, because his overdue confession wouldn't
be complete or satisfying so long as he kept hidden what he had done to his daughter. About

that he knew he could never open his mouth, so he felt that no matter what he did manage to say there would always be some disgusting thing left unsaid, some further sin to confess, and this he found utterly depressing.

Frank was standing behind the counter near the cash register, paring his fingernails with his knife blade when the grocer, his face pale, the skin of it loose, his neck swimming in his shirt collar, his dark eyes unfriendly, entered the store through the hall door.

The clerk tipped his cap and edged away from the cash register.

"Glad to see you back again, Morris," he said, regretting he hadn't once gone up to see him in all the days the grocer had been upstairs. Morris nodded coldly and went into the rear. Frank followed him in, fell on one knee, and lit the radiator.

"It's pretty cold here, so I better light this up. I've been keeping it shut off to save on the gas bill."

"Frank," Morris said firmly, "I thank you that you helped me when I took in my lungs so much gas, also that you kept the store open when I was sick, but now you got to go."

"Morris," answered Frank, heavy-hearted, "I swear I never stole another red cent after that last time, and I hope God will strike me dead right here if it isn't the truth."

"This ain't why I want you to go," Morris answered.

"Then why do you?" asked the clerk, flushing.

"You know," the grocer said, his eyes downcast.

"Morris," Frank said, at agonizing last, "I have something important I want to tell you. I tried to

tell you before only I couldn't work my nerve up.
Morris, don't blame me now for what I once did,
because I am now a changed man, but I was one
of the guys that held you up that night. I swear to
God I didn't want to once I got in here, but I
couldn't get out of it. I tried to tell you about it—
that's why I came back here in the first place, and
the first chance I got I put my share of the money
back in the register—but I didn't have the guts
to say it. I couldn't look you in the eye. Even
now I feel sick about what I am saying, but I'm
telling it to you so you will know how much I
suffered on account of what I did, and that I am
very sorry you were hurt on your head—even
though not by me. The thing you got to understand is I am not the same person I once was. I
might look so to you, but if you could see what's
been going on in my heart you would know I have
changed. You can trust me now, I swear it, and
that's why I am asking you to let me stay and help
you."

Having said this, the clerk experienced a moment of extraordinary relief—a treeful of birds
broke into song; but the song was silenced when
Morris, his eyes heavy, said, "This I already know,
you don't tell me nothing new."

The clerk groaned. "How do you know it?"

"I figured out when I was laying upstairs in bed.
I had once a bad dream that you hurt me, then I
remembered—"

"But I didn't hurt you," the clerk broke in emo-
tionally. "I was the one that gave you the water to
drink. Remember?"

"I remember. I remember your hands. I remember your eyes. This day when the detective

brought in here the hold-upnik that he didn't hold
me up I saw in your eyes that you did something
wrong. Then when I stayed behind the hall door
and you stole from me a dollar and put in in your
pocket, I thought I saw you before in some place
but I didn't know where. That day you saved me
from the gas I almost recognized you; then when I
was laying in bed I had nothing to think about,
only my worries and how I threw away my life in
this store, then I remembered when you first
came here, when we sat at this table, you told me
you always did the wrong thing in your life; this
minute when I remembered this I said to myself,
'Frank is the one that made on me the holdup.' "

"Morris," Frank said hoarsely, "I am sorry."

Morris was too unhappy to speak. Though he
pitied the clerk, he did not want a confessed criminal around. Even if he had reformed, what good
would it do to keep him here—another mouth to
feed, another pair of eyes to the death watch?

"Did you tell Helen what I did?" sighed Frank.

"Helen ain't interested in you."

"One last chance, Morris," the clerk pleaded.

"Who was the antisimeet that he hit me on the
head?"

"Ward Minogue," Frank said after a minute.
"He's sick now."

"Ah," sighed Morris, "the poor father."

"We meant to hold Karp up, not you. Please let
me stay one more month. I'll pay for my own food
and also my rent."

"With what will you pay if I don't pay you—with
my debts?"

"I have a little job at night after the store
closes. I make a few odd bucks."

"No," said the grocer.

"Morris, you need my help here. You don't know how bad everything is."

But the grocer had set his heart against his assistant and would not let him stay.

Frank hung up his apron and left the store. Later, he bought a suitcase and packed his few things. When he returned Nick's radio, he said good-by to Tessie.

"Where are you going now, Frank?"

"I don't know."

"Are you ever coming back?"

"I don't know. Say good-by to Nick."

Before leaving, Frank wrote a note to Helen, once more saying he was sorry for the wrong he had done her. He wrote she was the finest girl he had ever met. He had bitched up his life. Helen wept over the note but had no thought of answering.

Although Morris liked the improvements Frank had made in the store he saw at once that they had not the least effect on business. Business was terrible. And with Frank's going the income shrank impossibly lower, a loss of ten terrible dollars from the previous week. He thought he had seen the store at its worst but this brought him close to fainting.

"What will we do?" he desperately asked his wife and daughter, huddled in their overcoats one Sunday night in the unheated back of the store.

"What else?" Ida said, "give right away in auction."

"The best thing is to sell even if we have to give away," Morris argued. "If we sell the store we can also make something on the house. Then I can pay my debts and have maybe a couple thousand dollars. But if we give in auction how can I sell the house?"

"So if we sell who will buy?" Ida snapped.

"Can't we auction off the store without going into bankruptcy?" Helen asked.

"If we auction we will get nothing. Then when the store is empty and it stays for rent, nobody will buy the house. There are already two places for rent on this block. If the wholesalers hear I went in auction they will force me in bankruptcy and take away the house also. But if we sell the store, than we can get a better price for the house."

"Nobody will buy," Ida said. "I told you when to sell but you wouldn't listen."

"Suppose you did sell the house and store," Helen asked, "what would you do then?"

"Maybe I could find a small place, maybe a candy store. If I could find a partner we could open up a store in a nice neighborhood."

Ida groaned. "Penny candy I won't sell. Also a partner we had already, he should drop dead."

"Couldn't you look for a job?" Helen said.

"Who will give me at my age a job?" Morris asked.

"You're acquainted with some people in the business," she answered. "Maybe somebody could get you a cashier's job in a supermarket."

"You want your father to stand all day on his feet with his varicose veins?" Ida asked.

"It would be better than sitting in the freezing back of an empty store."

"So what will we do?" Morris asked, but nobody answered.

Upstairs, Ida told Helen that things would be better if she got married.

"Who should I marry, Mama?"

"Louis Karp," said Ida.

The next evening she visited Karp when he was alone in the liquor store and told him their troubles. The liquor dealer whistled through his teeth.

Ida said, "You remember last November you wanted to send us a man by the name Podolsky, a refugee he was interested to go in the grocery business?"

"Yes. He said he would come here but he caught a cold in his chest."

"Did he buy some place a store?"

"Not yet," Karp said cautiously.

"He still wants to buy?"

"Maybe. But how could I recommend him a store like yours?"

"Don't recommend him the store, recommend him the price. Morris will sell now for two thousand cash. If he wants the house we will give him a good price. The refugee is young, he can fix up the business and give the goyim a good competition."

"Maybe I'll call him sometime," Karp remarked. He casually inquired about Helen. Surely she would be getting married soon?

Ida faced the way she hoped the wind was blowing. "Tell Louis not to be so bashful. Helen is lonely and wants to go out with somebody."

Karp coughed into his fist. "I don't see your clerk any more. How is that?" He spoke offhandedly, walking carefully, knowing the size of his big feet.

"Frank," Ida said solemnly, "don't work for us any more. Morris told him to leave, so he left last week."

Karp raised bushy brows. "Maybe," he said slowly, "I will call Podolsky and tell him to come tomorrow night. He works in the day."

"In the morning is the best time. Comes in then a few Morris' old customers."

"I will tell him to take off Wednesday morning," Karp said.

He later told Louis what Ida had said about Helen, but Louis, looking up from clipping his fingernails, said she wasn't his type.

"When you got gelt in your pocket any woman is your type," Karp said.

"Not her."

"We will see."

The next afternoon Karp came into Morris's and speaking as if they were the happiest of friends, advised the grocer; "Let Podolsky look around here but not too long. Also keep your mouth shut about the business. Don't try to sell him anything. When he finishes in here he will come to my house and I will explain him what's what."

Morris, hiding his feelings, nodded. He felt he had to get away from the store, from Karp, before he collapsed. Reluctantly he agreed to do as the liquor dealer suggested.

Early Wednesday morning Podolsky arrived, a shy young man in a thick greenish suit that looked as if it had been made out of a horse blanket. He

wore a small foreign-looking hat and carried a
loose umbrella. His face was innocent and his eyes
glistened with good will.

Morris, uneasy at what he was engaged in, invited Podolsky into the back, where Ida nervously awaited him, but the refugee tipped his hat and
said he would stay in the store. He slid into the
corner near near the door and nothing could drag
him out. Luckily, a few customers dribbled in,
and Podolsky watched with interest as Morris pro-
fessionally handled them.

When the store was empty, the grocer tried to
make casual talk from behind the counter, but
Podolsky, though constantly clearing his throat,
had little to say. Overwhelmed by pity for the
poor refugee, at what he had in all probability
lived through, a man who had sweated blood to
save a few brutal dollars, Morris, unable to stand
the planned dishonesty, came from behind the
counter, and taking Podolsky by the coat lapels,
told him earnestly that the store was rundown
but that a boy with his health and strength, with
modern methods and a little cash, could build it
up in a reasonable time and make a decent living
out of it.

Ida shrilly called from the kitchen she needed
the grocer to help her peel potatoes, but Morris
kept on talking till he was swimming in his sea of
woes; then he recalled Karp's warning, and though
he felt more than ever that the liquor dealer was
thoroughly an ass, abruptly broke off the story he
was telling. Yet before he could tear himself away
from the refugee, he remarked, "I could sell for two
thousand, but for fifteen-sixteen cash, anybody

who wants it can take the store. The house we will talk about later. Is this reasonable?"

"Why not?" Podolsky murmured, then again clammed up.

Morris retreated into the kitchen. Ida looked at him as if he had committed murder but did not speak. Two or three more people appeared, then after ten-thirty the dry trickle of customers stopped. Ida grew fidgety and tried to think of ways to get Podolsky out of the place but he stayed on. She asked him to come into the back for a glass of tea; he courteously refused. She remarked that Karp must now be anxious to see him; Podolsky bobbed his head and stayed. He tightened the cloth around his umbrella stick. Not knowing what else to say she absently promised to leave him all her recipes for salads. He thanked her, to her surprise, profusely.

From half past ten to twelve nobody approached the store. Morris went down to the cellar and hid. Ida sat dully in the back. Podolsky waited in his corner. Nobody saw as he eased himself and his black umbrella out of the grocery and fled.

On Thursday morning Morris spat on his shoebrush and polished his shoes. He was wearing his suit. He rang the hall bell for Ida to come down, then put on his hat and coat, old but neat because he rarely used them. Dressed, he rang up "no sale" and hesitantly pocketed eight quarters.

He was on his way to Charlie Sobeloff, an old partner. Years ago, Charlie, a cross-eyed but clever conniver, had come to the grocer with a meager thousand dollars in his pocket, borrowed money, and offered to go into partnership with him—Morris to furnish four thousand—to buy a grocery Charlie had in mind. The grocer disliked Charlie's nervousness and pale cross-eyes, one avoiding what the other looked at; but he was persuaded by the man's nagging enthusiasm and they bought the store. It was a good business, Morris thought, and he was satisfied. But Charlie, who had taken accountancy in night school, said he would handle the books, and Morris, in spite of Ida's warnings, consented, because, the grocer argued, the books were always in front of his eyes for inspection. But Charlie's talented nose had sniffed the right sucker. Morris never looked at the books until, two years after they had bought the place, the business collapsed.

The grocer, stunned, heartbroken, could not at first understand what had happened, but Charlie had figures to prove that the calamity had been bound to occur. The overhead was too high—they had paid themselves too high wages—his fault, Charlie admitted; also profits were low, the price of goods increasing. Morris now knew that his partner had, behind his back, cheated, manipulated, stolen whatever lay loose. They sold the place for a miserable price, Morris going out dazed, cleaned out, whereas Charlie in a short time was able to raise the cash to repurchase and restock the store, which he gradually worked into a thriving self-service business. For years the two had not met, but within the last four or five years, the ex-partner, when he returned from his winters in Miami, for reasons unknown to Morris, sought out the grocer and sat with him in the back, his eyes roving, his ringed fingers drumming on the table as he talked on about old times when they were young. Morris, through the years, had lost his hatred of the man, though Ida still could not stand him, and it was to Charlie Sobeloff that the grocer, with a growing sense of panic, had decided to run for help, a job—anything.

When Ida came down and saw Morris, in his hat and coat, standingly moodily by the door, she said in surprise, "Morris, where you going?"

"I go to my grave," the grocer said.

Seeing he was overwrought, she cried out, clasping her hands to her bosom, "Where do you go, tell me?"

He had the door open. "I go for a job."

"Come back," she cried in anger. "Who will give you?"

But he knew what she would say and was already in the street.

As he went quickly past Karp's he noticed that Louis had five customers—drunkards all—lined up at the counter and was doing a thriving business in brown bottles. *He* had sold only two quarts of milk in four hours. Although it shamed him, Morris wished the liquor store would burn to the ground.

At the corner he paused, overwhelmed by the necessity of choosing a direction. He hadn't remembered that space provided so many ways to go. He chose without joy. The day, though breezy, was not bad—it promised better, but he had little love left for nature. It gave nothing to a Jew. The March wind hastened him along, prodding the shoulders. He felt weightless, unmanned, the victim in motion of whatever blew at his back; wind, worries, debts, Karp, holdupniks, ruin. He did not go, he was pushed. He had the will of a victim, no will to speak of.

"For what I worked so hard for? Where is my youth, where did it go?"

The years had passed without profit or pity. Who could he blame? What fate didn't do to him he had done to himself. The right thing was to make the right choice but he made the wrong. Even when it was right it was wrong. To understand why, you needed an education but he had none. All he knew was he wanted better but had not after all these years learned how to get it. Luck was a gift. Karp had it, a few of his old friends had it, well-to-do men with grandchildren already, while his poor daughter, made in his image, faced—if not actively sought—old-maidhood. Life was meager, the world changed for the worse. America had become too complicated. One man counted for nothing. There were too many stores, depressions, anxieties. What had he escaped to here?

The subway was crowded and he had to stand till a pregnant woman, getting off, signaled him to her seat. He was ashamed to take it but nobody else moved, so he sat down. After a while he began to feel at ease, thought he would be satisfied to ride on like this, provided he never got to where he was going. But he did. At Myrtle Avenue he groaned softly, and left the train.

Arriving at Sobeloff's Self-Service Market, Morris, although he had heard of the growth of the place from Al Marcus, was amazed at its size. Charlie had tripled the original space by buying the building next door and knocking out the wall between the stores, later running an extension three-quarters of the way into the back yards. The result was a huge market with a large number of stalls and shelved sections loaded with groceries. The supermarket was so crowded with people that to Morris, as he peered half-scared through the window, it looked like a department store. He felt a pang, thinking that part of this might now be his if he had taken care of what he had once owned. He would not envy Charlie Sobeloff his dishonest wealth, but when he thought of what he could do for Helen with a little money his regret deepened that he had nothing.

He spied Charlie standing near the fruit stalls, the balabos, surveying the busy scene with satisfaction. He wore a gray Homburg and blue serge suit, but under the unbuttoned suit jacket he had tied a folded apron around his silk-shirted paunch, and wandered around, thus attired, overseeing. The grocer, looking through the window, saw himself opening the door and walking the long half block to where Charlie was standing.

He tried to speak but was unable to, until after so much silence the boss said he was busy, so say it.

"You got for me, Charlie," muttered the grocer, "a job? Maybe a cashier or something? My business is bad, I am going in auction."

Charlie, still unable to look straight at him, smiled. "I got five steady cashiers but maybe I can use you part time. Hang up your coat in the locker downstairs and I'll give you directions what to do."

Morris saw himself putting on a white duck jacket with "Sobeloff's Self-Service" stitched in red over the region of the heart. He would stand several hours a day at the checking, adding, ringing up the cash into one of Charlie's massive chromium registers. At quitting time, the boss would come over to check his money.

"You're short a dollar, Morris," Charlie said with a little chuckle, "but we will let it go."

"No," the grocer heard himself say. "I am short a dollar, so I will pay a dollar."

He took several quarters out of his pants pocket, counted four, and dropped them into his ex-partner's palm. Then he announced he was through, hung up his starched jacket, slipped on his coat and walked with dignity to the door. He joined the one at the window and soon went away.

Morris clung to the edge of a silent knot of men who drifted along Sixth Avenue, stopping at the employment agency doors to read impassively the list of jobs chalked up on the blackboard signs. There were openings for cooks, bakers, waiters, porters, handymen. Once in a while one of the men would secretly detach himself from the others and go into the agency. Morris followed along with them to Forty-fourth Street, where he noted a job listed for countermen behind a steam counter in a cafeteria. He went one flight up a narrow staircase and into a room that smelled of tobacco smoke. The grocer stood there, uncomfortable, until the big-faced owner of the agency happened to look up over the roll-top desk he was sitting at.

"You looking for something, mister?"

"Counterman," Morris said.

"You got experience?"

"Thirty years."

The owner laughed. "You're the champ but they want a kid they can pay twenty a week."

"You got something for a man my experience?"

"Can you slice sandwich meat nice and thin?"

"The best."

"Come back next week, I might have something for you."

The grocer continued along with the crowd. At Forty-seventh Street he applied for a waiter's job in a kosher restaurant but the agency had filled the job and forgotten to erase it from their sign.

"So what else you got for me?" Morris asked the manager.

"What work do you do?"

"I had my own store, grocery and delicatessen."

"So why do you ask for waiter?"

"I didn't see for counterman anything."

"How old are you?"

"Fifty-five."

"I should live so long till you see fifty-five again," said the manager. As Morris turned to go the man offered him a cigarette but the grocer said his cough kept him from smoking.

At Fiftieth he went up a dark staircase and sat on a wooden bench at the far end of a long room.

The boss of the agency, a man with a broad back and a fat rear, holding a dead cigar butt between stubby fingers, had his heavy foot on a chair as he talked in a low voice to two gray-hatted Filipinos.

Seeing Morris on the bench he called out, "Whaddye want, pop?"

"Nothing. I sit on account I am tired."

"Go home," said the boss.

He went downstairs and had coffee at a dish-laden table in the Automat.

America.

Morris rode the bus to East Thirteenth Street, where Breitbart lived. He hoped the peddler would be home but only his son Hymie was. The boy was sitting in the kitchen, eating cornflakes with milk and reading the comics.

"What time comes home papa?" Morris asked.

"About seven, maybe eight," Hymie mumbled.

Morris sat down to rest. Hymie ate, and read the comics. He had big restless eyes.

"How old are you?"

"Fourteen."

The grocer got up. He found two quarters in his pocket and left them on the table. "Be a good boy. Your father loves you."

He got into the subway at Union Square and rode to the Bronx, to the apartment house where Al Marcus lived. He felt sure Al would help him find something. He would be satisfied, he thought, with little, maybe a night watchman's job.

When he rang Al's bell, a well-dressed woman with sad eyes came to the door.

"Excuse me," said Morris. "My name is Mr. Bober. I am an old-time customer Al Marcus's. I came to see him."

"I am Mrs. Margolies, his sister-in-law."

"If he ain't home I will wait."

"You'll wait a long time," she said, "they took him to the hospital yesterday."

Though he knew why he couldn't help asking.

"Can you go on living if you're already dead?"

When the grocer got home in the cold twilight

Ida took one look at him and began to cry.

"What did I tell you?"

That night Morris, alone in the store after Ida
had gone up to soak her poor feet, felt an uncon-
trollable craving for some heavy sweet cream.
He remembered the delicious taste of bread
dipped in rich milk when he was a boy. He found
a half-pint bottle of whipping cream in the refrigerator and took it, guiltily, with a loaf of stale
white bread, into the back. Pouring some cream
into a saucer, he soaked it up with bread, greedily
wolfing the cream-laden bread.

A noise in the store startled him. He hid the
cream and bread in the gas range.

At the counter stood a skinny man in an old hat
and a dark overcoat down to his ankles. His nose
was long, throat gaunt, and he wore a wisp of red
beard on his bony chin.

"A gut shabos," said the scarecrow.

"A gut shabos," Morris answered, though shabos
was a day away.

"It smells here," said the skinny stranger, his
small eyes shrewd, "like a open grave."

"Business is bad."

The man wet his lips and whispered, "Insurinks
you got—fire insurinks?"

Morris was frightened. "What is your business?"

"How much?"

"How much what?"

"A smart man hears one word but he understand two. How much you got insurinks?"

"Two thousand for the store."

"Feh."

"Five thousand for the house."

"A shame. Should be ten."

"Who needs ten for this house?"

"Nobody knows."

"What do you want here?" Morris asked, irir-tated.

The man rubbed his skinny, red-haired hands. "What does a macher want?"

"What kind of macher? What do you make?"

He shrugged slyly. "I make a living." The macher spoke soundlessly. "I make fires."

Morris drew back.

The macher waited with downcast eyes. "We are poor people," he murmured.

"What do you want from me?"

"We are poor people," the macher said, apolo-getically. "God loves the poor people but he helps the rich. The insurinks companies are rich. They take away your money and what they give you? Nothing. Don't feel sorry for the insurinks com-panies."

He proposed a fire. He would make it swiftly, safely, economically—guaranteed to collect.

From his coat pocket he produced a strip of cel-luloid. "You know what is this?"

Morris, staring at it, preferred not to say.

"Celluloy," hissed the macher. He struck a large yellow match and lit the celluloid. It flared instantly. He held it a second then let it fall to the counter, where it quickly burned itself out. With a *poof* he blew away nothing. Only the stench re-mained, floating in air.

"Magic," he hoarsely announced. "No ashes. This is why we use celluloy, not paper, not rags. You push a piece in a crack, and the fire burns in a minute. Then when comes the fire marshal and insurinks investigator, what they find?—nothing. For nothing they pay cash—two thousand for the store, five for the house." A smile crawled over his face.

Morris shivered. "You want me I should burn down my house and my store to collect the insurance?"

"I want," said the macher slyly, "tsu you want?"

The grocer fell silent.

"Take," said the macher persuasively, "your family and go for a ride to Cunyiland. When you come back is the job finished. Cost—five hun-hundred." He lightly dusted his fingers.

"Upstairs lives two people," muttered the grocer.

"When they go out?"

"Sometimes to the movies, Friday night." He spoke dully, not sure why he was revealing secrets to a total stranger.

"So let be Friday night. I am not kosher."

"But who's got five hundred dollars?"

The macher's face fell. He sighed deeply. "I will make for two hundred. I will do a good job. You will get six—seven thousand. After, pay me another three hundred."

But Morris had decided. "Impossible."

"You don't like the price?"

"I don't like fires. I don't like monkey business."

The macher argued another half hour and departed reluctantly.

The next night a car pulled up in front of the door, and the grocer watched Nick and Tessie, dressed for a party, get in and drive off. Twenty minutes later Ida and Helen came down to go to a movie. Helen had asked her mother to go with her, and Ida said yes, seeing how restless her daughter was. When he realized that the house was deserted, Morris felt suddenly agitated.

After ten minutes, he went up the stairs, and searched in a camphor-smelling trunk in the small room for a celluloid collar he had once worn. Ida saved everything, but he couldn't locate it. He searched in Helen's bureau drawer and found an envelope full of picture negatives. Discarding several of her as a school girl, Morris took some of boys in bathing suits, nobody he recognized. Hurrying down, he found matches and went into the cellar. He thought that one of the bins would be a good place to start the fire but settled instead on the air shaft. The flames would shoot up in an instant, and through the open toilet window into the store. Gooseflesh crept over him. He figured he could start the fire and wait in the hall. Once the flames had got a good start, he would rush into the street and ring the alarm. He could later say he had fallen asleep on the couch and had been awakened by the smoke. By the time the fire engines came, the house would be badly damaged. The hoses and axes would do the rest.

Morris inserted the celluloid strips into a crack between two boards, on the inside of the dumbwaiter. His hand shook and he whispered to himself as he touched the match to the negatives. Then the flame shot up in a stupefying stench and at once crawled up the wall of the dumb-waiter. Morris watched, hypnotized, then let out a terrible cry. Slapping frantically at the burning negatives, he knocked them to the cellar floor. As he hunted for something with which to beat out the fire in the dumb-waiter, he discovered that the bottom of his apron was burning. He smacked the flames with both hands and then his sweater sleeves began to blaze. He sobbed for God's mercy, and was at once roughly seized from behind and flung to the ground.

Frank Alpine smothered the grocer's burning clothes with his overcoat. He banged out the fire in the dumb-waiter with his shoe.

Morris moaned.

"For Christ sake," Frank pleaded, "take me back here."

But the grocer ordered him out of the house.

Saturday night, about one A.M., Karp's store began to burn.

In the early evening, Ward Minogue had knocked on Frank's door and learned from Tessie that the clerk had moved.

"Where to?"

"I don't know. Ask Mr. Bober," Tessie said, anxious to get rid of him.

Downstairs, Ward peered through the grocery window and seeing Morris, hurriedly withdrew. Though alcohol nauseated him lately, his thirst for a drink was killing him. He thought if he could get a couple of swigs past the nausea he would feel better. But all he had in his pocket was a dime, so he went into Karp's and begged Louis to trust him to a cheap fifth of anything.

"I wouldn't trust you for a fifth of sewer water," Louis said.

Ward grabbed a bottle of wine from the counter and flung it at Louis' head. He ducked but the wine smashed some bottles on the shelf. As Louis, yelling murder, rushed into the street, Ward snatched a bottle of whiskey and ran out of the store and up the block. He had gone past the butcher's when the bottle slipped from under his arm and broke on the sidewalk. Ward looked back with anguish but kept on running.

By the time the cops came Ward had disappeared. After supper that night, Detective Minogue, roaming the cold streets, saw his son in Earl's bar, standing over a beer. The detective went in by the side door but Ward saw him in the mirror and bolted out the front. Although short of breath, driven by great fear, he ran toward the coal yard. Hearing his father behind him, Ward leaped across the rusted chain stretched in front of the loading platform and sped over the cobblestones toward the back of the yard. He scrambled under one of the trucks in the shed.

The detective, calling him filthy names, hunted him in the dark for fifteen minutes. Then he took out his pistol and fired a shot into the shed. Ward, thinking he would be killed, crawled out from under the truck and ran into his father's arms.

Though he pleaded with the detective not to hurt him, crying he had diabetes and would surely get gangrene, his father beat him mercilessly with his billy until Ward collapsed.

Bending over him, the detective yelled, "I told you to stay the hell out of this neighborhood. This is my last warning to you. If I ever see you again, I'll murder you." He dusted his coat and left the coal yard.

Ward lay on the cobblestones. His nose had been gushing blood but it soon stopped. Getting up, he felt so dizzy he wept. He staggered into the shed and climbed into the cab of one of the coal trucks, thinking he would sleep there. But when he lit a cigarette he was overcome with nausea. Ward threw the butt out and waited for the nau-

sea to leave him. When it did he was thirsty again.
If he could climb the coal yard fence, then some
of the smaller ones beyond it, he would land up in
Karp's back yard. He knew from having cased the
place once that the liquor store had a barred window in the back, but that the rusty iron bars were
old and loose. He thought that if he got his
strength back he could force them apart.

He dragged himself over the coal yard fence,
then more slowly over the others until he stood at
last in Karp's weedy back yard. The liquor store
had been closed since midnight and there were no
lights burning in the house. Above the dark grocery one of Bober's windows was lit, so he had to
be careful or the Jew might hear him.

Twice, at intervals of ten minutes, he tried to
bend the bars but failed. The third time, straining
till he shook, he slowly forced the inside two
apart. The window was unlocked. Ward got his
fingertips under it and lifted it with care because
it squeaked. When it was open, he squeezed
through the bent bars, squirming into the back of
the liquor store. Once in there he laughed a little
to himself and moved around freely, knowing
Karp was too cheap to have a burglar alarm. From
the stock in the rear Ward sampled and spat out
three different brands of whiskey. Forcing himself,
he gurgled down a third of a bottle of gin. In a
couple of minutes he forgot his aches and pains
and lost the sorrow he had been feeling for himself. He snickered when he imagined Louis' comic
puss as he found the empty bottles all over the
floor in the morning. Remembering the cash register, Ward staggered out front and rang it open. It
was empty. He angrily smashed a whiskey bottle

on it. A feeling of nausea gagged him and with a croak he threw up over Karp's counter. Feeling better, he began by the light of the street lamp to smash the whiskey bottles against the cash register.

Mike Papadopolous, whose bedroom was right above the front part of the liquor store, was awakened by the noise. After five minutes he figured something was wrong so he got up and dressed. Ward had, in the meantime, destroyed a whole shelf of bottles, when he felt a hunger to smoke. It took him two minutes to get a match struck and the light touching his butt. He tasted the smoke with pleasure as the flame briefly lit his face, then he shook the match and flipped it over his shoulder. It landed, still burning, in a puddle of alcohol. The fire flew up with a zoom. Ward, lit like a flaming tree, flailed at himself. Screaming, he ran through the back and tried to get out of the window but was caught between the bars and, exhausted, died.

Smelling smoke, Mike came down in a rush and seeing fire in the store, raced to the drugstore corner to turn in the alarm. As he was running back, the plate glass window of the liquor store exploded and a roaring flame boiled up in the place. After Mike had got his mother and the up-stairs tenants out of the house, he ran into Bober's hall, shouting there was a fire next door. They were all up—Helen, who had been reading when the window crashed, had run up to call Nick and Tessie. They left the house, bundled in sweaters and overcoats, and stood across the street, hud-dled together with some passers-by, watching the fire destroy Karp's once prosperous business, then devour the house. Despite the heavy streams of water the firemen poured into the flames, the fire, fed by the blazing alcohol, rose to the roof, and when it was at last smothered, all that was left of Karp's property was a gutted, dripping shell.

As the firemen began with grappling hooks to tear out the burned fixtures and heave them onto the sidewalk, everybody fell silent. Ida moaned softly, with shut eyes thinking of Morris's burned sweater that she had found in the cellar, and the singed hair she had noticed on his hands. Sam Pearl, lost without his bifocals, mumbled to himself. Nat, hatless, an overcoat on over pajamas, edged close to Helen until he stood by her side. Morris was fighting a tormenting emotion.

A car drew up and parked beyond the drugstore. Karp got out with Louis and they crossed the hose-filled street to their store. Karp took one unbearable look at his former gesheft, and though it was for the most part insured, tottered forward and collapsed. Louis yelled at him to wake up. Two of the firemen carried the stricken liquor dealer to his car, and Louis frantically drove him home.

Afterward Morris couldn't sleep. He stood at his bedroom window in his long underwear, looking down at the pile of burned and broken fixtures on the sidewalk. With a frozen hand the grocer clawed at a live pain in his breast. He felt an overwhelming hatred of himself. He had wished it on Karp—just this. His anguish was terrible.

Sunday, the last of March, was overcast at eight A.M., and there were snow flurries in the air. Winter still spits in my face, thought the weary grocer. He watched the fat wet flakes melt as they touched the ground. It's too warm for snow, he thought, to-morrow will come April. Maybe. He had awaken-ed with a wound, a gap in his side, a hole in the ground he might fall through if he stepped out-side where the liquor store had been. But the earth held him up and the odd feeling wore off. It went as he reflected it was no use mourning Karp's loss; his pocketbook would protect him from too much pain. Pain was for poor people. For Karp's tenants the fire was a tragedy, and for Ward Minogue, dead young; maybe also for the detec-tive, but not for Julius Karp. Morris could have used the fire, so Karp had got it for free. Every-thing to him who has.

As the grocer was thinking this, the liquor deal-er, apparently the victim of a sleepless night, ap-peared in the falling snow and entered the gro-cery. He wore a narrow-brimmed hat with a foolish little feather in the band and a double-breasted overcoat, but despite his stylish appear-ance, his eyes, with dark bags under them, were filled with gloom, his complexion pasty, lips blue. Where his forehead had smacked the sidewalk last night he wore a plaster patch—an unhappy figure, the loss of his business the worst that could hap-pen to him. He couldn't stand the vision of dol-lars he might be taking in, flying daily away. Karp seemed embarrassed, ill. The grocer, his shame awakened, invited him into the back for tea. Ida, also up early, made a fuss over him.

Karp took a hot sip or two of tea, but after set-ting the cup down, hadn't the strength to lift it from the saucer. After a fidgety silence he spoke. "Morris, I want to buy your house. Also the store." He drew a deep, trembly breath.

Ida let out a stifled cry. Morris was stupefied.

"What for? The business is terrible."

"Not so terrible," cried Ida.

"Don't interest me the grocery business," Karp gloomily replied. "Only the location. Next door," he said, but couldn't go on.

They understood.

He explained it would take months to rebuild his house and place of business. But if he took over Morris's store he could have it refixtured, painted, stocked in a couple of weeks, thus keeping to a minimum his loss of trade.

Morris couldn't believe his ears. He was filled with excitement and dread that somebody would tell him he had just dreamed a dream, or that Karp, fat fish, would turn into a fat bird and fly away, screeching, "Don't you believe me," or in some heartbreaking way change his mind.

So he put his foot on anticipation and kept his mouth shut, but when Karp asked him to name his price the grocer had one ready. "Nine thousand for the house—three down, my equity—and for the store twenty-five hundred cash. After all, bad as it was, the grocery was a going business, and for the refrigerator alone he had paid nine hundred dollars. With trepidation he figured a fair fifty-five hundred in cash in his hands, enough after he had paid his debts to look for a new business. Seeing Ida's astonished expression, he was surprised at his nerve and thought Karp would surely laugh him in the face and offer less—which he would grab anyway; but the liquor dealer listlessly nodded. "I will give you twenty-five hundred for the store, less the auction price of stock and fixtures."

"This is your business," Morris replied.

Karp could not bear to discuss the terms any further. "My lawyer will draw the contract."

When he left the grocery, the liquor dealer vanished in the swirling snow. Ida wept joyfully, while Morris, still stunned, reflected that his luck had changed. So had Karp's, for what Karp had lost he had in a sense gained, as if to make up for the misery the man had caused him in the past. Yesterday he wouldn't have believed how things would balance out today.

The spring snow moved Morris profoundly. He watched it falling, seeing in it scenes of his childhood, remembering things he thought he had forgotten. All morning he watched the shifting snow. He thought of himself, a boy running in it, whooping at blackbirds as they flew from the snowy trees; he felt an irresistible thirst to be out in the open.

"I think I will shovel the snow," he told Ida at lunchtime.

"Go better to sleep."

"It ain't nice for the customers."

"What customers—who needs them?"

"People can't walk in such high snow," he argued.

"Wait, tomorrow it will be melted."

"'It's Sunday, it don't look so nice for the goyim that they go to church."

Her voice had an edge to it. "You want to catch pneumonia, Morris?"

"It's spring," he murmured.

"It's winter."

"I will wear my hat and coat."

"Your feet will get wet. You have no galoshes."

"Only five minutes."

"No," she said flatly.

Later, he thought.

All afternoon the snow came softly down and by evening it had reached a depth of six inches. When the snowing stopped, a wind rose and blew clouds of it through the streets. He watched at the front window.

Ida hung over him all day. He didn't get out till late. After closing he had sat relentlessly over a piece of store paper, writing a long list, until she grew impatient.

"Why do you stay so late?"

"I figure the stock for the auctioneer."

"This is Karp's business."

"I must help, he don't know the prices."

Talk of the store's sale relieved her. "Come up soon," she yawned.

He waited until he felt she was asleep, then went down to the cellar for the shovel. He put on his hat and a pair of old gloves and stepped out into the street. To his surprise the wind wrapped him in an icy jacket, his apron flapping noisily. He had expected, the last of March, a milder night. The surprise lingered in his mind but the shoveling warmed him. He kept his back to Karp's burned hole, though with the black turned white it wasn't too hard to look at.

Scooping up a shovelful of snow he heaved it into the street. It turned to dust in mid-air and whirled whitely away.

He recalled the hard winters when he had first come to America. After about fifteen years they turned mild but now they were hard again. It had been a hard life, but now with God's help he would have an easier time.

He flung another load of snow into the street. "A better life," he muttered.

Nick and Tessie came home from somewhere.

"At least put something warm on, Mr. Bober," advised Tessie.

"I'm almost finished," Morris grunted.

"It's your health," said Nick.

The first floor window shot up. Ida stood there in her flannel nightgown, her hair down.

"Are you crazy?" she shouted to the grocer.

"Finished," he answered.

"Without a coat—are you crazy?"

"Took me ten minutes."

Nick and Tessie went into the house.

"Come up now," Ida shouted.

"Finished," Morris cried. He heaved a last angry shovelful into the gutter. A little of the sidewalk remained to be cleaned but now that she was nagging he felt too tired to do it.

Morris dragged the wet shovel into the store. The warmth struck him across the head. He felt himself reeling and had a momentary fright but after a glass of hot tea with lemon felt rested.

As he was drinking the tea it began to snow again. He watched a thousand flakes push at the window, as if they wanted to snow through the glass and in the kitchen. He saw the snow as a moving curtain, and then he saw it in lit single flakes, not touching each other.

Ida banged hard on the floor, so he finally closed and went upstairs.

She was sitting in her bathrobe with Helen in the living room, her eyes dark with anger. "Are you a baby you had to go out in the snow? What's the matter with such a man?"

"I had my hat on. What am I, tissue paper?"

"You had pneumonia," she shouted.

"Mama, lower your voice," Helen said, "they'll hear upstairs."

"Who asked him to shovel snow, for God's sakes?"

"For twenty-two years stinks in my nose this store. I wanted to smell in my lungs some fresh air."

"Not in the ice cold."

"Tomorrow is April."

"Anyway," Helen said, "don't tempt fate, Papa."

"What kind of winter can be in April?"

"Come to sleep." Ida marched off to bed.

He sat with Helen on the couch. Since hearing of Karp's visit that morning she had lost her moodiness, looked again like a happy girl. He thought with sadness how pretty she was. He wanted to give her something—only good.

"How do you feel that I am selling the house and store?" he asked her.

"You know how I feel."

"Tell me anyway."

"Refreshed."

"We will move to a better neighborhood like you like. I will find a better parnusseh. You will keep your wages."

She smiled at him.

"I remember when you were a little baby," Morris said.

She kissed his hand.

"I want the most you should be happy."

"I will be." Her eyes grew wet. "If you only knew all the good things I'd like to give you, Papa."

"You gave me."

"I'll give you better."

"Look how it snows," said Morris.

They watched the snow through the moving windows, then Morris said good night.

"Sleep well," Helen said.

But he lay in bed restless, almost dejected. There was so much to do, so many changes to make and get used to. Tomorrow was the day Karp would bring the deposit. Tuesday the auctioneer would come and they would go over the goods and fixtures. Wednesday they could hold the auction. Thursday, for the first time in almost a generation, he would be without a place of business. Such a long time. After so many years in one place he hated the thought of having to get used to another. He disliked leaving the neighborhood though he hadn't liked it. It made him uncomfortable to be in a strange place. He thought uneasily of having to locate, appraise, and buy a new store. He would prefer to live above the store, but Helen wanted them to take a small apartment, so let it be a small apartment. Once he had the store he would let them look for a place to live. But the store he would have to find himself. What he feared most was that he would make another mistake and again settle in a prison. The possibility of this worried him intensely. Why would the owner want to sell? Would he be an honest man or, underneath, a thief? And once he had bought the place, would business keep up or go down? Would times stay good? Would he make a living? His

thoughts exhausted him. He could feel his poor
heart running a race against the merciless future.

He fell heavily asleep but awoke in a couple of
hours, drenched in hot sweat. Yet his feet were
freezing and he knew that if he kept his thoughts
on them he would break into shivering. Then his
right shoulder began to hurt, and when he forced
himself to take a deep breath, his left side pained
him. He knew he was sick and was miserably disappointed. He lay in the dark, trying not to think
how stupid it had been to shovel the snow. He
must have caught a chill. He thought he would
not. He thought he was entitled, after twenty-two
years, to a few minutes of freedom. Now his plans
would have to wait, although Ida could finish the
business with Karp and make arrangements with
the auctioneer. Gradually he accepted the thought
that he had a cold—maybe flu. He considered
waking her to call a doctor but who could they
call without a telephone? And if Helen got
dressed and used Sam Pearl's phone, what an embarrassment that would be, waking up a whole
family when she rang their bell; also arousing a
doctor out of his precious sleep, who would say
after examining him, "Mister, what's all the excitement? You got the flu, so stay in bed." For
such advice he didn't need to call a doctor in his
nightshirt. He could wait a few hours till morning. Morris dozed but felt fever shake him in his
sleep. He awoke with his hair stiff. Maybe he had
pneumonia? After a while he grew calmer. He
was sick but sickness was nothing new to him.
Probably if he hadn't shoveled snow he would
have got sick anyway. In the last few days he
hadn't felt so well—headachy, weak in the knees.

Yet though he tried to resign himself to what had happened, he felt enormously bitter that he had become ill. So he had shoveled snow in the street, but did it have to snow in April? And if it did, did he have to get sick the minute he stepped out into the open air? It frustrated him hopelessly that every move he made seemed to turn into an inevitable thing.

He dreamed of Ephraim. He had recognized him when the dream began by his brown eyes, clearly his father's. Ephraim wore a beanie cut from the crown of an old hat of Morris's, covered with buttons and shiny pins, but the rest of him was in rags. Though he did not for some reason expect otherwise, this and that the boy looked hungry shocked the grocer.

"I gave you to eat three times a day, Ephraim," he explained, "so why did you leave so soon your father?"

Ephraim was too shy to answer, but Morris, in a rush of love for him—a child was so small at that age—promised him a good start in life.

"Don't worry, I'll give you a fine college education."

Ephraim—a gentleman—averted his face as he snickered.

"I give you my word . . ."

The boy disappeared in the wake of laughter.

"Stay alive," his father cried after him.

When the grocer felt himself awaking, he tried to get back into the dream but it easily evaded him. His eyes were wet. He thought of his life with sadness. For his family he had not provided, the poor man's disgrace. Ida was asleep at his side.

He wanted to awaken her and apologize. He thought of Helen. It would be terrible if she became an old maid. He moaned a little, thinking of Frank. His mood was of regret. I gave away my life for nothing. It was the thunderous truth.

Was the snow still falling?

Morris died in the hospital, three days later, and was buried the day after in an enormous cemetery —it went on for miles—in Queens. He had been a member of a burial society since coming to America and the services took place in the Society's funeral parlor on the Lower East Side, where the grocer had lived as a young man. At noon in the chapel's antechamber, Ida, gray-faced and in mourning, every minute on the edge of fainting, sat in a high-backed tapestried chair, rocking her head. At her side, wasted, red-eyed from weeping, sat Helen. Landsleit, old friends, drawn by funeral notices in the Jewish morning papers, lamented aloud as they bent to kiss her, dropping pulpy tears on her hands. They sat on folding chairs facing the bereaved and talked in whispers. Frank Alpine stood for a moment, his hat uncomfortably on, in a corner of the room. When the place grew crowded he left and seated himself among the handful of mourners already assembled in the long narrow chapel, dimly lit by thick, yellow wall lamps. The rows of benches were dark and heavy. In the front of the chapel, on a metal stand, lay the grocer's plain wooden coffin.

At one P.M., the gray-haired undertaker, breathing heavily, escorted the widow and her daughter to the front row on the left, not far from the

coffin. A wailing began among the mourners. The
chapel was a little more than half-full of old
friends of the grocer, a few distant relatives, burial
society acquaintances, and one or two customers.
Breitbart, the bulb peddler, sat, stricken, against
the right wall. Charlie Sobeloff, grown heavy-
faced and stout, appeared, with Florida tan and
sad crossed eye, together with his stylish wife, who
sat staring at Ida. The entire Pearl family was present, Betty with her new husband, and Nat, sober,
concerned for Helen, wearing a black skull cap.
A few rows behind them was Louis Karp, alone
and ill at ease among strangers. Also Witzig, the
baker, who had served Morris bread and rolls for
twenty years. And Mr. Giannola, the barber, and
Nick and Tessie Fuso, behind whom Frank Alpine
sat. When the bearded rabbi entered the chapel
through a side door, Frank took off his hat but
quickly put it on again.

The secretary of the Society appeared, a soft-
voiced man with little hair, his glasses lit with re-
flections of the wall lamps, and read from a hand-
written paper praise for Morris Bober and lamen-
tation for his loss. When he announced the body
could be seen, the undertaker and his assistant, a
man in a chauffeur's cap, lifted the coffin lid and a
few people came forward. Helen wept profusely
at her father's waxen, berouged image, the head
wrapped in a prayer shawl, the thin mouth slightly
twisted.

Ida flung up both arms, crying in Yiddish at the
corpse, "Morris, why didn't you listen to me? You
went away and left me with a child, alone in the
world. Why did you do it?" She broke into rack-
ing sobs and was gently escorted by Helen and the

breathless undertaker to her seat, where she pressed her wet face against her daughter's shoulder. Frank went up last. He could see, where the prayer shawl fell back a little, the scar on the grocer's head, but outside of that it wasn't Morris. He felt a loss but it was an old one.

The rabbi then prayed, a stocky man with a pointed black beard. He stood on the podium near the coffin, wearing an old Homburg, a faded black frock coat over brown trousers, and bulbous shoes. After his prayer in Hebrew, when the mourners were seated, in a voice laden with sorrow he spoke of the dead man.

"My dear friends, I never had the pleasure to meet this good grocery man that he now lays in his coffin. He lived in a neighborhood where I didn't come in. Still and all I talked this morning to people that knew him and I am now sorry I didn't know him also. I would enjoy to speak to such a man. I talked to the bereaved widow, who lost her dear husband. I talked to his poor beloved daughter Helen, who is now without a father to guide her. To them I talked, also to landsleit and old friends, and each and all told me the same, that Morris Bober, who passed away so untimely—he caught double pneumonia from shoveling snow in front of his place of business so people could pass by on the sidewalk—was a man who couldn't be more honest. Such a person I am sorry I didn't meet sometime in my life. If I met him somewhere, maybe when he went to visit in a Jewish neighborhood—maybe at Rosh Hashana or Pesach—I would say to him, 'God bless you, Morris Bober.' Helen, his dear daughter, remembers from when she was a small girl that her father ran two blocks in the snow to give back to a poor Italian lady a nickel that she forgot on the counter. Who runs in wintertime without hat or coat, without rubbers to protect his feet, two blocks in the snow to give back five cents that a customer forgot? Couldn't he wait till she comes in tomorrow? Not Morris Bober, let him rest in peace. He didn't want the poor woman to worry, so he ran after her in the snow. This is why the grocer had so many friends who admi-red him."

The rabbi paused and gazed over the heads of the mourners.

"He was also a very hard worker, a man that never stopped working. How many mornings he got up in the dark and dressed himself in the cold, I can't count. After, he went downstairs to stay all day in the grocery. He worked long long hours. Six o'clock every morning he opened and he closed after ten every night, sometimes later. Fifteen, sixteen hours a day he was in the store, seven days a week, to make a living for his family. His dear wife Ida told me she will never forget his steps going down the stairs each morning, and also in the night when he came up so tired for his few hours' sleep before he will open again the next day the store. This went on for twenty-two years in this store alone, day after day, except the few days when he was too sick. And for this reason that he worked so hard and bitter, in his house, on his table, was always something to eat. So besides honest he was a good provider."

The rabbi gazed down at his prayer book, then looked up.

"When a Jew dies, who asks if he is a Jew? He is a Jew, we don't ask. There are many ways to be a

Jew. So if somebody comes to me and says, 'Rabbi, shall we call such a man Jewish who lived and worked among the gentiles and sold them pig meat, trayfe, that we don't eat it, and not once in twenty years comes inside a synagogue, is such a man a Jew, rabbi?' To him I will say, 'Yes, Morris Bober was to me a true Jew because he lived in the Jewish experience, which he remembered, and with the Jewish heart.' Maybe not to our formal tradition—for this I don't excuse him—but he was true to the spirit of our life—to want for others that which he wants also for himself. He followed the Law which God gave to Moses on Sinai and told him to bring to the people. He suffered, he endu-red, but with hope. Who told me this? I know. He asked for himself little—nothing, but he wanted for his beloved child a better existence than he had. For such reasons he was a Jew. What more does our sweet God ask his poor people? So let Him now take care of the widow, to comfort and protect her, and give to the fatherless child what her father wanted her to have. 'Yaskadal v'yiskadash shmey, rabo. B'olmo divro . . .' "

The mourners rose and prayed with the rabbi.

Helen, in her grief, grew restless. He's overdone it, she thought. I said Papa was honest but what was the good of such honesty if he couldn't exist in this world? Yes, he ran after this poor woman to give her back a nickel but he also trusted cheaters who took away what belonged to him. Poor Papa; being naturally honest, he didn't believe that others come by their dishonesty naturally. And he couldn't hold onto those things he had worked so hard to get. He gave away, in a sense, more than he owned. He was no saint; he was in a way weak, his only true strength in his sweet nature and his understanding. He knew, at least, what was good. And I didn't say he had many friends who admired him. That's the rabbi's invention. People liked him, but who can admire a man passing his life in such a store? He buried himself in it; he didn't have the imagination to know what he was missing. He made himself a victim. He could, with a little more courage, have been more than he was.

Helen prayed for peace on the soul of her dead father.

Ida, holding a wet handkerchief to her eyes, thought, So what if we had to eat? When you eat you don't want to worry whose money you are eating—yours or the wholesalers'. If he had money he had bills; and when he had more money he had more bills. A person doesn't always want to worry if she will be in the street tomorrow. She wants sometimes a minute's peace. But maybe it's my fault, because I didn't let him be a druggist.

She wept because her judgment of the grocer was harsh although she loved him. Helen, she thought, must marry a professional.

When the prayer was done the rabbi left the chapel through the side door, and the coffin was lifted by some of the Society members and the undertaker's assistant, carried on their shoulders outside, and placed in the hearse. The people in the chapel filed out and went home, except Frank Alpine, who sat alone in the funeral parlor.

Suffering, he thought, is like a piece of goods. I bet the Jews could make a suit of clothes out of it. The other funny thing is that there are more of them around than anybody knows about.

In the cemetery it was spring. The snow had melted on all but a few graves, the air was warm, fragrant. The small group of mourners following the grocer's coffin were hot in their overcoats. At the Society's plot, crowded with tombstones, two gravediggers had dug a fresh pit in the earth and were standing back, holding their shovels. As the rabbi prayed over the empty grave—from up close his beard was thick with gray—Helen rested her head against the coffin held by the pallbearers.

"Good-by, Papa."

Then the rabbi prayed aloud over the coffin as the gravediggers lowered it to the bottom of the grave.

"Gently . . . gently."

Ida, supported by Sam Pearl and the secretary of the Society, sobbed uncontrollably. She bent forward, shouting into the grave, "Morris, take care of Helen, you hear me, Morris?"

The rabbi, blessing it, tossed in the first shovelful of earth.

"Gently."

Then the diggers began to push in the loose earth around the grave and as it fell on the coffin the mourners wept aloud.

Helen tossed in a rose.

Frank, standing close to the edge of the grave, leaned forward to see where the flower fell. He lost his balance, and though flailing his arms, landed feet first on the coffin.

Helen turned her head away.

Ida wailed.

"Get the hell out of there," Nat Pearl said.

Frank scrambled out of the grave, helped by the

diggers. I spoiled the funeral, he thought. He felt
pity on the world for harboring him.

At last the coffin was covered, the grave full,
running over. The rabbi said a last short Kaddish.
Nat took Helen by the arm and led her away.

She gazed back once, with grief, then went with
him.

Louis Karp was waiting for them in the dark
hallway when Ida and Helen returned from the
cemetery.

"Excuse me for bothering you on this sad occa-
sion," he said, holding his hat in his hand, "but I
wanna tell you why my father couldn't get to the
funeral. He's sick and has to lay flat on his back
for the next six weeks or so. The other night when
he passed out at the fire, we found out later he
had a heart attack. He's lucky he's still alive."

"Vey is mir," muttered Ida.

"The doctor says he's gonna have to retire from
here on in," Louis said, with a shrug, "so I don't
think he'll wanna buy your house any more. Myself," he added, "I got a job of salesman for a liquor concern."

He said good-by and left them.

"Your father is better off dead," said Ida.

As they toiled up the stairs they heard the dull
cling of the register in the store and knew the
grocer was the one who had danced on the grocer's coffin.

Frank lived in the back, his clothes hung in a bought closet, sleeping under his overcoat on the couch. He had used their week of mourning, when mother and daughter were confined upstairs, to get the store going. Staying open kept it breathing, but beyond that things were rocky. If not for his thirty-five weekly dollars in the register he would have had to close up. Seeing he paid his little bills, the wholesalers extended credit. People stopped in to say they were sorry Morris was dead. One man said the grocer was the only storekeeper that had ever trusted him for anything. He paid Frank back eleven dollars that he owed Morris. Frank told anybody who asked that he was keeping the business going for the widow. They approved of that.

He gave Ida twelve dollars a week rent and promised her more when times got better. He said when they did, he might buy the store from her, but it would have to be on small installments because he had no money for a down payment. She didn't answer him. She was worried about the future and feared she might starve. She lived on the rent he paid her, plus Nick's rent, and Helen's salary. Ida now had a little job sewing epaulettes for military uniforms, a bag of which Abe Rubin, a landsman of Morris's, delivered in his car every Monday morning. That brought in another twenty-eight to thirty a month. She rarely went down to the store. To speak to her, Frank had to go upstairs and knock on her door. Once, through Rubin, someone came to look at the grocery and Frank was worried, but the man soon left.

He lived in the future, to be forgiven. On the stairs one morning he said to Helen, "Things are changed. I am not the same guy I was."

"Always," she answered, "you remind me of everything I want to forget."

"Those books you once gave me to read," he said, "did you understand them yourself?"

Helen waked from a bad dream. In the dream she had got up to leave the house in the middle of the night to escape Frank waiting on the stairs; but there he stood under the yellow lamp, fondling his lascivious cap. As she approached, his lips formed, "I love you."

"I'll scream if you say it."

She screamed and woke.

At a quarter to seven she forced herself out of bed, shut off the alarm before it rang and drew off her nightgown. The sight of her body mortified her. What a waste, she thought. She wanted to be a virgin again and at the same time a mother.

Ida was still asleep in the half-empty bed that had for a lifetime served two. Helen brushed her hair, washed, and put on coffee. Standing at the kitchen window, she gazed out at the back yards in flower, feeling sorrow for her father lying in his immovable grave. What had she ever given him, ever done to make his poor life better? She wept for Morris, thinking of his compromises and surrenders. She felt she must do something for herself, accomplish some worthwhile thing or suffer his fate. Only by growing in value as a person could she make Morris's life meaningful, in the sense that she was of him. She must, she thought, in some way eventually earn her degree. It would take years—but was the only way.

Frank stopped waiting for her in the hall. She had cried out one morning, "Why do you force yourself on me?" and it had struck him that his penitence was a hammer, so he withdrew. But he watched her when he could, through an opening in the tissue paper backing of the store window. He watched as if he were seeing for the first time her slender figure, high small breasts, the slim roundness of her hips and the exciting quality of her slightly bowed legs. She always looked lonely. He tried to think what he could ever do for her and all he could think of was to give her something she had no use for, that would end up in the garbage.

The idea of doing something for her seemed as futile as his other thoughts till one day, the tissue paper held a little aside as he watched her impassively entering the house, he had a thought so extraordinary it made the hair on the back of his neck stiffen. He figured the best thing he could do was help her get the college education she had always wanted. There was nothing she wanted more. But where, if she agreed to let him—he doubted it every minute it was in his mind—could he get the money unless he stole it? The more he pondered this plan, the more it excited him until he couldn't stand the possibility it might be impossible.

He carried in his wallet the note Helen had once written him, that she would come up to his room if Nick and Tessie went to the movies, and he read it often.

One day he got another idea. He pasted a sign in the window: "Hot Sandwiches And Hot Soups To Go." He figured he could use his short-order cooking experience to advantage in the grocery. He had some handbills printed, advertising these new things and paid a kid half a buck to deliver them to places where there were working men. He followed the boy for a couple of blocks to see that he didn't dump the papers into a sewer. Before the end of the week a few new people were coming in at lunch and suppertime. They said this was the first time you could get any hot food to take out in the neighborhood. Frank also tried his hand at ravioli and lasagna once a week, making them from recipes he got out of a cookbook in the library. He experimented with baking small pizzas in the gas stove, which he sold for two bits apiece. The pasta and pizzas sold better than the hot sandwiches. People came in for them. He considered putting a table or two in the grocery but there was no room, so all the food had to go.

He got another little break. The milkman told him the two Norwegians had taken to yelling at each other in front of their customers. He said they were making less than they had expected. The store was fine for one man but not for two, so they each wanted to buy the other out. Pederson's nerves couldn't stand the fighting, and Taast

bought him out at the end of May and had the
place all to himself. But he found that the long
hours alone were killing his feet. His wife came
in to help out around suppertime; however Taast
couldn't stand being away from his family every
night, when everyone else was free and at home,
so he decided to close at seven-thirty and stop
fighting Frank until almost ten. These couple of
hours all to himself at night helped Frank. He got
back some of the customers who came home from
work late, and also the housewives who at the last
minute needed something for breakfast. And
Frank noticed, from peering into Taast's window
after he was closed, that he was no longer so gen-
erous with the specials.

The weather turned hot in July. People cooked
less, lived more on delicatessen, canned goods,
bottled drinks. He sold a lot of beer. His pastas
and pizzas went very well. He heard that Taast
had tried making pizzas but they were too doughy.
Also, instead of using canned soups, Frank made a
minestrone of his own that everybody praised; it
took time to cook up, but the profit was better.
And the new things he was selling pushed other
goods along. He now paid Ida ninety a month for
rent and the use of her store. She was earning
more money on her epaulettes, and did not think
so often that she would starve.

"Why do you give me so much?" she asked him
when he raised the money to ninety.

"Maybe Helen could keep some of her wages?"
he suggested.

"Helen isn't interested any more in you," she
said sternly.

He didn't answer her.

But that night after supper—he had treated himself to ham and eggs and now smoked a cigar —Frank cleared the table and sat down to figure out how much it would cost to support Helen in college if she would quit her job and give all her time to education. When he had figured out the tuition from the college catalogues he had collected, he saw he couldn't do it. His heart was heavy. Later he thought maybe he could work it if she went to a free college. He could give her enough for her daily expenses and also to make up whatever money she now gave her mother. He figured that to do it would be a rocky load on his head, but he *had* to do it, it was his only hope; he could think of no other. All he asked for himself was the privilege of giving her something she couldn't give back.

The big thing, exciting yet frightening, was to talk to her, say what he hoped to do. He always had it in mind to say but found it very hard. To speak to her, after all that had happened to them, seemed impossible—opening on peril, disgrace, physical pain. What was the magic word to begin with? He despaired he could ever convince her. She was remote, sinned against, unfeeling, or if she felt, it was disgust of him. He cursed himself for having conceived this mess he couldn't now bring himself to speak of.

One August night after he had seen her come home from work in the company of Nat Pearl, sick of the misery of unmotion, Frank made himself move. He was standing behind the counter piling bottles of beer into a woman's market bag

when he caught sight of Helen going by with some
books on her arm. She was wearing a new summer
dress, red trimmed with black, and the sight of
her struck him with renewed hunger. All summer
she had wandered at night alone in the neighborhood, trying to outwalk her loneliness. He had
been tempted to close up and follow her, but until he had his new idea he could not think what he
dared say that she wouldn't run from. Hurrying
the customer out of the store, Frank washed,
slicked back his hair and quickly changed into a
fresh sport shirt. He locked the store and hurried
in the direction Helen had gone. The day had been
hot but was cooling now and still. The sky was
golden green, though below the light was dark.
After running a block he remembered something
and trudged back to the store. He sat in the back
listening to his heart hammering in his ears. In
ten minutes he lit a lamp in the store window. The
globe drew a ragged moth. Knowing how long she
lingered among books, he shaved. Then locking
the front door again, he went toward the library.
He figured he would wait across the street till she
came out. He would cross over and catch up with
her on her way home. Before she could even see
him, he would speak his piece and be done with it.
Yes or no, she could say, and if no, he would shut
the joint tomorrow and skiddoo.

He was nearing the library when he glanced up
and saw her. She was about half a block away and
walking toward him. He stood there not knowing
which way to go, dreading to be met by her as
lovely as she looked, standing like a crippled dog
as she passed him. He thought of running back the
way he had come, but she saw him, turned and

went in haste the other way; so, reviving an old habit, he was after her, and before she could deny him, had touched her arm. They shivered. Giving her no time to focus her contempt, he blurted out what he had so long saved to say but could not now stand to hear himself speak.

When Helen realized what he was offering her, her heart moved violently. She had known he would follow and speak, but she could never in a thousand years have guessed he would say *this*. Considering the conditions of his existence, she was startled by his continuing ability to surprise her, make God-knows-what-next-move. His staying power mystified and frightened her, because she felt in herself, since the death of Ward Minogue, a waning of outrage. Although she detested the memory of her experience in the park, lately it had come back to her how she had desired that night to give herself to Frank, and might have if Ward hadn't touched her. She had wanted him. If there had been no Ward Minogue, there would have been no assault. If he had made his starved leap in bed she would have returned passion. She had hated him, she thought, to divert hatred from herself.

But her response to his offer was an instantaneous no. She said it almost savagely, to escape any possibility of being directly obligated to him, of another entrapment, nausea.

"I couldn't think of it."

He was astonished to have got this far, to be walking at her side—only it was a night in a different season, and her summer face was gentler than her winter one, her body more womanly; yet it all added up to loss, the more he wanted her the more he had lost.

"In your father's name," he said. "If not for you, then for him."

"What has my father got to do with it?"

"It's his store. Let it support you to go to college like he wanted you to."

"It can't without you. I don't want your help."

"Morris did me a big favor. I can't return it to him but I might to you. Also because I lost myself that night—"

"For God's sake, don't say it."

He didn't, was dumb. They walked dumbly on. To her horror they were coming to the park. Abruptly she went the other way.

He caught up with her. "You could graduate in three years. You wouldn't have any worry about expenses. You could study all you want."

"What would you expect to get from this—virtue?"

"I already said why—I owe something to Morris."

"For what? Taking you into his stinking store and making a prisoner out of you?"

What more could he say? To his misery, what he had done to her father rose in his mind. He had often imagined he would someday tell her, but not now. Yet the wish to say it overwhelmed him. He tried wildly to escape it. His throat hurt, his stomach heaved. He clamped his teeth tight but the words came up in blobs, in a repulsive stream.

He spoke with pain. "I was the one that held him up that time. Minogue and me. Ward picked on him after Karp ran away, but it was my fault too on account of I went in with him."

She screamed and might have gone on screaming but strangers were staring.

"Helen, I swear—"

"You criminal. How could you hit such a gentle
person? What harm did he ever do you?"

"I didn't hit him, Ward did. I gave him a drink
of water. He saw I didn't want to hurt him. After,
I came to work for him to square up what I did
wrong. For Christ's sake, Helen, try to understand
me."

With contorted face she ran from him.

"I confessed it to him," he shouted after her.

He had managed well in the summer and fall,
but after Christmas business dragged, and though
his night salary had been raised five bucks, he
found it impossible to meet all his expenses. Every
penny looked as big as the moon. Once he spent an
hour searching for a two-bit piece he had dropped
behind the counter. He tore up a loose floor board
and was elated to recover more than three dollars
in green and grimy coins that Morris had lost
during the years.

For himself he spent only for the barest neces-
sities, though his clothes were falling apart. When
he could no longer sew up the holes in his un-
dershirts he threw them away and wore none. He
soaked his laundry in the sink and hung it to dry
in the kitchen. He was, as a rule, prompt in his payment of jobbers and wholesalers, but during the
winter he kept them waiting. One man he held
off his neck by threatening to go bankrupt. Another he promised tomorrow. He slipped a
couple of bucks to his most important salesman, to
calm them at the office. Thus he kept going. But

he never missed a payment of rent to Ida. He valued his payments to her because Helen had returned to night college in the fall, and if he didn't give the ninety to Ida, Helen wouldn't have enough for her own needs.

He was always tired. His spine ached as if it had been twisted like a cat's tail. On his night off from the Coffee Pot he slept without moving, dreaming of sleep. In the dead hours at the Coffee Pot, he sat with his head on his arms at the counter, and during the day in the grocery he took catnaps whenever he could, trusting the buzzer to rouse him, although other noises did not. When he awoke, his eyes were hot and watery, his head like porous lead. He grew thin, his neck scrawny, face bones prominent, his broken nose sharp. He saw life from a continual wet-eyed yawn. He drank black coffee till his stomach turned sour. In the evening he did nothing—read a little. Or he sat in the back with the lights out, smoking, listening to the blues on the radio.

He had other worries, had noticed Nat was hanging around Helen more. A couple of times a week the law student drove her home from work. Now and then, over the week end, they went for a ride at night. Nat would toot his horn in front of the door and she came out dressed up and smiling, neither of them noticing Frank, in open sight. And she had had a new telephone put in upstairs, and once or twice a week he heard it ring. The phone made him jumpy, jealous of Nat. Once on his night off from the Coffee Pot, Frank woke abruptly when Helen and somebody came into the hall. Sneaking into the store and listening at the side door, he could hear them whispering;

then they were quiet and he imagined them neck-ing. For hours after, he couldn't get back to sleep, desiring her so. The next week, listening at the door, he discovered the guy she was kissing was Nat. His jealousy ate him good.

She never entered the store. To see her he had to stand at the front window.

"Jesus," he said, "why am I killing myself so?" He gave himself many unhappy answers, the best being that while he was doing this he was doing nothing worse.

But then he took to doing things he had prom-ised himself he never would again. He did them with dread of what he would do next. He climbed up the air shaft to spy on Helen in the bathroom. Twice he saw her disrobe. He ached for her, for the flesh he had lived in a moment. Yet he hated her for having loved him, for to desire what he had once had, and hadn't now, was torture. He swore to himself that he would never spy on her again, but he did. And in the store he took to cheating customers. When they weren't watching the scale he short-weighted them. A couple of times he shortchanged an old dame who never knew how much she had in her purse.

Then one day, for no reason he could give, though the reason felt familiar, he stopped climb-ing up the air shaft to peek at Helen, and he was honest in the store.

One night in January Helen was waiting at the curb for a trolley. She had been studying with a girl in her class and afterward had listened to some records, so she had left later than she had planned. The trolley was late in coming, and though she was cold, she was considering walking home, when she began to feel she was being watched. Looking into the store before which she was standing, she saw nobody there but the counterman resting his head on his arms. As she observed him, trying to figure out why she felt so strange, he raised his sleepy head and she saw in surprise that it was Frank Alpine. He gazed with burning eyes in a bony face, with sad regret, at his reflection in the window, then went drunkenly back to sleep. It took her a minute to realize he hadn't seen her. She felt the momentary return of an old misery, yet the winter night seemed clear and beautiful.

When the trolley came, she took a seat in the rear. Her thoughts were heavy. She remembered Ida saying Frank worked some place at night but the news had meant nothing to her. Now that she had seen him there, groggy from overwork, thin, unhappy, a burden lay on her, because it was no mystery who he was working for. He had kept them alive. Because of him she had enough to go to school at night.

In bed, half-asleep, she watched the watcher. It came to her that he had changed. It's true, he's not the same man, she said to herself. I should have known by now. She had despised him for the evil he had done, without understanding the why or aftermath, or admitting there could be an end to the bad and a beginning of good.

It was a strange thing about people—they could look the same but be different. He had been one thing, low, dirty, but because of something in himself—something she couldn't define, a memory perhaps, an ideal he might have forgotten and

then remembered—he had changed into somebody else, no longer what he had been. She should
have recognized it before. What he did to me he
did wrong, she thought, but since he has changed
in his heart he owes me nothing.

On her way to work one morning a week later,
Helen, carrying her brief case, entered the grocery and found Frank hidden behind the tissue
paper of the window, watching her. He was embarrassed, and she was curiously moved by the
sight of his face.

"I came in to thank you for the help you're giving us," she explained.

"Don't thank me," he said.

"You owe us nothing."

"It's just my way."

They were silent, then he mentioned his idea of
her going to day college. It would be more satisfying to her than at night.

"No, thank you," Helen said, blushing. "I
couldn't think of it, especially not with you working so hard."

"It's no extra trouble."

"No, please."

"Maybe the store might get better, then I could
do it on what we take in here?"

"I'd rather not."

"Think about it," Frank said.

She hesitated, then answered she would.

He wanted to ask her if he still had any chance
with her but decided to let that wait till a later
time.

Before she left, Helen, balancing the brief case
on her knee, unsnapped it and took out a leather-

bound book. "I wanted you to know I'm still using your Shakespeare."

He watched her walk to the corner, a good-looking girl, carrying his book in her brief case. She was wearing flat-heeled shoes, making her legs slightly more bowed, which for some reason he found satisfying.

The next night, listening at the side door, he heard a scuffle in the hall and wanted to break in and assist her but held himself back. He heard Nat say something harsh, then Helen slapped him and he heard her run upstairs.

"You bitch," Nat called after her.

One morning in the middle of March the grocer was sleeping heavily after a night off from the Coffee Pot, when he was awakened by a pounding on the front door. It was the Polish nut wanting her three-cent roll. She came later these days but still too early. The hell with all that, he thought, I need my sleep. But after a few minutes he grew restless and began to dress. Business still wasn't so hot. Frank washed his face before the cracked mirror. His thick hair needed cutting but it could wait one more week. He thought of growing himself a beard but was afraid it would scare some of the customers away, so he settled for a mustache. He had been letting one grow for two weeks and was surprised at the amount of red in it. He sometimes wondered if his old lady had been a redhead.

Unlocking the door, he let her in. The Polish dame complained he had kept her waiting too long in the cold. He sliced a roll for her, wrapped it, and rang up three cents.

At seven, standing by the window, he saw Nick,

a new father, come out òf the hall and run around
the corner. Frank hid behind the paper and soon
saw him return, carrying a bag of groceries he had
bought in Taast's store. Nick ducked into the
hallway and Frank felt bad.

"I think I will make this joint into a restaurant."

After he had mopped the kitchen floor and
swept the store, Breitbart appeared, dragging his
heavy boxes. Lowering the cartons of bulbs to the
floor, the peddler took off his derby and wiped his
brow with a yellowed handkerchief.

"How's it going?" Frank asked.

"Schwer."

Breitbart drank the tea and lemon that Frank
cooked up for him, meanwhile reading his *Forward*. After about ten minutes he folded the
newspaper into a small, thick square and pushed
it into his coat pocket. He lifted the bulbs onto
his itchy shoulders and left.

Frank had only six customers all morning. To
keep from getting nervous he took out a book he
was reading. It was the Bible and he sometimes
thought there were parts of it he could have written himself.

As he was reading he had this pleasant thought.
He saw St. Francis come dancing out of the woods
in his brown rags, a couple of scrawny birds flying
around over his head. St. F. stopped in front of the
grocery, and reaching into the garbage can,
plucked the wooden rose out of it. He tossed it
into the air and it turned into a real flower that he
caught in his hand. With a bow he gave it to Hel-
en, who had just come out of the house. "Little
sister, here is your little sister the rose." From him

she took it, although it was with the love and best wishes of Frank Alpine.

One day in April Frank went to the hospital and had himself circumcised. For a couple of days he dragged himself around with a pain between his legs. The pain enraged and inspired him. After Passover he became a Jew.